D1564077

The Making of a Saint

THE MAKING OF A SAINT

THE MAKING OF A SAINT

SAINT

BY

WILLIAM SOMERSET MAUGHAM

LONDON

T. FISHER UNWIN

PATERNOSTER SQUARE

1898

Quanto e bella giovinezza,
    Che si fugge tuttavia ;
Chi vuol esser lieto, sia,
    Di doman non c'e certezza.

Youth—how beautiful is youth !
    But, alas, elusive ever !
Let him be light of heart who would be so,
    For there's no surety in the morrow.

The Making of a Saint

INTRODUCTION

THESE are the memoirs of the Beato Giuliano,
brother of the Order of St Francis of Assisi, known
in his worldly life as Filippo Brandolini; of which
family I, Giulo Brandolini, am the last descendant.
On the death of Fra Giuliano the manuscript was given
to his nephew Leonello, on whom the estates devolved;
and has since been handed down from father to son,
as the relic of a member of the family whose piety
and good works still shed lustre on the name of
Brandolini.

It is perhaps necessary to explain how the resolu-
tion to give these memoirs to the world has eventually been arrived at. For my part, I should have
allowed them to remain among the other papers of
the family; but my wife wished otherwise. When
she deserted her home in the New World to become
the Countess Brandolini, she was very naturally interested at finding among my ancestors a man who had
distinguished himself in good works, so as to be
granted by the Pope the title of Beatus, which was
acquired for him by the influence of his great-nephew

A

not very long after his death; and, indeed, had our house retained the prosperity which it enjoyed during the fifteenth and sixteenth centuries, he would undoubtedly have been canonised, for it was a well certified fact that the necessary miracles had been performed by his remains and that prayers had been regularly offered at his tomb, but our estates had dwindled, so that we could not afford the necessary expenditure; and now, when my wife has restored its ancient magnificence to our house, times, alas! have changed. The good old customs of our fathers have fallen into disuse, and it is impossible to create a saint for ready money. However, my wife desired to publish an account of her pious ancestor. But a difficulty arose in the fact that there were no materials whatever for any relation of the life which Fra Giuliano led when he had entered the Franciscan monastery of Campomassa, and it was obvious that, even if there had been good works, prayer and fasting could not have afforded a very interesting story; and so we have been constrained to leave untold his pieties and recount instead his sins, for which there was every facility in the memoirs he had himself left behind him.

Not content with writing the story of his own life, Fra Giuliano begins with a mythical Consul of the Roman Republic, who is supposed to have founded the family by a somewhat discreditable union with somebody else's wife. He then carries the story through countless ages till he arrives at his own conception, and the prodigies attending his birth, which he describes with great minuteness. He gives very amply the history of his childhood and boyhood, the period he spent as page at the Court of the Bentivogli of Bologna, and his adventures in the Neapolitan armies under the Duke of Calabria; but the whole story is narrated at such length, with so many digressions and details, and is sometimes so vague, incoherent and disjointed that, with whatever editing, it was considered impossible to make a clear and continuous narrative.

Fra Giuliano himself divided his life into two parts: the one he named the Time of Honey, being the period of expectation; the other the Time of Gall, being that of realisation. The second half commences with his arrival at the town of Forli, in the year 1488, and it is this part which we have decided to publish; for, notwithstanding its brevity, this was the most eventful period of his life, and the account of it seems to hang together in a sufficiently lucid fashion, centring round the conspiracy which resulted in the assassination of Girolamo Riario, and finishing with the author's admission to the Order of St Francis. This, then, I have given exactly as he wrote it, neither adding nor suppressing a word. I do not deny that it would have pleased me a little to falsify the history, for the Anglo-Saxons are a race of idealists, as is shown in all their dealings, international and commercial; and truth they have always found a little ugly. I have a friend who lately wrote a story of the London poor, and his critics were properly disgusted because his characters dropped their aitches and often used bad language, and did not behave as elegantly as might be expected from the example they were continually receiving from their betters; while some of his readers were

shocked to find that people existed in this world who
did not possess the delicacy and refinement which
they felt palpitating in their own bosoms. The
author forgot that truth is a naked lady, and that
nudity is always shameful, unless it points a moral.
If Truth has taken up her abode at the bottom of a
well, it is clearly because she is conscious that she is
no fit companion for decent people.

I am painfully aware that the persons of this
drama were not actuated by the moral sentiments,
which they might have acquired by education at a
really good English public school ; but one may find
excuse for them in the recollection that their deeds
took place four hundred years ago, and that they
were not wretched paupers, but persons of the very
highest rank. If they sinned, they sinned elegantly,
and much may be forgiven to people whose pedigree
is above suspicion. And the writer, as if unwilling
to wound the susceptibilities of his readers, has taken
care to hurl contempt at the only character whose
family was distinctly not respectable.

Before making my bow and leaving the reader
with Filippo Brandolini, I will describe his appearance, shown in a portrait painted in the same year,
1488, and till the beginning of this century in the
possession of my family, when it was sold, with many
other works of art, to travellers in Italy. My wife has
succeeded in buying back the portraits of several of
my ancestors, but this particular one is in the collec-
tion of an English nobleman, who has refused to
part with it, though kindly allowing a copy to
be made, which now hangs in the place formerly
occupied by the original.

It represents a middle-sized man, slim and graceful, with a small black beard and moustache; an oval face, olive coloured, and from his fine dark eyes he is looking straight out into the world with an expression of complete happiness. It was painted soon after his marriage. He is dressed in the costume of the period, and holds a roll of parchment in his hand. At the top right hand corner are the date and the arms of the family; or a griffin rampant. Gules. Crest: a demiswan issuing from a coronet. The motto: *Felicitas.*

I

'ALLOW me to present to you my friend Filippo Brandolini, a gentleman of Citta di Castello.'

Then, turning to me, Matteo added, 'This is my cousin, Checco d'Orsi.'

Checco d'Orsi smiled and bowed.

'Messer Brandolini,' he said, 'I am most pleased to make your acquaintance; you are more than welcome to my house.'

'You are very kind,' I replied; 'Matteo has told me much of your hospitality.'

Checco bowed courteously, and asked his cousin, 'You have just arrived, Matteo?'

'We arrived early this morning. I wished to come here directly, but Filippo, who suffers from a very insufferable vanity, insisted on going to an inn and spending a couple of hours in the adornment of his person.'

'How did you employ those hours, Matteo?' asked Checco, looking rather questioningly at his cousin's dress and smiling.

Matteo looked at his boots and his coat.

'I am not elegant! But I felt too sentimental to attend to my personal appearance, and I had to

6

restore myself with wine. You know, we are very proud of our native Forli wine, Filippo.'

'I did not think you were in the habit of being sentimental, Matteo,' remarked Checco.

'It was quite terrifying this morning, when we arrived,' said I; 'he struck attitudes and called it his beloved country, and wanted to linger in the cold morning and tell me anecdotes about his childhood.'

'You professional sentimentalists will never let anyone sentimentalise but yourselves.'

'I was hungry,' said I, laughing, 'and it didn't become you.   Even your horse had his doubts.'

'Brute!' said Matteo. 'Of course, I was too excited to attend to my horse, and he slipped over those confounded stones and nearly shot me off— and Filippo, instead of sympathising, burst out laughing.'

'Evidently you must abandon sentiment,' said Checco.

'I'm afraid you are right. Now, Filippo can be romantic for hours at a stretch, and, what is worse, he is—but nothing happens to him. But on coming back to my native town after four years, I think it was pardonable.'

'We accept your apology, Matteo,' I said.

'But the fact is, Checco, that I am glad to get back. The sight of the old streets, the Palazzo, all fill me with a curious sensation of joy—and I feel—I don't know how I feel.'

'Make the utmost of your pleasure while you can ; you may not always find a welcome in Forli,' said Checco, gravely.

'What the devil do you mean?' asked Matteo.

'Oh, we'll talk of these things later. You had better go and see my father now, and then you can rest yourselves. You must be tired after your journey. To-night we have here a great gathering, where you will meet your old friends. The Count has deigned to accept my invitation.'

'Deigned?' said Matteo, lifting his eyebrows and looking at his cousin.

Checco smiled bitterly.

'Times have changed since you were here, Matteo' he said ; 'the Forlivesi are subjects and courtiers now.'

Putting aside Matteo's further questions, he bowed to me and left us.

'I wonder what it is?' said Matteo. 'What did you think of him?'

I had examined Checco d'Orsi curiously—a tall dark man, with full beard and moustache, apparently about forty. There was a distinct likeness between him and Matteo: they both had the same dark hair and eyes ; but Matteo's face was broader, the bones more prominent, and the skin rougher from his soldier's life. Checco was thinner and graver, he looked a great deal more talented ; Matteo, as I often told him, was not clever.

'He was very amiable,' I said, in reply to the question.

'A little haughty, but he means to be courteous. He is rather oppressed with his dignity of head of the family.'

'But his father is still alive.'

'Yes, but he's eighty-five, and he's as deaf as a post and as blind as a bat ; so he remains quietly in his room while Checco pulls the strings, so that we

poor devils have to knuckle under and do as he bids
us.'

'I'm sure that must be very good for you,' I said.
'I'm curious to know why Checco talks of the Count
as he did; when I was here last they were bosom
friends. However, let us go and drink, having done
our duty.'

We went to the inn at which we had left our
horses and ordered wine.

'Give us your best, my fat friend,' cried Matteo
to mine host. 'This gentleman is a stranger, and
does not know what wine is; he was brought up
on the sickly juice of Citta di Castello.'

'You live at Citta di Castello?' asked the innkeeper.

'I wish I did,' I answered.

'He was ejected from his country for his country's
good,' remarked Matteo.

'That is not true,' I replied, laughing. 'I left of
my own free will.'

'Galloping as hard as you could, with four-and-
twenty horsemen at your heels.'

'Precisely! And so little did they want me to go,
that when I thought a change of air would suit me
they sent a troop of horse to induce me to return.'

'Your head would have made a pretty ornament
stuck on a pike in the grand piazza.'

'The thought amuses you,' I answered, 'but the
comedy of it did not impress me at the time.'

I remembered the occasion when news was
brought me that the Vitelli, the tyrant of Castello,
had signed a warrant for my arrest; whereupon,
knowing the rapid way he had of dealing with his

enemies, I had bidden farewell to my hearth and home with somewhat indecent haste. . . . But the old man had lately died, and his son, proceeding to undo all his father's deeds, had called back the Fuorusciti, and strung up from the Palace windows such of his father's friends as had not had time to escape. I had come to Forli with Matteo, on my way home to take possession of my confiscated property, hoping to find that the intermediate proprietor, who was dangling at a rope's end some hundred feet from the ground, had made sundry necessary improvements.

'Well, what do you think of our wine?' said Matteo. 'Compare it with that of Citta di Castello.'

'I really haven't tasted it yet,' I said, pretending to smile agreeably. 'Strange wines I always drink at a gulp—like medicine.'

'*Brutta bestia!*' said Matteo. 'You are no judge.'

'It's passable,' I said, laughing, having sipped it with great deliberation.

Matteo shrugged his shoulders.

'These foreigners!' he said scornfully. 'Come here, fat man,' he called to the innkeeper. 'Tell me how Count Girolamo and the gracious Caterina are progressing? When I left Forli the common people struggled to lick the ground they trod on.'

The innkeeper shrugged his shoulders.

'Gentlemen of my profession have to be careful in what they say.'

Don't be a fool, man; I am not a spy.'

'Well, sir, the common people no longer struggle to lick the ground the Count treads on.'

'I see!'

'You understand, sir. Now that his father is dead—'

'When I was here last Sixtus was called his uncle.'

'Ah, they say he was too fond of him not to be his father, but, of course, I know nothing. Far be it from me to say anything in disparagement of his Holiness, past or present.'

'However, go on.'

'Well, sir, when the Pope died the Count Girolamo found himself short of money—and so the taxes that he had taken off he put on again.'

'And the result is—'

'Well, the people are beginning to murmur about his extravagance; and they say that Caterina behaves as if she were a queen; whereas we all know that she is only the bastard of old Sforza of Milan. But, of course, it has nothing to do with me!'

Matteo and I were beginning to feel sleepy, for we had been riding hard all night; and we went upstairs, giving orders to be called in time for the night's festivity. We were soon fast asleep.

In the evening Matteo came to me, and began examining my clothes.

'I have been considering, Filippo,' he said, 'that it behoves me on my first appearance before the eyes of my numerous lady loves to cut the best figure I can.'

'I quite agree with you,' I answered; 'but I don't see what you are doing with my clothes.'

'Nobody knows you, and it is unimportant how you look; and, as you have some very nice things here, I am going to take advantage of your kindness and—'

'You're not going to take my clothes!' I said, springing out of bed. Matteo gathered up in his arms various garments and rushed out of the room, slamming the door and locking it on the outside, so that I was left shut in, helpless.

I shouted abuse after him, but he went away laughing, and I had to manage as best I could with what he had left me. In half an hour he came to the door. 'Do you want to come out?' he said.

'Of course I do,' I answered, kicking the panel.

'Will you promise not to be violent?'

I hesitated.

'I shan't let you out unless you do.'

'Very well!' I answered, laughing.

Matteo opened the door and stood bolt upright on the threshold, decked out from head to foot in my newest clothes.

'You villain!' I said, amazed at his effrontery.

'You don't look bad, considering,' he answered, looking at me calmly.

II

WHEN we arrived at the Palazzo Orsi, many of the guests had already come. Matteo was immediately surrounded by his friends; and a score of ladies beckoned to him from different parts of the room, so that he was torn away from me, leaving me rather disconsolate alone in the crowd. Presently I was attracted to a group of men talking to a woman whom I could not see; Matteo had joined them, and they were laughing at something he had said. I had turned away to look at other people when I heard Matteo calling me.

'Filippo,' he said, coming towards me, 'come and be introduced to Donna Giulia; she has asked me to present you.'

He took me by the arm, and I saw that the lady and her admirers were looking at me.

'She's no better than she should be,' he whispered in my ear; 'but she's the loveliest woman in Forli!'

'Allow me to add another to your circle of adorers, Donna Giulia,' said Matteo, as we both bowed—'Messer Filippo Brandolini, like myself, a soldier of distinction.'

I saw a graceful little woman, dressed in some

13

Oriental brocade; a small face, with quite tiny
features, large brown eyes, which struck me at the
first glance as very soft and caressing, a mass of
dark, reddish-brown hair, and a fascinating smile.

'We were asking Matteo where his wounds
were,' she said, smiling on me very graciously. 'He
tells us they are all in the region of his heart.'

'In that case,' I answered, 'he has come to a more
deadly battlefield than any we saw during the
war.'

'What war?' asked a gentleman who was standing
by. 'Nowadays we are in the happy state of having
ten different wars in as many parts of the country.'

'I was serving under the Duke of Calabria,' I
replied.

'In that case, your battles were bloodless.'

'We came, we saw, and the enemy decamped,'
said Matteo.

'And now, taking advantage of the peace, you
have come to trouble the hearts of Forli,' said
Donna Giulia.

'Who knows how useful your swords may not
be here!' remarked a young man.

'Be quiet, Nicolo!' said another, and there was
an awkward silence, during which Matteo and I
looked at one another in surprise; and then everyone burst out talking, so that you could not hear
what was said.

Matteo and I bowed ourselves away from Donna
Giulia, and he took me to Checco, standing in a
group of men.

'You have recovered from your fatigue?' he asked
kindly.

'You have been travelling, Matteo?' said one of the company.

'Yes, we rode sixty miles yesterday,' he replied.

'Sixty miles on one horse; you must have good steeds and good imaginations,' said a big, heavy-looking man—an ugly, sallow-faced person, whom I hated at first sight.

'It was only once in a way, and we wanted to get home.'

'You could not have come faster if you had been running away from a battlefield,' said the man.

I thought him needlessly disagreeable, but I did not speak. Matteo had not cultivated the golden quality.

'You talk as one who has had experience,' he remarked, smiling in his most amiable manner.

I saw Checco frown at Matteo, while the bystanders looked on interestedly.

'I only said that,' added the man, shrugging his shoulders, 'because the Duke of Calabria is rather celebrated for his retreative tactics.'

I entertained a very great respect for the Duke, who had always been a kind and generous master to me.

'Perhaps you do not know very much about tactics,' I remarked as offensively as I could.

He turned and looked at me, as if to say, 'Who the devil are you!' He looked me up and down contemptuously, and I began to feel that I was almost losing my temper.

'My good young man,' he said, 'I imagine that I was engaged in war when your battles were with your nursemaid.'

'You have the advantage of me in courtesy as well
as in years, sir,' I replied. 'But I might suggest that
a man may fight all his life, and have no more idea
of war at the end than at the beginning.'

'It depends on the intelligence,' remarked Matteo.

'Exactly what I was thinking,' said I.

'What the devil do you mean?' said the man,
angrily.

'I don't suppose he means anything at all, Ercole,'
put in Checco, with a forced laugh.

'He can answer for himself, I suppose,' said the
man. A flush came over Checco's face, but he did
not answer.

'My good sir,' I said, 'you have to consider whether
I choose to answer.'

'Jackanapes!'

I put my hand to my sword, but Checco caught
hold of my arm. I recovered myself at once.

'I beg your pardon, Messer Checco,' I said; then,
turning to the man, 'You are safe in insulting me
here. You show your breeding! Really, Matteo,
you did not tell me that you had such a charming
fellow-countryman.'

'You are too hard on us, Filippo,' answered my
friend, 'for such a monstrosity as that Forli is not
responsible.'

'I am no Forlivese, thank God! Neither the
Count nor I.' He looked round scornfully. 'We
offer up thanks to the Almighty every time the fact
occurs to us. I am a citizen of Castello.'

Matteo was going to burst out, but I anticipated
him. 'I, too, am a citizen of Castello; and allow me
to inform you that I consider you a very insolent

fellow, and I apologise to these gentlemen that a countryman of mine should forget the courtesy due to the city which is sheltering him.'

'You a Castelese! And, pray, who are you?'

'My name is Filippo Brandolini.'

'I know your house. Mine is Ercole Piacentini.'

'I cannot return the compliment; I have never heard of yours.'

The surrounders laughed.

'My family is as good as yours, sir,' he said.

'Really, I have no acquaintance with the middle-classes of Castello; but I have no doubt it is respectable.'

I noticed that the listeners seemed very contented, and I judged that Messer Ercole Piacentini was not greatly loved in Forli; but Checco was looking on anxiously.

'You insolent young boy!' said the man, furiously 'How dare you talk to me like that. I will kick you!'

I put my hand to my sword to draw it, for I was furious too; I pulled at the hilt, but I felt a hand catch hold of mine and prevent me. I struggled; then I heard Checco in my ear.

'Don't be a fool,' he said. 'Be quiet!'

'Let me be!' I cried.

'Don't be a fool! You'll ruin us.' He held my sword, so that I could not draw it.

Ercole saw what was going on; his lips broke into a sarcastic smile.

'You are being taught the useful lesson of discretion, young man. You are not the only one who has learnt it.' He looked round at the bystanders. . . .

B

At that moment a servant came to Checco and announced,—

'The Count!'

The group broke up, and Checco advanced to the further end of the hall, with Ercole Piacentini and several other gentlemen. Matteo and I lingered where we were. There was a rustle, and the Count and Countess appeared attended by their suite.

First of all my eyes were attracted to Caterina; she was wonderfully beautiful. A tall, well-made woman, holding herself proudly, her head poised on the neck like a statue.

'One would think she was a king's daughter!' said Matteo, looking at her with astonishment.

'It is almost Francesco's face,' I said.

We both had an immense admiration for Francesco Sforza, the King of Condottieri, who had raised himself from a soldier of fortune to the proudest duchy in the world. And Caterina, his natural daughter, had the same clear, strong features, the strong piercing eyes, but instead of the Sforza's pock-marked skin, she had a complexion of rare delicacy and softness; and afterwards she proved that she had inherited her father's courage as well as his appearance. . . . She was dressed in a gorgeous robe of silver cloth, glittering and shimmering as she walked, and her hair was done in her favourite manner, intertwined with gold and silver threads; but the wonderful chestnut outshone the brilliant metals, seeming to lend them beauty rather than to borrow it. I heard her speak, and her voice was low and full like a man's.

Matteo and I stood looking at her for a minute; then we both broke out 'Per Bacco, she is beautiful!'

I began thinking of the fairy stories I had heard of Caterina at Rome, where she had enchanted every-one by her loveliness; and Sixtus had squandered the riches of the Church to satisfy her whims and fancies: banquets, balls, pageants and gorgeous ceremonies; the ancient city had run red with wine and mad with delight of her beauty.

Suddenly Matteo said to me, 'Look at Girolamo!'

I lifted my eyes, and saw him standing quite close to me—a tall man, muscular and strong, with big heavy face, and prominent jaw bones, the nose long and hooked, small keen eyes, very mobile. His skin was unpleasant, red and coarse; like his wife, he was dressed with great magnificence.

'One sees the sailor grandfather in him,' I said, remembering that Sixtus's father, the founder of the family, was a common sailor at Rovese.

He was talking to Checco, who was apparently speaking to him of us, for he turned and stepped forward to Matteo.

'The prodigal has returned,' he said. 'We will not fail to kill the fatted calf. But this time you must stay with us, Matteo; we can give you service as well as the Duke of Calabria.'

Matteo smiled grimly; and the Count turned to me.

'Checco has told me of you also, sir; but I fear there is no chance of keeping you, you are but a bird of passage—still, I hope you will let us make you welcome at the Palace.'

All the time he was speaking his eyes kept moving rapidly up and down, all round me, and I felt he was taking in my whole person. . . . After these few words he smiled, a harsh, mechanical smile, meant to be gracious, and with a courteous bow moved on. I turned to Matteo and saw him looking after the Count very sourly.

'What is it,' I asked.

'He is devilish condescending,' he answered. 'When last I was here it was hail fellow, well met, but, good God! he's put on airs since then!'

'Your cousin said something to the same effect,' I remarked.

'Yes, I understand what he meant now.'

We strolled round the room, looking at the people and talking.

'Look,' I said, 'there's a handsome woman!' pointing to a voluptuous beauty, a massive creature, full-brested and high-coloured.

'Your eye is drawn to a handsome woman like steel to a magnet, Filippo,' answered Matteo, laughing.

'Introduce me,' I said, 'if she is not ferocious.'

'By no means; and she has probably already fixed her eyes upon you. But she is wife to Ercole Piacentini.'

'I don't care. I mean to kill the man afterwards; but that is no reason why I should not make myself pleasant to his spouse.'

'You will do her a service in both ways,' he replied; and, going up to her, 'Claudia,' he said, 'your fatal eyes have transfixed another heart.'

Her sensual lips broke into a smile.

'Have they that power?' She fixed them on me, and made room on the couch on which she was sitting. Neither Matteo nor I were slow to take the hint, for I took my place and he his leave. 'I wonder you have not already fallen victim to Madonna Giulia,' said Claudia, looking languorously at me, and glancing over to the other lady.

'One does not worship the moon when the sun is shining,' I replied politely.

'Giulia is more like the sun, for she gathers all men in her embrace. I am more modest.'

I understood that the rival beauties were not good friends.

'You boast that you are cruel,' I replied. She did not answer, but sighed deeply, smiling, and fixed on me her great, liquid eyes.

'Oh, there is my husband.' I looked up and saw the great Ercole glaring viciously at me. I laughed within myself.

'He must be very jealous of so beautiful a wife?' I asked.

'He torments me to death.'

Under these circumstances I thought I would pursue my advantage; I pressed closer to her.

'I can understand it: the first moment I saw you, I felt my head whirl.'

She gave me a very long glance from beneath her eyelashes. I seized her hand.

'Those eyes!' I said, looking into them fervently.

'Ah!' she sighed again.

'Madam,' said a pageboy, coming up to her, 'Messer Piacentini begs that you will come to him.'

She gave a little cry of annoyance.

'My husband!' Then, rising from her seat, she turned to me, holding out her hand; I immediately offered my arm, and we solemnly crossed the room to Ercole Piacentini. Here she bowed very graciously to me, and I smiled on the happy husband with the utmost sweetness, while he looked very grim and took not the faintest notice of me; then I marched off, feeling particularly pleased with myself.

The Count and Countess were on the point of taking their departure: they were followed by Ercole and his wife; the remaining guests soon went, and in a little while there were left only Matteo and myself, two other men and Checco.

III

CHECCO led us to a smaller room, at some distance from the great hall of the reception; then, turning to a man I did not know, he said, 'Did you hear the Piacentini?'

'Yes!' he answered; and for a moment they looked at one another silently.

'He would not have been so bold without good cause,' added the man.

I was told that his name was Lodovico Pansecchi, and that he was a soldier in the Count's pay.

Checco turned round and looked at me sharply. Matteo understood what he meant, and said, 'Have no fear of Filippo; he is as safe as myself.'

Checco nodded, and made a sign to a youth, who immediately rose and carefully closed the door. We sat still for a while; then Checco stood up and said impatiently, 'I cannot understand it.' He walked up and down the room, stopping at last in front of me.

'You had never seen that man before?'

'Never!' I answered.

'The quarrel was brought on solely by Ercole

23

himself,' said the youth, whom I found to be
Alessandro Moratini, a brother of Giulia dall'
Aste.

'I know,' said Checco, 'but he would never have
dared to behave thus unless he knew of some design
of Girolamo.' He paused a moment to think, then
turning to me again, 'You must not challenge
him.'

'On the contrary,' I replied, 'I must challenge
him; he has insulted me.'

'I don't care about that. I will not have you
challenge him.'

'This concerns myself alone.'

'Nonsense! You are a guest of my house, and
for all I know it is just such an opportunity as this
that Girolamo is seeking.'

'I don't understand,' I said.

'Listen,' said Checco, sitting down again. 'When
Sixtus obtained possession of Forli for his nephew,
Girolamo Riario, I, like the fool I was, did all I
could to bring the town to his allegiance. My father
was against the plan, but I bore down his opposition
and threw the whole power of my house on his side.
Without me he would never have been Lord of
Forli.'

'I remember,' said Matteo. 'You used Sixtus to
keep the Ordelaffi out; and you thought Girolamo
would be a catspaw in our hands.'

'I did not give the city for love of a person I had
never seen in my life. . . . Well, this was eight
years ago. Girolamo took off the heaviest taxes,
granted favours to the town and entered in solemn
state with Caterina.'

'Amid shouts and cheers,' remarked Alessandro.

'For a while he was more popular than ever the Ordelaffi had been, and when he went out the people ran to kiss the hem of his garment. He spent the great part of his time in Rome, but he employed the riches of the Pope in beautifying Forli, and when he came it was one round of feasts and balls and gaiety.

'Then Pope Sixtus died, and Girolamo settled here for good in the palace which he had commenced building on his accession. The feasts and balls and gaiety continued. Whenever a distinguished stranger passed through the town, he was welcomed by the Count and his wife with the most lavish hospitality; so that Forli became renowned for its luxury and riches.

'The poets ransacked Parnassus and the ancients for praises of their rules, and the people echoed the panegyrics of the poet. . . .

'Then came the crash. I had often warned Girolamo, for we were intimate friends—then. I told him that he could not continue the splendour which he had used when the wealth of Christendom was at his command, when he could spend the tribute of a nation on a necklace for Caterina. He would not listen. It was always, "I cannot be mean and thrifty," and he called it policy. "To be popular," he said, "I must be magnificent." The time came when the Treasury was empty, and he had to borrow. He borrowed in Rome and Florence and Milan— and all the time he would not retrench, but rather, as his means became less, the extravagance became greater; but when he could borrow no more outside, he came to the citizens of Forli, first, of course, to me, and I repeatedly lent him large sums. These were not enough, and he sent for the richest men of Forli and asked them to lend him money. Naturally they could not refuse. But he squandered their money as he had squandered his own; and one fine day he assembled the Council.'

'Ah, yes,' said Alessandro, 'I was there then. I heard him speak.'

Checco stopped as if for Alessandro.

'He came to the Council chamber, clad as usual in the richest robes, and began talking privately to the senators, very courteously—laughing with them, shaking their hands. Then, going to his place, he began to speak. He talked of his liberality towards them, and the benefits he had conferred on the town; showed them his present necessities, and finally asked them to re-impose the taxes which he had taken off at the beginning of his reign. They were all prejudiced against him, for many of them had already lent him money privately, but there was such a charm in his discourse, he was so persuasive, that one really could not help seeing the reasonableness of his demand. I know I myself would have granted him whatever he asked.'

'He can make one do anything he likes when he once begins talking,' said Lodovico.

'The Council unanimously voted the re-imposition of the taxes, and Girolamo offered them his thanks in his most gracious manner.'

There was a silence, broken by Matteo.

'And then?' he asked.

'Then,' answered Checco, 'he went to Imola, and

commenced spending there the money that he was gathering here.'

'And what did they think of it in Forli?'

'Ah, when the time came to pay the taxes they ceased their praises of Girolamo. First they murmured beneath their breath, then out loud; and soon they cursed him and his wife. The Count heard of it and came back from Imola, thinking, by his presence, to preserve the town in its allegiance. But the fool did not know that the sight of him would redouble the anger of the populace. They saw his gorgeous costumes, the gold and silver dresses of his wife, the jewels, the feasting and riotry, and they knew that it came out of their pockets; the food of their children, all that they had toiled and worked for, was spent on the insane luxury of this papal favourite and his bastard wife.'

'And how has he treated us?' cried Lodovico, beating his fist violently down on the table. 'I was in the pay of the Duke of Calabria, and he made me tempting offers, so that I left the armies of Naples to enter the papal service under him. And now, for four years, I have not received a penny of my salary, and when I ask him, he puts me aside with gentle words, and now he does not even trouble to give me them. A few days back I stopped him in the piazza, and, falling on my knees, begged for what he owed me. He threw me violently away, and said he could not pay me—and the jewel on his breast was worth ten times the money he owed me. And now he looks at me with frowns, me who have served him faithfully as a dog. I will not endure it; by God! I will not.' He clenched his fists as he spoke, trembling with rage.

'And you know how he has served me,' said Checco. 'I have lent him so much that he has not the face to ask for more; and how do you think he has rewarded me? Because I have not paid certain dues I owe the Treasury, he sent a sheriff to demand them, and when I said I would not pay them at that moment, he sent for me, and himself asked for the money.'

'What did you do?'

'I reminded him of the money he owed me, and he informed me that a private debt had nothing to do with a debt to the State, and said that I must pay or the law should take its course.'

'He must be mad,' said Matteo.

'He is mad, mad with pride, mad in his extravagance.'

'I tell you,' said Lodovico, 'it cannot be endured.'

'And they tell me that he has said my tongue must be silenced,' added Checco. 'The other day he was talking to Giuseppe Albicina, and he said "Let Checco beware; he may go too far and find the hand of the master not so gentle as the hand of the friend!"'

'I, too, have heard him say things which sounded like threats,' said Alessandro.

'We have all heard it,' added Lodovico. 'When his temper overcomes him, he cares not what he says, and one discovers then what he and his silent wife have been plotting between them.'

'Now, sir,' interrupted Checco, speaking to me, 'you see how things stand: we are on thin ground, and the fire is raging beneath us. You must promise not to seek further quarrel with this countryman of yours, this Ercole Piacentini. He is one of Girolamo's chiefest favourites, and he would not bear to see him touched ; if you happened to kill him, the Count would take the opportunity to have us all arrested, and we should suffer the fate of the Pazzi at Florence. Will you promise?'

'I promise,' I answered, smiling, 'to defer my satisfaction to a fitter opportunity.'

'Now, gentlemen,' said Checco, 'we can separate.'

We bade one another Good-night ; Alessandro, as he was going, said to Matteo, 'You must bring your friend to my sister to-morrow ; she will be glad to see you both.'

We said we should be enchanted, and Alessandro and Lodovico Pansecchi left us.

Matteo looked at Checco meditatively.

'Cousin,' he said, 'all this looks very like conspiracy.'

Checco started.

'I cannot help it, if the people are dissatisfied with Girolamo.'

'But you?' pursued Matteo. 'I imagine you do not greatly care whether the people are taxed or no. You knew the taxes would have to come on again sooner or later.'

'Has he not insulted me by sending a sheriff to demand his dues?'

'Is there nothing further than that?' asked Matteo, looking at his cousin steadily.

Checco lifted his eyes and gazed back into Matteo's.

'Yes,' he said at last ; 'eight years ago I was Girolamo's equal, now I am his servant. I was his friend, he loved me like a brother—and then his wife came, the daughter of Francesco Sforza, the bastard—and gradually he has lifted himself up from me. He has been cold and reserved; he begins to show himself master; and now I am nothing more than a citizen among citizens—the first, but not the equal of the master.'

Checco kept silence for a moment, and in his quietness I could see the violence of his emotion.

'This concerns you as well as me, Matteo. You are an Orsi, and the Orsi are not made to be servants. I will be no man's servant. When I think of this man—this bastard of a pope—treating me as beneath him, by God! I cannot breathe. I could roll on the floor and tear my hair with rage. Do you know that the Orsi have been great and rich for three hundred years? The Medici pale before them, for they are burghers and we have been always noble. We expelled the Ordelaffi because they wished to give us a bastard boy to rule over us, and shall we accept this Riario? I swear I will not endure it.'

'Well said!' said Matteo.

'Girolamo shall go as the Ordelaffi went. By God! I swear it.'

I looked at Matteo, and I saw that suddenly a passion had caught hold of him; his face was red, his eyes staring wide, and his voice was hoarse and thick.

'But do not mistake again, Checco,' he said; 'we want no foreign rulers. The Orsi must be the only Lords of Forli.'

Checco and Matteo stood looking at one another; then the former, shaking himself as if to regain his calmness, turned his back on us and left the room. Matteo strode up and down for a while in thought, and then, turning to me, said, ' Come.'

We went out and returned to our hostelry.

IV

NEXT day we went to Donna Giulia's.

'Who is she?' I asked Matteo, as we walked along.

'A widow!' he answered shortly.

'Further?' I asked.

'The scandal of Forli!'

'Most interesting; but how has she gained her reputation?'

'How do I know?' he answered, laughing; 'how do women usually gain their reputations? She drove Giovanni dall' Aste into his grave; her rivals say she poisoned him—but that is a cheerful libel, probably due to Claudia Piacentini.'

'How long has she been a widow?'

'Five or six years.'

'And how has she lived since then?'

Matteo shrugged his shoulders.

'As widows usually live!' he answered. 'For my part, I really cannot see what inducement a woman in that position has to be virtuous. After all, one is only young once, and had better make the best use of one's youth while it lasts.'

'But has she no relations?'

'Certainly; she has a father and two brothers. But they hear nothing or care nothing. Besides, it may be only scandal after all.'

'You talked as if it were a fact,' I said.

'Oh, no; I only say that if it is not a fact she is a very foolish woman. Now that she has a bad reputation, it would be idiotic not to live up to it.'

'You speak with some feeling,' I remarked, laughing.

'Ah,' answered Matteo, with another shrug of the shoulders, 'I laid siege to the fort of her virtue—and she sallied and retired, and mined and counter-mined, advanced and drew back, so that I grew weary and abandoned the attack. Life is not long enough to spend six months in politeness and flattery, and then not be sure of the reward at the end.'

'You have a practical way of looking at things.'

'With me, you know, one woman is very like another. It comes to the same in the end; and after one has kicked about the world for a few years, one arrives at the conclusion that it it does not much matter if they be dark or fair, fat or thin. . . .'

'Did you tell all this to Donna Giulia?' I asked.

'More or less.'

'What did she think of it?'

'She was cross for a while. She wished she had yielded sooner, when it was too late; it served her right!'

We had arrived at the house, and were ushered in. Donna Giulia greeted us very politely, gave me a glance, and began talking again to her friends. One could see that the men round her were more or less

C

in love, for they followed every motion with their
eyes, disputing her smiles, which she scattered in
profusion, now upon one, now upon another. . . .   I
saw she delighted in adulation, for the maker of any
neat compliment was always rewarded with a softer
look and a more charming smile.

Matteo surpassed the others in the outrageousness
of his flattery; I thought she must see that he was
laughing at her, but she accepted everything he said
quite seriously, and was evidently much pleased.

'Are you not glad to be back in Forli?' she said
to him.

'We all delight to tread the ground you walk on.'

'You have grown very polite during your absence.'

'What other result could have been, when I spent
my time thinking of the lovely Giulia.'

'I am afraid you had other thoughts in Naples:
they say that there the women are all beautiful.'

'Naples! My dear lady, I swear that during all
the time I have been away I have never seen a face
to compare with yours.'

Her eyes quite shone with pleasure. I turned
away, finding the conversation silly. I thought I
would do without the pleasant looks of Madonna
Giulia, and I decided not to come to her again.
Meanwhile, I began talking to one of the other
ladies in the room and passed the time agreeably
enough. . . . In a little while Giulia passed me,
leaning on the arm of one of her admirers. I
saw her glance at me, but I took no notice. Immediately afterwards she came again, hesitating a moment,
as if she wished to say something, but passed on
without speaking. I thought she was piqued at my

inattention to her, and, with a smile, redoubled my
attentions to the lady with whom I was talking.'

'Messer Filippo!' Donna Giulia called me, 'if you
are not too engaged, will you speak to me for one
moment?'

I approached her smiling.

'I am anxious to hear of your quarrel with Ercole
Piacentini. I have heard quite ten different stories.'

'I am surprised that the insolence of an ill-bred
fellow should rouse such interest.'

'We must talk of something in Forli. The only
thing I hear for certain is that he insulted you, and
you were prevented from getting satisfaction.'

'That will come later.'

She lowered her voice and took my arm.

'But my brother tells me that Checco d'Orsi has
made you promise to do nothing.'

'I shall get my revenge—having to wait for it will
only make it sweeter.'

Then, supposing she had nothing further to say to
me, I stood still, as if expecting her to leave me.
She looked up suddenly.

'Am I incommoding you?' she said.

'How could you!' I replied gallantly.

'I thought you wanted to get rid of me.'

'How can such an idea have entered your head?
Do you not see that all men lie humble at your
feet, attentive to every word and gesture?'

'Yes,' she answered, 'but not you!'

Of course I protested.

'Oh,' she said, 'I saw very well that you avoided
me. When you came in here—you hardly came
near me.'

'I did not think you would notice my inattention.'

'Certainly I noticed it; I was afraid I had offended you. I could not think how.'

'My dear lady, you have certainly done nothing to offend me.'

'Then, why do you avoid me?' she asked petulantly.

'Really,' I said, 'I don't. Perhaps in my modesty I thought it would be a matter of indifference to you whether I was at your side or not. I am sorry I have annoyed you.'

'I don't like people not to like me,' she said in a plaintive way.

'But why should you think I do not like you? Indeed, without flattery, I can assure you that I think you one of the most beautiful women I have ever seen.'

A faint blush came over her cheeks, and a smile broke out on her lips; she looked up at me with a pretty reproachful air.

'Then, why don't you let me see it more plainly?'

I smiled, and, looking into her eyes, was struck by their velvet softness. I almost thought she was as charming as she was beautiful.

'Do you really wish to know?' I said, in reply to her question.

'Do tell me!' she said, faintly pressing my arm.

'I thought you had so many admirers that you could well do without me.'

'But, you see,' she answered charmingly, 'I cannot!'

'And then I have a certain dislike to losing myself in a crowd. I did not wish to share your smiles with twenty others.'

'And would you for that refuse them altogether?'

'I have always avoided the woman who is the object of general admiration. I think I am too proud to struggle for favours; I would rather dispense with them.'

'But, then, supposing the lady wishes to favour you especially, you do not give her the opportunity.'

'That is so rare,' I replied, 'that it is not worth while breaking the rule.'

'But it may happen.'

I shrugged my shoulders. She paused a moment, and then said,—

'You do like me, then, after all?'

I saw a slight trembling of the lip, perhaps the eyes were a little moist. I felt sorry for what I had done.

'I fear I have given you pain,' I said.

'You have a little,' she replied.

'I am sorry. I thought you did not care.'

'I like people to love me and be pleased with me.'

'I do both!'

'Then you must show it,' she replied, a smile breaking through the beginning of tears.

I really had been brutal, and I was very sorry that I had caused a cloud to gather over her sunshiny nature. She was indeed very sweet and charming.

'Well, we are good friends now, aren't we?' she said.

'Of course.'

'And you'll come and see me often?'

'As often as you will allow me to,' I answered.

She gave me her hand to kiss, and a bright, happy smile lit up her face.

'*A rivederci !*' she said.

We went home, and Matteo found waiting for him a message from Checco, bidding him leave the inn and take up his quarters with me at the Palazzo Orsi. On arriving, we found Checco excitedly walking up and down a long corridor lined with statues and pictures.

'I am glad you have come,' he said to Matteo, taking his hand and nodding. 'You must stay here; we must all keep together now, for anything may happen.'

'What do you mean?' asked Matteo.

'The catastrophe nearly came to-day.'

We both looked at him with astonishment, not comprehending. Checco stood still abruptly.

'He tried to arrest me to-day—Girolamo!' Then, speaking very quickly, as if labouring under great excitement, 'I had to go to the Palace on business. I found him in the audience chamber, and we began to talk certain matters over, and I grew rather heated. Suddenly I noticed that the place had emptied itself. I stopped in the midst of my sentence and looked up at Girolamo. I saw he was not attending to me; his eyes were fixed on the door.'

Checco was silent, and drops of perspiration were standing on his forehead.

'Yes! Yes!' we both said eagerly.

'The door opened, and the Master of the Guard walked in. "By God!" I thought, "I'm trapped!" "I have been waiting for you, Andrea," said Girolamo. Then he turned to me, and said, "Come into the

Room of the Nymphs, Checco. I have some papers there to show you." He took hold of my arm. I loosed myself. " I pray you, excuse me," I said, " I have some very urgent business." I walked to the door. Andrea glanced at his master, and I thought he was going to bar my way; I think he was waiting for some sign, but before it came I had seen through the open door Paolo Bruni, and I called out, " Paolo, Paolo, wait for me. I want to talk to you urgently." Then I knew I was safe; he dared not touch me; and I turned round and said again, " I pray you, excuse me; my business with Paolo is a matter of life or death." I brushed past Andrea and got out. By Heaven! how I breathed when I found myself in the piazza!'

'But are you sure he meant to arrest you?' said Matteo.

'Certain; what else?'

'Andrea might have come in by accident. There may have been nothing in it at all.'

'I was not deceived,' answered Checco, earnestly. 'Their looks betrayed them—Andrea's questioning glance. I know he wants to kill me.'

'But would he dare seize you in cold blood?'

'He cares for nothing when he has an object in view. Besides, when he had me in his power, what could have been done? I know Girolamo too well. There would have been a mock trial, and I should have been condemned. Or else he would have me strangled in my cell, and when I had gone you would have been helpless—my father is too old, and there would have been no leader to the party but you— and what could you do alone?'

We all remained silent for a while, then Checco broke out.

'I know he wants to rid himself of me. He has threatened before, but has never gone so far as this.'

'I agree with you,' said Matteo; 'things are becoming grave.'

'It is not so much for myself I care; but what would happen to my children? My father is safe—he is so old and helpless that they would never think of touching him—but my boys? Caterina would throw them into prison without a scruple.'

'Well,' said Matteo, 'what will you do?'

'What can I do?' he answered. 'I have been racking my brains, and I see no way of safety. I can wear a coat of mail to preserve me from the stray knife of an assassin, but that will not help me against a troop of soldiers. I can leave Forli, but that is to abandon everything.'

'No, you must not leave Forli—anything but that!'

'What can I do? What can I do?' he stamped his foot on the ground as if almost in desperation.

'One thing,' said Matteo, 'you must not go about alone—always with at least two friends.'

'Yes, I have thought of that. But how will it all turn out; it cannot last. What can I do?'

He turned to me.

'What do you think?' he said. 'He means to kill me.'

'Why not anticipate him?' I answered quietly.

They both started up with a cry.

'Kill him!'

'Assassination! I dare not, I dare not,' said Checco, very excitedly. 'I will do all I can by fair means, but assassination—'

I shrugged my shoulders.

'It seems a matter of self-preservation,' I said.

'No, no; I won't speak of it! I won't think of it.' He began again to walk excitedly up and down the room. 'I won't think of it, I tell you. I could not.'

Neither Matteo nor I spoke.

'Why don't you speak?' he said to Matteo, impatiently.

'I am thinking,' he answered.

'Not of that; I forbid you to think of that. I will not have it.' Then, after a pause, abruptly, as if he were angry with us and with himself, 'Leave me!'

V

A FEW days later, Matteo came to me as I was dressing, having rescued my clothes from him.

'I wonder you're not ashamed to go out in those garments,' he remarked, 'people will say that you wear my old things.'

I took no notice of the insult.

'Where are you going?' he asked.

'To Madonna Giulia.'

'But you went there yesterday!'

'That is no reason why I should not go to-day. She asked me to come.'

'That's very obliging of her, I'm sure.' Then, after a pause, during which I continued my toilet, 'I have been gathering the news of Forli.'

'Oh!'

'Madonna Giulia has been affording a great deal of interest. . . .'

'You have been talking to the lady whom you call the beautiful Claudia,' I said.

'By the way, why have you not been to her?'

'I really don't know,' I said. 'Why should I?'

'You told me you had progressed a long way in

42

her favours during the half-hour's talk you had with her the other night; have you not followed up the advantage?'

I shrugged my shoulders.

'I don't think I like a woman to make all the advances.'

'Don't you?' said Matteo. 'I do!'

'Besides, I don't care for the type; she is too massive.'

'She feels very much hurt at your neglect. She says you have fallen in love with Giulia.'

'That is absurd,' I replied; 'and as to her being hurt at my neglect, I am very sorry, but I don't feel any obligation to throw myself into the arms of every woman who chooses to open them.'

'I quite agree with you; neither she nor Giulia are a bit better than they should be. I'm told Giulia's latest lover is Amtrogio della Treccia. It seems one day he was almost caught by old Bartolomeo, and had to slip out of the window and perform feats worthy of a professional acrobat to get out of the way.'

'I don't think I attach belief to all the scandal circulating on the subject of that lady.'

'You're not in love with her?' asked Matteo, quickly.

I laughed.

'Certainly not. But still—'

'That's all right; because, of course, you know it's notorious that she has had the most disgraceful amours. And she hasn't even kept them to her own class; all sorts of people have enjoyed her favours.'

'She does not look very much like a Messalina,'
I said, sneering a little.

'Honestly, Filippo, I do think she is really very
little better than a harlot.'

'You are extremely charitable,' I said. 'But don't
you think you are somewhat prejudiced by the fact
that you yourself did not find her one. Besides, her
character makes no particular difference to me; I
really care nothing if she's good or bad; she is agree-
able, and that is all I care about. She is not going
to be my wife.'

'She may make you very unhappy; you won't be
the first.'

'What a fool you are!' I said, a little angrily.
'You seem to think that because I go and see a
woman I must be dying of love for her. You are
absurd.'

I left him, and soon found myself at the Palazzo
Aste, where Donna Giulia was waiting for me. I
had been to see her nearly every day since my
arrival in Forli, for I really liked her. Naturally, I
was not in love with her as Matteo suggested, and
I had no intention of entering into that miserable
state. I had found her charmingly simple, very
different from the monster of dissipation she was
supposed to be. She must have been three or four-
and-twenty, but in all her ways she was quite girlish,
merry and thoughtless, full of laughter at one moment,
and then some trifling thing would happen to dis-
compose her and she would be brought to the verge
of tears; but a word or caress, even a compliment,
would make her forget the unhappiness which had
appeared so terrible, and in an instant she would be

wreathed in smiles. She seemed so delightfully
fragile, so delicate, so weak, that one felt it necessary
to be very gentle with her. I could not imagine how
anyone could use a hard word to her face.

Her eyes lit up as she saw me.

'How long you've been,' she said. 'I thought
you were never coming.'

She always seemed so glad so see you that you
thought she must have been anxiously awaiting you,
and that you were the very person of all others that
she wished to have with her. Of course, I knew it
was an affectation, but it was a very charming one.

'Come and sit by me here,' she said, making room
for me on a couch; then when I had sat down, she
nestled close up to me in her pretty childish way, as
if seeking protection. 'Now, tell me all you've been
doing.'

'I've been talking to Matteo,' I said.

'What about?'

'You.'

'Tell me what he said.'

'Nothing to your credit, my dear,' I said, laughing.

'Poor Matteo,' she answered. 'He's such a clumsy,
lumbering creature, one can see he's spent half his
life in camps.'

'And I? I have spent the same life as Matteo.
Am I a clumsy, lumbering creature?'

'Oh, no,' she answered, 'you are quite different.'
She put the pleasantest compliments in the look of
her eyes.

'Matteo told me all sorts of scandal about you.'
She blushed a little.

'Did you believe it?'

'I said I did not much care if it were true or not.'

'But do you believe it?' she asked, insisting.

'If you'll tell me it is not true, I will believe absolutely what you say.'

The little anxious look on her face gave way to a bright smile.

'Of course, it is not true.'

'How beautiful you are when you smile,' I remarked irrelevantly. 'You should always smile.'

'I always do on you,' she answered. She opened her mouth, as if about to speak, held back, as if unable to make up her mind, then said, 'Did Matteo tell you he made love to me once, and was very angry because I would not pick up the handkerchief which he had condescended to throw.'

'He mentioned it.'

'Since then, I am afraid he has not had very much good to say of me.'

I had thought at the time that Matteo was a little bitter in his account of Donna Giulia, and I felt more inclined to believe her version of the story than his.

'He has been beseeching me not to fall in love with you,' I said.

She laughed.

'Claudia Piacentini has been telling everyone that it is too late, and she is horribly jealous.'

'Has she? Matteo also seemed certain I was in love with you.'

'And are you?' she asked suddenly.

'No!' I replied with great promptness.

'*Brutta bestia!*' she said, throwing herself to the end of the couch, and beginning to pout.

'I am very sorry,' I said, laughing, 'but I cannot help it.'

'I think it is horrid of you,' she remarked.

'You have so many adorers,' I said in expostulation.

'Yes, but I want more,' she smiled.

'But what good can it do you to have all these people in love with you?'

'I don't know,' she said, 'it is a pleasant sensation.

'What a child you are!' I answered, laughing.

She bent forward seriously.

'But are you not at all in love with me?'

I shook my head. She came close up to me, so that her hair brushed lightly against my cheek; it sent a shiver through me. I looked at her tiny ear; it was beautifully shaped, transparent as a pink shell. Unconsciously, quite without intention, I kissed it. She pretended to take no notice, and I was full of confusion. I felt myself blushing furiously.

'Are you quite sure?' she said gravely.

I got up to go, foolishly, rather angry with myself.

'When shall I see you again?' I asked.

'I am going to confession to-morrow. Be at San Stefano at ten, and we can have a little talk in the church when I have finished.'

VI

THERE had been a great commotion in Forli during the last two days; for it had become known that the country people of the Count's domain had sent a petition for the removal of certain taxes which pressed so heavily upon them, that the land was speedily going to ruin. The proprietors were dismissing their labourers, the houses of the peasants were falling into decay, and in certain districts the poverty had reached such a height that the farmers had not even grain wherewith to sow their fields, and all around the ground was lying bare and desolate. A famine had been the result, and if the previous year the countrymen had found it difficult to pay their taxes, this year they found it impossible. Girolamo had listened to their arguments, and knew them to be true. After considering with his councillors, he had resolved to remit certain of the more oppressive taxes; but in doing this he was confronted with the fact that his Treasury was already empty, and that if the income were further diminished it would be impossible for him to meet the demands of the coming year.

It was clear that the country could not pay, and it was clear that the money must be procured. He set his eyes on the town, and saw that it was rich and flourishing, but he dared not, on his own initiative, propose any increase in its burdens. He called a council, showed the state of his affairs, and asked the elders for advice. No one stirred or spoke. At last Antonio Lassi, a creature of the Count, whom he had raised to the council from a humble position, rose to his feet and gave utterance to the plan which his master had suggested to him. The pith of it was to abrogate the taxes on the country people, and in compensation place others on certain food-stuffs and wines, which had previously gone free. Girolamo answered in a studied speech, pretending great unwillingness to charge what were the necessaries of life, and asked several of the more prominent members what they thought of the suggestion. They had met Antonio Lassi's speech with silence, and now applauded Girolamo's answer; they agreed with him that such taxes should not be. Then the Count changed his tone. He said it was the only means of raising the money, and gathering anger from their sullen looks and their silence, he told them that if they would not give their sanction to the decree, he would do without their sanction. Then, breaking short, he asked them for their answer. The councillors looked at one another, rather pale but determined; and the reply came from one after the other, quietly,—

'No—no—no!'

Antonio Lassi was cowed, and dared not give his answer at all. The Count, with an oath, beat his fist

D

on the table and said, ' I am determined to be lord
and master here; and you shall learn, all of you, that
my will is law.'

With that he dismissed them.

When the people heard the news, there was great
excitement. The murmurs against the Count, which
had hitherto been cautiously expressed, were now
cried out in the market-place; the extravagance of
the Countess was bitterly complained of, and the
townsmen gathered together in groups, talking
heatedly of the proposed exaction, occasionally breaking out into open menace. It was very like sedition. .

On the day after the council, the head of the
customs had been almost torn to pieces by the
people as he was walking towards the Palace, and
on his way back he was protected by a troop of
soldiers. Antonio Lassi was met everywhere with
hoots and cries, and Checco d'Orsi, meeting him in
the loggia of the piazza, had assailed him with
taunts and bitter sarcasms. Ercole Piacentini interposed and the quarrel nearly ended in a brawl; but
Checco, with difficulty restraining himself, withdrew
before anything happened. . . .

On leaving Donna Giulia, I walked to the piazza
and found the same restlessness as on the preceding
days. Through all these people a strange commotion seemed to pass, a tremor like the waves of
the sea; everywhere little knots of people were
listening eagerly to some excited speaker; no one
seemed able to work; the tradesmen were gathered
at their doors talking with one another; idlers were
wandering to and fro, now joining themselves to one
group, now to another.

Suddenly there was a silence; part of the crowd began looking eagerly in one direction, and the rest in their curiosity surged to the end of the piazza to see what was happening. Then it was seen that Caterina was approaching. She entered the place, and all eyes were fixed upon her. As usual, she was magnificently attired; her neck and hands and arms, her waistband and headgear, shone with jewels; she was accompanied by several of her ladies and two or three soldiers as guard. The crowd separated to let her pass, and she walked proudly between the serried rows of people, her head uplifted and her eyes fixed straight in front, as if she were unaware that anyone was looking at her. A few obsequiously took off their hats, but most gave no greeting; all around her was silence, a few murmurs, an oath or two muttered under breath, but that was all. She walked steadily on, and entered the Palace gates. At once a thousand voices burst forth, and after the deadly stillness the air seemed filled with confused sounds. Curses and imprecations were hurled on her from every side; they railed at her pride, they called her foul names. . . . Six years before, when she happened to cross the streets, the people had hurried forward to look at her, with joy in their hearts and blessings on their lips. They vowed they would die for her, they were in ecstasies at her graciousness.

I went home thinking of all these things and of Donna Giulia. I was rather amused at my unintentional kiss; I wondered if she was thinking of me. . . . She really was a charming creature, and

I was glad at the idea of seeing her again on the morrow. I liked her simple, fervent piety. She was in the habit of going regularly to mass, and happening to see her one day, I was struck with her devout air, full of faith; she also went to confessional frequently. It was rather absurd to think she was the perverse being people pretended. . . .

When I reached the Palazzo Orsi I found the same excitement as outside in the piazza. Girolamo had heard of the dispute in the loggia, and had sent for Checco to hear his views on the subject of the tax. The audience was fixed for the following morning at eleven, and as Checco never went anywhere without attendants, Scipione Moratini, Giulia's second brother, and I were appointed to accompany him. Matteo was not to go for fear of the presence of the two most prominent members of the family tempting the Count to some sudden action.

The following morning I arrived at San Stefano at half-past nine, and to my surprise found Giulia waiting for me.

'I did not think you would be out of the confessional so soon,' I said. 'Were your sins so small this week?'

'I haven't been,' she answered. 'Scipione told me that you and he were to accompany Checco to the Palace, and I thought you would have to leave here early, so I postponed the confessional.'

'You have preferred earth and me to Heaven and the worthy father?'

'You know I would do more for you than that,' she answered.

'You witch!'

She took my arm.

'Come,' she said, 'come and sit in one of the transept chapels; it is quiet and dark there.'

It was deliciously cool. The light came dimly through the coloured glass, clothing the marble of the chapel in mysterious reds and purples, and the air was faintly scented with incense. Sitting there she seemed to gain a new charm. Before, I had never really appreciated the extreme beauty of the brown hair tinged with red, its wonderful quality and luxuriance. I tried to think of something to say, but could not. I sat and looked at her, and the perfumes of her body blended with the incense.

'Why don't you speak?' she said.

'I'm sorry; I have nothing to say.'

She laughed.

'Tell me of what you are thinking.'

'I daren't,' I said.

She looked at me, repeating the wish with her eyes.

'I was thinking you were very beautiful.'

She turned to me and leant forward so that her face was close to mine; her eyes acquired a look of deep, voluptuous languor. We sat without speaking, and my head began to whirl.

The clock struck ten.

'I must go,' I said, breaking the silence.

'Yes,' she answered, 'but come to-night and tell me what has happened.'

I promised I would, then asked whether I should lead her to another part of the church.

'No, leave me here,' she said. 'It is so good and quiet. I will stay and think.'

'Of what?' I said.

She did not speak, but she smiled so that I understood her answer.

VII

I HURRIED back to the Palazzo and found Scipione
Moratini already arrived. I liked him for his sister's
sake, but in himself he was a pleasant person.

Both he and his brother had something of Giulia in
them—the delicate features, the fascination and the
winning ways which in them seemed almost effemi-
nate. Their mother had been a very beautiful
woman—report said somewhat gay—and it was from
her the sons had got the gallantry which made them
the terror of husbands in Forli, and Giulia the coquetry
which had given rise to so much scandal. The father,
Bartolomeo, was quite different. He was a rugged,
upright man of sixty, very grave and very digni-
fied, the only resemblance of feature to his children
being the charming smile, which the sons possessed
as well as Giulia; though in him it was rarely seen.
What I liked most in him was the blind love for his
daughter, leading him to unbend and become a youth
to flatter her folly. He was really devoted to her, so
that it was quite pathetic to see the look of intense
affection in his eyes as he followed her movements.
He, of course, had never heard a word of the rumours
circulating about Giulia; he had the utmost faith in

. 55

her virtue, and I, it seems to me, had gained faith from him.

After talking a while with Scipione, Checco came, and we started for the Palazzo. The people in Forli know everything, and were well aware of Checco's mission. As we walked along we were met by many kind greetings, good luck, and God speed were wished us, and Checco, beaming with joy, graciously returned the salutations.

We were ushered into the council chamber, where we found the councillors and many of the more prominent citizens, and several gentlemen of the Court; immediately the great folding doors were opened and Girolamo entered with his wonted state, accompanied by his courtiers and men-at-arms, so that the hall was filled with them. He took his seat on a throne, and graciously bowed to the left and to the right. His courtiers responded, but the citizens preserved a severe aspect, quite unsympathetic towards his condescension.

Girolamo rose to his feet and made a short speech, in which he extolled Checco's wisdom and knowledge and patriotism, saying he had heard of a controversy between him and Antonio Lassi on the subject of the proposed tax, and consequently had sent for him to hear his opinion on the subject.

He stopped and looked round; his courtiers obsequiously applauded. Then, at opposite ends of the room, doors opened, and through each filed a string of soldiers; the citizens looked at one another, wondering. A flourish of trumpets was heard in the piazza outside, and the tramp of soldiers. Girolamo waited; at last he proceeded,—

'A good prince owes this to his subjects—to do nothing against their will freely expressed; and though I could command, for I am placed here by the Vicar of Christ himself, with absolute power over your lives and fortunes, yet such is my love and affection towards you that I do not disdain to ask your advice.'

The courtiers broke out into a murmur of surprise and self-congratulation at his infinite graciousness; the trumpets flourished again, and in the succeeding silence could be heard cries of command from the officers in the square, while from the soldiers standing about the hall there was a clank of swords and spurs.

Checco rose from his seat. He was pale and he almost seemed to hesitate; I wondered if the soldiers had had the effect which Girolamo intended. Then he began to speak, quietly, in even, well-turned sentences, so that one could see the speech had been carefully thought out.

He called to mind his own affection for Girolamo, and the mutual friendship which had solaced many hours of doubt and difficulty, and assured him of his unalterable fidelity to himself and his family; then he reminded him of the love borne by the people towards their ruler, and their consciousness of an equal love on the part of the Count towards themselves. He drew a picture of the joy in Forli when first Girolamo came to it, and of the enthusiasm caused by the sight of him or his wife walking through the streets.

There was a little applause, chiefly from the Count's suite; Checco paused as if he had come to the end of his preface, and were gathering himself up

for the real matter of his speech. There was deadly
silence in the hall, all eyes were fixed on him, and all
minds were asking themselves, 'What will he say?'
Girolamo was leaning forward, resting his chin on his
hand, looking anxious. I wondered if he regretted
that he had called the meeting.

Checco resumed his speech.

'Girolamo,' he said, 'the people from the country
districts lately sent you a petition, in which they
showed their sufferings from rain and storm and
famine, their poverty and misery, the oppressiveness
of the taxes. They bade you come and look at their
untilled fields, their houses falling to ruin, themselves
dying by the roadside, naked and hungry, children
expiring at their mothers' breasts, parents lying un-
buried in the ruin of their home. They bade you
come and look at the desolation of the land, and
implored you to help them while there was yet time,
and lighten from their backs the burdens you had
laid upon them.

'You turned an eye of pity on them ; and now the
land smiles, the people have shaken themselves from
their sleep of death, and awakened to new life, and
everywhere prayers are offered and blessings rained
on the head of the most high and magnificent prince,
Girolamo Riario.

'And we too, my Lord, join in the thanks and
·praise ; for these to whom you have given new life
are our cousins and brothers, our fellow-countrymen.'

What was coming? The councillors looked at one
another questioningly. Could Checco have made
terms with the Count, and was it a comedy they
were playing? Girolamo also was surprised ; he

had not for long heard praise from any but his
courtiers.

'Eight years ago, when you acquired the sovereignty of Forli, you found the town weighed down
under the taxes which the Ordelaffi had imposed.
Depression had seized hold of the merchants and
tradesmen; they were burdened so that they could
not buy nor sell; they had given up effort, and the
town was lying numb and cold, as if dying from a
pestilence. The streets were deserted; such people
as there were moved sadly, and with downturned
faces. The inhabitants were becoming fewer; there
was no motion, no life; a few years more and Forli
would have become a city of the dead!

'But you came, and with you life; for your first
deed was to remove the most oppressive imposts.
As the bow, doubled up, when the string is loosened
shoots back with a sudden impulse which propels the
arrow to its mark, so Forli rebounded from the weight
it had borne before. The Goddess of Plenty reigned
in the land; it was the sunlight after storm; everywhere life and activity! The merchant wrote busily
at his desk, the tradesman spread his wares anew and
laughed in the joy of his heart. The mason, the
builder, the blacksmith returned to their work, and
through the city was heard the sound of hammering
and building. The news spread of a beneficent lord,
and the goldsmith and silversmith, the painter, the
sculptor, came to the city in throngs. The money
passed from hand to hand, and in its passage seemed
to increase by magic. On the faces of all was happiness; the apprentice sang as he worked, and mirth
and joy were universal; Forli became known as the

home of delight; Italy rang with its feasts and cele-
brations—and every citizen was proud to be a
Forlivese.

'And everywhere prayers were offered and blessings rained on the head of the most high and magnificent prince, Girolamo Riario.'

Checco paused again. An inkling of his meaning
was coming to his hearers, but they dared not think
he would say what was in all their minds.

'Then,' Checco went on, 'you re-imposed the taxes
which you had taken off.'

'That is a lie!' interrupted Girolamo. 'They were
imposed by the council.'

Checco shrugged his shoulders, smiling ironically.

'I remember quite well. You called a meeting
of the Ancients, and showing them your necessities, suggested that they should re-impose the
taxes.

'I forget if you reminded them that you could
command, and that you were placed here by the
Vicar of Christ on earth.

'And you forebore to let us hear the ring of
trumpets and the tramp of soldiery in the square.
Nor did you think so numerous a suite necessary
for your dignity.'

He looked round at the soldiers, thoughtfully
stroking his beard.

'Proceed!' said Girolamo, impatiently; he was
beginning to get angry.

Checco, in talking, had recovered the assurance
which at first seemed to fail him. He smiled politely
at the Count's command, and said,—

'I will come to the point at once.

'You replaced the taxes which you had taken away, and thereby undid the benefit you had done. The town soon felt the effect of the change; its prosperity is already declining, and it is not doubtful that a few years more will bring it to the condition in which you found it. And who knows, perhaps its last state may be worse than its first?

'And now you propose to make the townspeople pay the duties which you have taken off the country-folk. You have sent for me to ask my advice on the subject, and here I give it you.

'Do not put on, but take off. In the name of the people, I beseech you to do away with the taxes you imposed four years ago, and return to the happy state of the first years of your rule.'

He paused a moment, then with outstretched arm, pointing to the Count, he added solemnly, 'Or Girolamo Riario, the magnificent prince, may share the fate of the Ordelaffi, who ruled the town for two centuries and now wander homeless about the land.'

There was a cry all round the room. They were astounded at his audacity. Girolamo had started in his chair—his eyes were staring, his face red; he was dumb with rage. He tried to speak, but the words died in his throat, and nothing was heard but an inarticulate murmur. The soldiers and courtiers were looking at one another in surprise; they did not know what to do or think; they looked at their master, but found no help in him. The citizens were bewildered, and by turns felt wonder, dismay, fear, pleasure; they could not understand . . .

'Oh, Girolamo!' said Checco, unmindful of the

excitement round him, 'I do not say these things in enmity to you. Come among your people yourself, and see their wants with your own eyes. Do not believe what your courtiers tell you—do not think the land in your charge is a captured town, which you can spoil at your pleasure. You have been placed here as a guardian in our perils and an assistance in our necessities.

'You are a stranger here; you do not know this people as I know it. They will be faithful, meek, obedient—but do not rob them of the money they have hardly earned, or they will turn against you. Forli has never supported an oppressor, and if you oppress them, beware of their wrath. What do you think are these soldiers of yours against the wrath of a people! And are you so sure of your soldiers? Will they take part for you against their fathers and brothers, their children?'

'Be quiet!' Girolamo had risen from his seat, and was standing with his arm threateningly upraised. He shouted so as to drown Checco, 'Be quiet! You have always been against me, Checco,' he cried. 'You have hated me because I have overwhelmed you with bounty. There has never been trouble between me and my people but you have come to make them more bitter against me.'

'You lie!' said Checco, passionately.

'Oh, I know you, Checco, and your pride! As Satan fell by pride, so may you, notwithstanding all your riches and power. You thought you were my equal, and because you found me your master you gnashed your teeth and cursed me.

'By God, you would kill me if you could!'

Checco lost his calm, and gesticulating wildly shouted back at Girolamo.

'I have hated you because you are a tyrant to this town. Are these not my fellow-citizens, my brothers, my friends? Have we not been together since childhood, and our fathers and grandfathers before us? And do you think I look upon them as you who are a stranger?

'No; so long as you obtained money from the rich, I said nothing. You know what sums I have myself lent you; all that I freely give you. I do not want a penny of it back—keep it all. But when you have extorted the uttermost from us, and you turn to the poor and needy and rob them of their little, then I will not keep silence. You shall not impose these taxes on the people! And why is it you want them? For your riotous, insane extravagance; so that you may build yourself new palaces, and deck yourself in gorgeous robes, and buy diamonds and precious stones for your wife.'

'Do not speak of my wife,' interrupted the Count.

'So that you may pile gold in the hands of the parasite who makes a sonnet in your praise. You came to us and begged for money; we gave it and you flung it away in feasts and riotry. The very coat you wear was made out of our riches. But you have no right to take the money of the people for these ignoble uses. You are not their master; you are their servant; their money is not yours, but yours is theirs. Your duty before God is to protect them, and, instead, you rob them.'

'Be silent!' broke in Girolamo. 'I will hear no more. You have outraged me as no man has ever done without repenting it. You think you are all-powerful, Checco, but by God you shall find that I am more powerful!

'Now go, all of you! I have had enough of this scene. Go!'

He waved his hand imperiously. Then, with a look of intense rage, he descended from his throne and, scowling, flung himself out of the room.

VIII

THE courtiers followed on their master's heels, but the soldiers stood undecided. ·Ercole Piacentini looked at us, and spoke in an undertone to the Captain of the Guard. I thought they were discussing the possibility of boldly arresting Checco on the spot, which they doubtless knew would be a step very acceptable to Girolamo; but he was surrounded by his friends, and evidently, whatever Ercole and the Captain wished, they dared nothing, for the former quietly left the chamber, and the soldiers, on a whispered order, slid silently from the room like whipped dogs.

Then the excitement of our friends knew no bounds. I, at the end of the speech, had seized his hand and said,—

'Well done.'

Now he was standing in the midst of all these people, happy and smiling, proud of the enthusiasm he had aroused, breathing heavily, so that a casual observer might have thought him drunk with wine.

'My friends,' he said, in answer to their praises, and his voice slightly trembled, so that his sincerity was conspicuous, 'whatever happens, be sure that I

E

will continue to uphold your rights, and that I will willingly give my life for the cause of justice and freedom.'

He was choked by the violence of his emotion, and could say nothing more.

The cries of approbation were renewed, and then, with an impulse to get into the open air, they surged out of the council chamber into the piazza. It was not exactly known what had passed in the Palace, but the people knew that Checco had braved the Count, and that the latter had broken up the meeting in anger. Wonderful rumours were going about : it was said that swords had been drawn, and there had almost been a battle; others said that the Count had tried to arrest Checco, and this story, gaining credence—some even saying that Checco was being kept a prisoner—had worked the citizens to fever height.

When Checco appeared, there was a great shout and a rush towards him. 'Bravo!' 'Well done!' I don't know what they did not find to say in praise of him. Their enthusiasm grew by its own fire; they went mad; they could not contain themselves, and they looked about for something on which to vent their feeling. A word, and they would have attacked the Palace or sacked the custom - house. They surrounded us, and would not let us pass. Bartolomeo Moratini pushed his way to Checco and said,—

'Quiet them quickly, before it is too late.'

Checco understood at once. 'Friends,' he said, 'let me pass quietly, for the love of God, and do you return to your work in peace. Let me pass!'

Moving forward, the crowd opened to him, and still shouting, yelling and gesticulating, allowed him to go through. When we arrived at the gate of his palace, he turned to me and said,—

'By God! Filippo, this is life. I shall never forget this day!'

The crowd had followed to the door, and would not go away. Checco had to appear on the balcony and bow his thanks. As he stood there, I could see that his head was whirling. He was pale, almost senseless with his great joy.

At last the people were persuaded to depart, and we entered the house.

We were in Checco's private room. Besides the cousins and myself were present Bartolomeo Moratini and his two sons, Fabio Oliva and Cesare Gnocchi, both related on the mother's side to the Orsi. We were all restless and excited, discussing the events that had occurred; only Bartolomeo was quiet and grave. Matteo, in the highest of spirits, turned to him.

'Why so silent, Messer Bartolomeo?' he said. 'You are like the skeleton at the banquet.'

'It is a matter for gravity,' he answered.

'Why?'

'Why! Good God, man, do you suppose nothing has happened!'

We stopped talking and stood round him, as if suddenly awakened.

'Our ships are burnt behind us,' he proceeded, 'and we must advance—must!'

What do you mean?' said Checco.

'Do you suppose Girolamo is going to allow things to go on as before? You must be mad, Checco!

'I believe I am,' was the answer. 'All this has turned my head. Go on.'

'Girolamo has only one step open to him now. You have braved him publicly; you have crossed the streets in triumph, amid the acclamation of the people, and they have accompanied you to your house with shouts of joy. Girolamo sees in you a rival—and from a rival there is only one safeguard.'

'And that—?' asked Checco.

'Is death!'

We were all silent for a moment; then Bartolomeo spoke again.

'He cannot allow you to live. He has threatened you before, but now he must carry his threats into effect. Take care!'

'I know,' said Checco, 'the sword is hanging over my head . But he dare not arrest me.'

'Perhaps he will try assassination. You must go out well guarded.'

'I do,' said Checco, 'and I wear a coat of mail. The fear of assassination has been haunting me for weeks. Oh God, it is terrible! I could bear an open foe. I have courage as much as anyone; but this perpetual suspense! I swear to you it is making me a coward. I cannot turn the corner of a street without thinking that my death may be on the other side; I cannot go through a dark corridor at night without thinking that over there in the darkness my murderer may be waiting for me. I start at the slightest sound, the banging of a door, a sudden step. And I awake in the night with a cry, sweating. I cannot stand it. I shall go mad if it continues. What can I do?'

Matteo and I looked at one another; we had the same thought. Bartolomeo spoke.

'Anticipate him!'

We both started, for they were my very words. Checco gave a cry.

'You too! That thought has been with me night and day! Anticipate him! Kill him! But I dare not think of it. I cannot kill him.'

'You must,' said Bartolomeo.

'Take care we are not heard,' said Oliva.

'The doors are well fastened.'

'You must,' repeated Bartolomeo. 'It is the only course left you. And what is more, you must make haste—for he will not delay. The lives of all of us are at stake. He will not be satisfied with you; after you are gone, he will easily enough find means to get rid of us.'

'Hold your peace, Bartolomeo, for God's sake! It is treachery.'

'Of what are you frightened? It would not be difficult.'

'No, we must have no assassination! It always turns out badly. The Pazzi in Florence were killed, Salviati was hanged from the Palace windows, and Lorenzo is all-powerful, while the bones of the conspirators rot in unconsecrated ground. And at Milan, when they killed the Duke, not one of them escaped.'

'They were fools. We do not mistake as in Florence; we have the people with us, and we shall not bungle it as they did.'

'No, no, it cannot be.'

'I tell you it must.   It is our only safety!'

Checco looked round anxiously.

'We are all safe,' said Oliva.   'Have no fear.'

'What do you think of it?' asked Checco.   'I know what you think, Filippo, and Matteo.'

'I think with my father!' said Scipione.

'I too!' said his brother.

'And I!'

'And I!'

'Every one of you,' said Checco; 'you would have me murder him.'

'It is just and lawful.'

'Remember that he was my friend.   I helped him to this power.   Once we were almost brothers.'

'But now he is your deadly enemy.   He is sharpening a knife for your heart—and if you do not kill him, he will kill you.'

'It is treachery.   I cannot!'

'When a man has killed another, the law kills him.   It is a just revenge.   When a man attempts another's life, the law permits him to kill that man in self-defence.   Girolamo has killed you in thought —and at this moment he may be arranging the details of your murder.   It is just and lawful that you take his life to defend your own and ours.'

'Bartolomeo is right,' said Matteo.

A murmur of approval showed what the others thought.

'But think, Bartolomeo,' said Checco, 'you are grey-headed; you are not so very far from the tomb; if you killed this man, what of afterwards?'

'I swear to you, Checco, that you would be a

minister of God's vengeance. Has he not madly oppressed the people? What right has he more than another? Through him men and women and children have died of want; unhappiness and misery have gone through the land—and all the while he has been eating and drinking and making merry.'

'Make up your mind, Checco. You must give way to us!' said Matteo. 'Girolamo has failed in every way. On the score of honesty and justice he must die. And to save us he must die.'

'You drive me mad,' said Checco. 'All of you are against me. You are right in all you say, but I cannot—oh God, I cannot!'

Bartolomeo was going to speak again, but Checco interrupted him.

'No, no, for Heaven's sake, say nothing more. Leave me alone. I want to be quiet and think.'

IX

IN the evening at ten I went to the Palazzo Aste.
The servant who let me in told me that Donna
Giulia was at her father's, and he did not know
when she would be back. I was intensely disappointed. I had been looking forward all day to
seeing her, for the time in church had been so
short. . . . The servant looked at me as if
expecting me to go away, and I hesitated; but
then I had such a desire to see her that I told
him I would wait.

I was shown into the room I already knew so
well, and I sat down in Giulia's chair. I rested
my head on the cushions which had pressed against
her beautiful hair, her cheek; and I inhaled the
fragrance which they had left behind them.

How long she was! Why did she not come?

I thought of her sitting there. In my mind I saw
the beautiful, soft brown eyes, the red lips; her mouth
was exquisite, very delicately shaped, with wonderful
curves. It was for such a mouth as hers that the
simile of Cupid's bow had been invented.

I heard a noise below, and I went to the door to

listen.   My heart beat violently, but, alas! it was not
she, and, bitterly disappointed, I returned to the chair.
I thought I had been waiting hours, and every hour
seemed a day.   Would she never come ?

At last!   The door opened, and she came in—so
beautiful.   She gave me both her hands.

' I am sorry you have had to wait,' she said, ' but I
could not help it.'

' I would wait a hundred years to see you for an
hour.'

She sat down, and I lay at her feet.

' Tell me,' she said, ' all that has happened to-day.'

I did as she asked; and as I gave my story, her
eyes sparkled and her cheeks flushed.   I don't know
what came over me ; I felt a sensation of swooning,
and at the same time I caught for breath.   And I had
a sudden impulse to take her in my arms and kiss her
many times.

' How lovely you are!' I said, raising myself to her
side.

She did not answer, but looked at me, smiling.   Her
eyes glistened with tears, her bosom heaved.

' Giulia ! '

I put my arm round her, and took her hands in mine.

' Giulia, I love you ! '

She bent over to me, and put forward her face ; and
then—then I took her in my arms and covered her
mouth with kisses.   Oh God!   I was mad, I had
never tasted such happiness before.   Her beautiful
mouth, it was so soft, so small, I gasped in the agony
of my happiness.   If I could only have died then !

Giulia ! Giulia !

The cock crew, and the night seemed to fade away into greyness. The first light of dawn broke through the windows, and I pressed my love to my heart in one last kiss.

'Not yet,' she said; 'I love you.'

I could not speak; I kissed her eyes, her cheeks, her breasts.

'Don't go,' she said.

'My love!'

At last I tore myself away, and as I gave her the last kiss of all, she whispered,—

'Come soon.'

And I replied,—

'To-night!'

I walked through the grey streets of Forli, wondering at my happiness; it was too great to realise. It seemed absurd that I, a poor, commonplace man, should be chosen out for this ecstasy of bliss. I had been buffeted about the world, an exile, wandering here and there in search of a captain under whom to serve. I had had loves before, but common, grotesque things—not like this, pure and heavenly. With my other loves I had often felt a certain ugliness about them; they had seemed sordid and vulgar; but this was so pure, so clean! She was so saintly and innocent. Oh, it was good! And I laughed at myself for thinking I was not in love with her. I had loved her always; when it began I did not know . . . and I did not care; all that interested me now was to think of myself, loving and beloved. I was not worthy of her; she was so good, so kind, and I a poor, mean wretch. I felt her a goddess, and I could have knelt down and worshipped her.

I walked through the streets of Forli with swinging steps ; I breathed in the morning air, and felt so strong, and well, and young. Everything was beautiful—all life ! The grey walls enchanted me ; the sombre carvings of the churches ; the market women, gaily dressed, entering the town laden with baskets of many-coloured fruit. They gave me greeting, and I answered with a laughing heart. How kind they were ! Indeed, my heart was so full of love that it welled over and covered everything and everybody, so that I felt a strange, hearty kindness to all around me. I loved mankind !

X

When I got home, I threw myself on my bed and enjoyed a delightful sleep, and when I awoke felt cool and fresh, and very happy.

'What is the matter with you?' asked Matteo.

'I am rather contented with myself,' I said.

'Then, if you want to make other people contented, you had better come with me to Donna Claudia.'

'The beautiful Claudia?'

'The same!'

'But can we venture in the enemy's camp?'

'That is exactly why I want you to come. The idea is to take no notice of the events of yesterday, and that we should all go about as if nothing had happened.'

'But Messer Piacentini will not be very glad to see us.'

'He will be grinding his teeth, and inwardly spitting fire; but he will take us to his arms and embrace us, and try to make us believe he loves us with the most Christian affection.'

'Very well; come on!'

Donna Claudia, at all events, was delighted to see

us, and she began making eyes and sighing, and
putting her hand to her bosom in the most affecting
manner.

'Why have you not been to see me, Messer Filippo?'
she asked.

'Indeed, madam, I was afraid of being intrusive.'

'Ah,' she said, with a sweeping glance, 'how could
you be! No, there was another reason for your
absence. Alas!'

'I dared not face those lustrous eyes.'

She turned them full on me, and then turned them
up, Madonna-wise, showing the whites.

'Are they so cruel, do you think?'

'They are too brilliant. How dangerous to the
moth is the candle; and in this case the candle is
twain.'

'But they say the moth as it flutters in the flame
enjoys a perfection of ecstasy.'

'Ah, but I am a very sensible moth,' I answered in
a matter-of-fact tone, 'and I am afraid of burning my
wings.'

'How prosaic!' she murmured.

'The muse,' I said politely, 'loses her force when
you are present.'

She evidently did not quite understand what I
meant, for there was a look of slight bewilderment
in her eyes; and I was not surprised, for I had not
myself the faintest notion of my meaning. Still she
saw it was a compliment.

'Ah, you are very polite!'

We paused a moment, during which we both looked
unutterable things at one another. Then she gave a
deep sigh.

'Why so sad, sweet lady?' I asked.

'Messer Filippo,' she answered, 'I am an unhappy woman.' She hit her breast with her hand.

'You are too beautiful,' I remarked gallantly.

'Ah no! ah no! I am unhappy.'

I glanced at her husband, who was stalking grimly about the room, looking like a retired soldier with the gout; and I thought that to be in the society of such a person was enough to make anyone miserable.

'You are right,' she said, following my eyes; 'it is my husband. He is so unsympathetic.'

I condoled with her.

'He is so jealous of me, and, as you know, I am a pattern of virtue to Forli!'

I had never heard her character so described, but, of course, I said,—

'To look at you would be enough to reassure the most violent of husbands.'

'Oh, I have temptation enough, I assure you,' she answered quickly.

'I can well believe that.'

'But I am as faithful to him as if I were old and ugly; and yet he is jealous.'

'We all have our crosses in this life,' I remarked sententiously.

'Heaven knows I have mine; but I have my consolations.'

So I supposed, and answered,—

'Oh!'

'I pour out my soul in a series of sonnets.'

'A second Petrarch!'

'My friends say some of them are not unworthy of that great name.'

' I can well believe it.'

Here relief came, and like the tired sentinel, I left the post of duty. I thought of my sweet Giulia, and wondered at her beauty and charm; it was all so much clearer and cleaner than the dross I saw around me. I came away, for I was pining for solitude, and then I gave myself up to the exquisite dreams of my love.

At last the time came, the long day had at last worn away, and the night, the friend of lovers, gave me leave to go to Giulia.

XI

I WAS so happy. The world went on; things happened in Forli, the rival parties agitated and met together and discussed; there was a general ferment—and to it all I was profoundly indifferent. What matter all the petty little affairs of life? I said. People work and struggle, plot, scheme, make money, lose it, conspire for place and honour; they have their ambitions and hopes; but what is it all beside love? I had entered into the excitement of politics in Forli; I was behind the veil and knew the intricacies, the ambitions, the emotions of the actors; but now I withdrew myself. What did I care about the prospects of Forli, whether taxes were put on or taken off, or whether A killed B or B killed A, it really seemed so unimportant. I looked upon them as puppets performing on a stage, and I could not treat their acts with seriousness. Giulia! That was the great fact in life. Nothing mattered to me but Giulia. When I thought of Giulia my heart was filled with ecstasy, and I spat with scorn on all the silly details of events.

I would willingly have kept myself out of the stream which was carrying along the others; but I could not help knowing what happened. And it was indeed ridiculous. After the great scene at the Palace people had begun to take steps as if for big events. Checco had sent a large sum of money to Florence for the Medici to take care of; Bartolomeo Moratini had made preparations; there were generally a stir and unrest. Girolamo was supposed to be going to take some step; people were prepared for everything; when they woke up in the morning they asked if aught had taken place in the night; and Checco wore a coat of mail. On the Count's side people were asking what Checco meant to do, whether the ovation he had received would encourage him to any violent step. All the world was agog for great events—and nothing happened. It reminded me of a mystery play in which, after great preparation of dialogue, some great stage effect is going to be produced—a saint is going to ascend to heaven, or a mountain is to open and the devil spring out. The spectators are sitting open-mouthed; the moment has come, everything is ready, the signal is given; the mob have already drawn their breath for a cry of astonishment—and something goes wrong and nothing happens.

The good Forlivesi could not understand it: they were looking. for signs and miracles, and behold! they came not. Each day they said to themselves that this would be one to be remembered in the history of the town; that to-day Girolamo would surely leave his hesitations; but the day wore on quite calmly. Everyone took his dinner and supper

F

as usual, the sun journeyed from east to west as it had done on the previous day, the night came, and the worthy citizen went to his bed at his usual hour, and slept in peace till the following sunrise. Nothing happened, and it seemed that nothing was going to happen. The troubled spirits gradually came to the conclusion that there was nothing to be troubled about, and the old quiet came over the town; there was no talk of new taxes, and the world wagged on. . . . Checco and Matteo and the Moratini resigned themselves to the fact that the sky was serene, and that they had better pursue their way without troubling their little heads about conspiracies and midnight daggers.

Meanwhile, I laughed, and admired their folly and my own wisdom. For I worried myself about none of these things; I lived in Giulia, for Giulia, by Giulia. . . . I had never enjoyed such happiness before; she was a little cold, perhaps, but I did not mind. I had passion that lived by its own flame, and I cared for nothing as long as she let me love her. And I argued with myself that it is an obvious thing that love is not the same on both sides. There is always one who loves and one who lets himself be loved. Perhaps it is a special decree of Nature; for the man loves actively, caresses and is passionate; while the woman gives herself to him, and is in his embrace like some sweet, helpless animal. I did not ask for such love as I gave; all I asked was that my love should let herself be loved. That was all I cared for; that was all I wanted. My love for Giulia was wonderful even to me. I felt I had lost myself in her. I had given my whole being into her hand.

Samson and Delilah! But this was no faithless Philistine. I would have given my honour into her keeping and felt it as sure as in my own. In my great love I felt such devotion, such reverence, that sometimes I hardly dared touch her; it seemed to me I must kneel and worship at her feet. I learnt the great delight of abasing myself to the beloved. I could make myself so small and mean in my humility; but nothing satisfied my wish to show my abject slavery. . . . Oh, Giulia! Giulia!

But this inaction on the part of Girolamo Riario had the effect of persuading his subjects of his weakness. They had given over expecting reprisals on his part, and the only conclusion they could come to was that he dared do nothing against Checco. It was inconceivable that he should leave unavenged the insults he had received; that he should bear without remark the signs of popularity which greeted Checco, not only on the day of the Council meeting, but since, every time he appeared in the streets. They began to despise their ruler as well as hate him, and they told one another stories of violent disputes in the Palace between the Count and Caterina. Everyone knew the pride and passion which came to the Countess with her Sforza blood, and they felt sure that she would not patiently bear the insults which her husband did not seem to mind; for the fear of the people could not stop their sarcasms, and when any member of the household was seen he was assailed with taunts and jeers; Caterina herself had to listen to scornful laughs as she passed by, and the town was ringing with a

song about the Count. It was whispered that
Girolamo's little son, Ottaviano, had been heard singing it in ignorance of its meaning, and had been
nearly killed by his father in a passion of rage. Evil
reports began to circulate about Caterina's virtue ;
it was supposed that she would not keep faithful to
such a husband, and another song was made in praise
of cuckoldry.

The Orsi would not be persuaded that this calm
was to be believed in. Checco was assured that
Girolamo must have some scheme on hand, and the
quiet and silence seemed all the more ominous.

The Count very rarely appeared in Forli; but one
Saint's day he went to the Cathedral, and as he came
back to the Palace, passing through the piazza, saw
Checco. At the same moment Checco saw him, and
stopped, uncertain what to do. The crowd suddenly
became silent, and they stood still like statues petri-
fied by a magic spell. What was going to happen ?
Girolamo himself hesitated a moment ; a curious
spasm crossed his face. Checco made as if to walk
on, pretending not to notice the Count. Matteo and
I were dumbfounded, absolutely at a loss. Then the
Count stepped forward, and held out his hand.

'Ah, my Checco ! how goes it ? '

He smiled and pressed warmly the hand which the
Orsi gave him. Checco was taken aback, pale as if
the hand he held were the hand of death.

'You have neglected me of late, dear friend,' said
the Count.

'I have not been well, my lord.'

Girolamo linked his arm in Checco's.

'Come, come,' he said, 'you must not be angry

because I used sharp words to you the other day. You know I am hot-tempered.'

'You have a right to say what you please.'

'Oh, no; I have only a right to say pleasant things.'

He smiled, but all the time the mobile eyes were shifting here and there, scrutinising Checco's face, giving occasional quick glances to me and Matteo. He went on,—

'You must show a forgiving spirit.' Then, to Matteo, 'We must all be good Christians if we can, eh, Matteo?'

'Of course!'

'And yet your cousin bears malice.'

'No, my lord,' said Checco. 'I am afraid I was too outspoken.'

'Well, if you were, I have forgiven you, and you must forgive me. But we will not talk of that. My children have been asking for you. It is strange that this ferocious creature, who tells me I am the worst among bad men, should be so adored by my children. Your little godson is always crying for you.'

'Dear child!' said Checco.

'Come and see them now. There is no time like the present.'

Matteo and I looked at one another. Was all this an attempt to get him in his hand, and this time not to let him go?

'I must pray you to excuse me, for I have some gentlemen coming to dine with me to-day, and I fear I shall be late already.'

Girolamo gave us a rapid look, and evidently saw

in our eyes something of our thoughts, for he said good-humouredly,—.

'You never will do anything for me, Checco. But I won't keep you ; I respect the duties of hospitality. However, another day you must come.'

He warmly pressed Checco's hand, and, nodding to Matteo and me, left us.

The crowd had not been able to hear what was said, but they had seen the cordiality, and as soon as Girolamo disappeared behind the Palace doors, broke out into murmurs of derision. The Christian sentiment clearly gained little belief from them, and they put down the Count's act to fear. It was clear, they said, that he found Checco too strong for him, and dared nothing. It was a discovery that the man they had so feared was willing to turn the other cheek when the one was smitten, and to all their former hate they added a new hate that he had caused them terror without being terrible. They hated him now for their own pusillanimity. The mocking songs gained force, and Girolamo began to be known as Cornuto, the Man of Horns.

Borne on this wave of contempt came another incident, which again showed the Count's weakness. On the Sunday following his meeting with Checco, it was known that Girolamo meant to hear mass at the church of San Stefano, and Jacopo Ronchi, commander of a troop, stationed himself, with two other soldiers, to await him. When the Count appeared, accompanied by his wife and children and his suite, Jacopo pressed forward and, throwing himself on his knees, presented a petition, in which he asked for the arrears of pay of himself and his fellows. The Count took it without speaking, and pursued his way. Then Jacopo took hold of his legs to stop him, and said,—

'For Heaven's sake, my lord, give me a hearing. I and these others have received nothing for months, and we are starving.'

'Let me go,' said the Count, 'your claim shall be attended to.'

'Do not dismiss me, my lord. I have presented three petitions before, and to none of them have you paid attention. Now I am getting desperate, and can wait no longer. Look at my tattered clothes. Give me my money!'

'Let me go, I tell you,' said Girolamo, furiously, and he gave him a sweeping blow, so that the man fell on his back to the ground. 'How dare you come and insult me here in the public place! By God! I cannot keep my patience much longer.'

He brought out these words with such violence of passion that it seemed as if in them exploded the anger which had been gathering up through this time of humiliation. Then, turning furiously on the people, he almost screamed,—

'Make way!'

They dared not face his anger, and with white faces, shrunk back, leaving a path for him and his party to walk through.

XII

I LOOKED at these events as I might have looked at a comedy of Plautus; it was very amusing, but perhaps a little vulgar. I was wrapped up in my own happiness, and I had forgotten Nemesis.

One day, perhaps two months from my arrival in Forli, I heard Checco tell his cousin that a certain Giorgio dall' Aste had returned. I paid no particular attention to the remark; but later, when I was alone with Matteo, it occurred to me that I had not heard before of this person. I did not know that Giulia had relations on her husband's side. I asked,—

'By the way, who is that Giorgio dall' Aste, of whom Checco was speaking?'

'A cousin of Donna Giulia's late husband.'

'I have never heard him spoken of before.'

'Haven't you? He enjoys quite a peculiar reputation, as being the only lover that the virtuous Giulia has kept for more than ten days.'

'Another of your old wives' tales, Matteo! Nature intended you for a begging friar.'

'I have often thought I have missed my vocation. With my brilliant gift for telling lies in a truthful

88

manner, I should have made my way in the Church
to the highest dignities. Whereas, certain antiquated
notions of honour having been instilled into me during
my training as a soldier, my gifts are lost; with the
result, that when I tell the truth people think I am
lying. But this is solemn truth!'

'All your stories are!' I jeered.

'Ask anyone. This has been going on for years.
When Giulia was married by old Tommaso, whom
she had never seen in her life before the betrothal,
the first thing she did was to fall in love with Giorgio.
He fell in love with her, but being a fairly honest
sort of man, he had some scruples about committing
adultery with his cousin's wife, especially as he lived
on his cousin's money. However, when a woman is
vicious, a man's scruples soon go to the devil. If
Adam couldn't refuse the apple, you can't expect us
poor fallen creatures to do so either. The result was
that Joseph did not run away from Potiphar's wife
so fast as to prevent her from catching him.'

'How biblical you are.'

'Yes,' answered Matteo; 'I'm making love to a
parson's mistress, and I am cultivating the style
which I find she is used to. . . . But, however,
Giorgio, being youthful, after a short while began to
have prickings of conscience, and went away from
Forli. Giulia was heart-broken, and her grief was so
great that she must have half the town to console
her. Then Giorgio's conscience calmed down, and
he came back, and Giulia threw over all her
lovers.'

'I don't believe a single word you say.'

'On my honour, it's true.'

'On the face of it, the story is false. If she really loves him, why do they not keep together now that there is no hindrance?'

'Because Giulia has the heart of a strumpet and can't be faithful to any one man. She's very fond of him, but they quarrel, and she takes a sudden fancy for somebody else, and for a while they won't see one another. But there seems some magical charm between them, for sooner or later they always come back to one another. I believe, if they were at the ends of the world, eventually they would be drawn together, even if they struggled with all their might against it. And, I promise you, Giorgio has struggled; he tries to part with her for good and all, and each time they separate he vows it shall be for ever. But there is an invisible chain and it always brings him back.'

I stood looking at him in silence. Strange, horrible thoughts passed through my head and I could not drive them away. I tried to speak quite calmly.

'And how is it when they are together?'

'All sunshine and storm, but as time goes on the storm gets longer and blacker; and then Giorgio goes away.'

'But, good God! man, how do you know?' I cried in agony.

He shrugged his shoulders.

'They quarrel?' I asked.

'Furiously! He feels himself imprisoned against his will, with the door open to escape, but not the strength to do it; and she is angry that he should love her thus, trying not to love her. It rather seems to me that it explains her own excesses; her other loves are partly to show him how much she is loved, and to persuade herself that she is lovable.'

I did not believe it. Oh, no, I swear I did not believe it, yet I was frightened, horribly frightened ; but I would not believe a single word of it.

'Listen, Matteo,' I said. 'You believe badly of Giulia; but you do not know her. I swear to you that she is good and pure, whatever she may have been in the past ; and I do not believe a word of these scandals. I am sure that now she is as true and faithful as she is beautiful.'

Matteo looked at me for a moment.

'Are you her lover ?' he asked.

'Yes !'

Matteo opened his mouth as if about to speak, then stopped, and after a moment's hesitation turned away.

That evening I went to Giulia. I found her lying full length on a divan, her head sunken in soft cushions. She was immersed in reverie. I wondered whether she was thinking of me, and I went up to her silently, and, bending over her, lightly kissed her lips. She gave a cry, and a frown darkened her eyes.

'You frightened me !'

'I am sorry,' I answered humbly. 'I wanted to surprise you.'

She did not answer, but raised her eyebrows, slightly shrugging her shoulders. I wondered whether something had arisen to vex her. I knew she had a quick temper, but I did not mind it ; a cross word was so soon followed by a look of repent-

ance and a word of love. I passed my hand over
her beautiful soft hair. The frown came again, and
she turned her head away.

'Giulia,' I said, 'what is it?' I took her hand;
she withdrew it immediately.

'Nothing,' she answered.

'Why do you turn away from me and withdraw
your hand?'

'Why should I not turn away from you and withdraw my hand?'

'Don't you love me, Giulia?'

She gave a sigh, and pretended to look bored.
I looked at her, pained at heart and wondering.

'Giulia, my dear, tell me what it is. You are
making me very unhappy.'

'Oh, don't I tell you, nothing, nothing, nothing!'

'Why are you cross?'

I put my face to her's, and my arms round her
neck. She disengaged herself impatiently.

'You refuse my kisses, Giulia!'

She made another gesture of annoyance.

'Giulia, don't you love me?' My heart was beginning to sink, and I remembered what I had heard
from Matteo. Oh, God! could it be true? . . .

'Yes, of course I love you, but sometimes I must
be left in peace.'

'You have only to say the word, and I will go
away altogether.'

'I don't want you to do that, but we shall like one
another much better if we don't see too much of one
another.'

'When one is in love, really and truly, one does
not think of such wise precautions.'

'And you are here so often that I am afraid of my good name.'

'You need have no fear about your character,' I answered bitterly. 'One more scandal will not make much difference.'

'You need not insult me!'

I could not be angry with her, I loved her too much, and the words I had said hurt me ten times more than they hurt her. I fell on my knees by her side and took hold of her arms.

'Oh, Giulia, Giulia, forgive me! I don't mean to say anything to wound you. But, for God's sake! don't be so cold. I love you, I love you. Be good to me.'

'I think I have been good to you. . . . After all, it is not such a very grave matter. I have not taken things more seriously than you.'

'What do you mean?' I cried, aghast.

She shrugged her shoulders.

'I suppose you found me a pretty woman, and thought you could occupy a few spare moments with a pleasant amour. You can hardly have expected me to be influenced by sentiments very different from your own.'

'You mean you do not love me?'

'I love you as much as you love me. I don't suppose either you are Lancelot, or I Guinevere.'

I still knelt at her side in silence, and my head felt as if the vessels in it were bursting. . . .

'You know,' she went on quite calmly, 'one cannot love for ever.'

'But I love you, Giulia; I love you with all my heart and soul! I have had loves picked up for the opportunity's sake, or for pure idleness; but my love for you is different. I swear to you it is a matter of my whole life.'

'That has been said to me so often. . . .'

I was beginning to be overwhelmed.

'But do you mean that it is all finished? Do you mean that you won't have anything more to do with me!'

'I don't say I won't have anything more to do with you.'

'But love? It is love I want.'

She shrugged her shoulders.

'But] why not?' I said despairingly. 'Why have you given it me at all if you want to take it away?'

'One is not master of one's love. It comes and goes.'

'Don't you love me at all?'

'No!'

'Oh, God! But why do you tell me this to-day?'

'I had to tell you some time.'

'But why not yesterday, or the day before? Why to-day particularly?'

She did not answer.

'Is it because Giorgio dall' Aste has just returned?'

She started up and her eyes flashed.

'What have they been telling you about him?'

'Has he been here to-day? Were you thinking of him when I came? Were you languorous from his embraces?'

'How dare you!'

'The only lover to whom you have been faithful, more or less!'

'You vowed you did not believe the scandals

about me, and now, when I refuse you the smallest
thing, you are ready to believe every word. What a
love is this! I thought I had heard you talk so often
of boundless confidence.'

'I believe every word I have heard against you.
I believe you are a harlot.'

She had raised herself from her couch, and we were
standing face to face.

'Do you want money? Look! I have as good
money as another. I will pay you for your love;
here, take it.'

I took gold pieces from my pocket and flung them
at her feet.

'Ah,' she cried in indignation, 'you cur! Go, go!'

She pointed to the door. Then I felt a sudden
revulsion. I fell on my knees and seized her hands.

'Oh, forgive me, Giulia. I don't know what I am
saying; I am mad. But don't rob me of your love;
it is the only thing I have to live for. For God's
sake, forgive me! Oh, Giulia, I love you, I love
you. I can't live without you.' The tears broke
from my eyes. I could not stop them.

'Leave me! leave me!'

I was ashamed of my abjectness; I rose up
indignant.

'Oh, you are quite heartless. You have no right
to treat me so. You were not obliged to give me
your love; but when once you have given it you cannot take it away. No one has the right to make
another unhappy as you make me. You are a bad,
evil woman. I hate you!'

I stood over her with clenched fists. She shrank
back, afraid.

'Don't be frightened,' I said; 'I won't touch you. I hate you too much.'

Then I turned to the crucifix, and lifted my hands.

'Oh, God! I pray you, let this woman be treated as she has treated me.' And to her, 'I hope to God you are as unhappy as I am. And I hope the unhappiness will come soon—you harlot!'

I left her, and in my rage slammed the door, so that the lock shattered behind me.

XIII

I WALKED through the streets like a man who has received sentence of death. My brain was whirling, and sometimes I stopped and pressed my head with both hands to relieve the insupportable pressure. I could not realise what had happened; I only knew it was terrible. I felt as if I were going mad; I could have killed myself. At last, getting home, I threw myself on my bed and tried to gather myself together. I cried out against that woman. I wished I had my fingers curling round her soft white throat, that I could strangle the life out of her. Oh, I hated her!

At last I fell asleep, and in that sweet forgetfulness enjoyed a little peace. When I woke I lay still for a moment without remembering what had happened; then suddenly it came back to me, and the blood flushed to my face as I thought of how I had humiliated myself to her. She must be as hard as stone, I said to myself, to see my misery and not take pity on me. She saw my tears and was not moved one jot. All the time I had been praying and beseeching, she had been as calm as a marble figure. She must have seen my agony and the passion of my love, and yet she was absolutely, absolutely indifferent. Oh, I despised her! I had known even when I adored her madly that it was only my love which gave her the qualities I worshipped. I had seen she was ignorant and foolish, and commonplace and vicious; but I did not care as long as I loved her and could have her love in return. But when I thought of her so horribly heartless, so uncaring to my unhappiness, I did more than hate her—I utterly despised her. I despised myself for having loved her. I despised myself for loving her still. . . .

I got up and went about my day's duties, trying to forget myself in their performance. But still I brooded over my misery, and in my heart I cursed the woman. It was Nemesis, always Nemesis! In my folly I had forgotten her; and yet I should have remembered that through my life all happiness had been followed by all misery. . . . I had tried to ward off the evil by sacrifice; I had rejoiced at the harm which befell me, but the very rejoicing seemed to render the hurt of no avail, and with the inevitableness of fate, Nemesis had come and thrown me back into the old unhappiness. But of late I had forgotten. What was Nemesis to me now when I thought my happiness so great that it could not help but last? It was so robust and strong that I never thought of its cessation. I did not even think the Gods were good to me at last. I had forgotten the Gods; I thought of nothing but love and Giulia.

Matteo came asking me to go to the Palace with him and Checco, at the particular desire of Girolamo, who wished to show them the progress of the decorations. I would not go. I wanted to be alone and think.

But my thoughts maddened me. Over and over again I repeated every word of the terrible quarrel, and more than ever I was filled with horror for her cold cruelty. What right have these people to make us unhappy? Is there not enough misery in the world already? Oh, it is brutal!

I could not bear myself; I regretted that I had not gone to the Palace. I detested this solitude.

The hours passed like years, and as my brain grew tired I sank into a state of sodden, passive misery.

At last they came back, and Matteo told me what had happened. I tried to listen, to forget myself. . . . It appeared that the Count had been extremely cordial. After talking to them of his house, and showing the beautiful things he had collected to furnish it with, he took them to Caterina's apartments, where they found the Countess surrounded by her children. She had been very charming and gracious, even deigning to compliment Matteo on his gallantry. How it interested me to know all this! The children had run to Checco as soon as they saw him, dragging him into their game. The others looked on while the Orsi played good-humouredly with the little boys, and Girolamo, laying his hand on Checco's shoulder, had remarked,—

'You see, dear friend, the children are determined that there should not be enmity between us. And when the little ones love you so dearly, can you think that I should hate you?'

And when they left he had accompanied them to the gates and been quite affectionate in his farewell.

At last the night came and I could shut myself up in my room. I thought with a bitter smile that it was the hour at which I was used to go to Giulia. And now I should never go to Giulia again. My unhappiness was too great for wrath; I felt too utterly miserable to think of my grievances, or of my contempt. I only felt broken-hearted. I could not keep the tears back, and burying my face in the pillows, I cried my heart out. It was years and years since I had wept, not since I was quite a boy, but this blow had taken from me all manliness, and I gave myself over to my grief, passionately, shamelessly. I did not care that I was weak; I had no respect for myself, or care for myself. The sobs came, one on the heels of another like waves, and the pain, as they tore my chest, relieved the anguish of my mind. Exhaustion came at last, and with it sleep.

But I knew I could not hide the change in me, and Matteo soon noticed it.

'What is the matter with you, Filippo?' he asked. I blushed and hesitated.

'Nothing,' I answered at last.

'I thought you were unhappy.'

Our eyes met, but I could not stand his inquiring glance and looked down. He came to me, and sitting on the arm of my chair, put his hand on my shoulder and said affectionately,—

'We're friends, aren't we, Filippo?'

'Yes,' I answered, smiling and taking his hand.

'Won't you trust me?'

After a pause I answered,—

'I should so much like to.' I felt as if indeed it would relieve me to be able to confide in somebody, I wanted sympathy so badly.

He passed his hand gently over my hair.

I hesitated a little, but I could not help myself, and I told him the whole story from beginning to end.

'Poverino!' he said, when I had finished; then, clenching his teeth, 'She is a beast, that woman!'

'I ought to have taken your warning, Matteo, but I was a fool.'

'Who ever does take warning!' he answered, shrugging his shoulders. 'How could you be expected to believe me?'

'But I believe you now. I am horrified when I think of her vice and cruelty.'

'Ah, well, it is over now.'

'Quite! I hate her and despise her. Oh, I wish I could get her face to face and tell her what I think of her.'

I thought my talk with Matteo had relieved me, I thought the worst was over; but at night melancholy came on me stronger than ever, and I groaned as I threw myself on my bed. I felt so terribly alone in the world. . . . I had no relation but a half-brother, a boy of twelve, whom I had hardly seen; and as I wandered through the land, an exile, I had been continually assailed by the hateful demon of loneliness. And sometimes in my solitude I had felt that I could kill myself. But when I found I was in love with Giulia, I cried aloud with joy. . . . I threw everything to the winds, gathering myself up for the supreme effort of passion. All the storm and stress were passed; I was no longer alone, for I had someone to whom I could give my love. I was like the ship that arrives in the harbour, and reefs her sails and clears her deck, settling down in the quietness of the waters.

And now all was over! Oh God, to think that my hopes should be shattered in so short a time, that the ship should be so soon tossed about in the storm, and the stars hidden by the clouds! And the past delight made the present darkness all the more bitter. I groaned. In my misery I uttered a prayer to God to help me. I could not think I should live henceforth. How could I go on existing with this aching void in my heart? I could not spend days and weeks and years always with this despair. It was too terrible to last. My reason told me that time would remedy it; but time was so long, and what misery must I go through before the wound was healed! And as I thought of what I had lost, my agony grew more unbearable. It grew vivid, and I felt Giulia in my arms. I panted as I pressed my lips against hers, and I said to her,—

'How could you!'

I buried my face in my hands, so as better to enjoy my dream. I smelt the perfume of her breath; I felt on my face the light touch of her hair. But it would not last. I tried to seize the image and hold it back, but it vanished and left me broken-hearted. . . .

I knew I did not hate her. I had pretended to,

but the words came from the mouth. In my heart
I loved her still, more passionately than ever. What
did I care if she was heartless and cruel and faithless
and vicious! It was nothing to me as long as I
could hold her in my arms and cover her with
kisses. I did despise her; I knew her for what
she was, but still I loved her insanely. Oh, if she
would only come back to me! I would willingly
forget everything and forgive her. Nay, I would
ask her forgiveness and grovel before her, if she
would only let me enjoy her love again.

I would go back to her and fall on my knees, and
pray her to be merciful. Why should I suppose she
had changed in the few days. I knew she would
treat me with the same indifference, and only feel a
wondering contempt that I should so abase myself.
It came like a blow in the face, the thought of her
cold cruelty and her calmness. No, I vowed I would
never subject myself to that again. I felt myself
blush at the remembrance of the humiliation. But
perhaps she was sorry for what she had done. I
knew her pride would prevent her from coming or
sending to me, and should I give her no opportunity?.
Perhaps, if we saw one another for a few moments
everything might be arranged, and I might be happy
again. An immense feeling of hope filled me. I
thought I must be right in my idea; she could not
be so heartless as to have no regret. How willingly
I would take her back! My heart leaped. But I
dared not go to her house. I knew I should find her
on the morrow at her father's, who was going to give
a banquet to some friends. I would speak to her
there, casually, as if we were ordinary acquaintances ;

and then at the first sign of yielding on her part, even if I saw but a tinge of regret in her eyes, I would burst out. I was happy in my plan, and I went to sleep with the name of Giulia on my lips and her image in my heart.

XIV

I WENT to the Moratini Palace, and with beating heart looked round for Giulia. She was surrounded by her usual court, and seemed more lively and excited than ever. I had never seen her more beautiful. She was dressed all in white, and her sleeves were sewn with pearls; she looked like a bride. She caught sight of me at once, but pretended not to see me, and went on talking.

I approached her brother Alessandro and said to him casually,—

'I am told a cousin of your sister has come to Forli. Is he here to-day?'

He looked at me inquiringly, not immediately understanding.

'Giorgio dall' Aste,' I explained.

'Oh, I didn't know you meant him. No, he's not here. He and Giulia's husband were not friends, and so—'

'Why were they not friends?' I interrupted, on the spur of the moment, not seeing the impertinence of the question till I had made it.

'Oh, I don't know. Relations always are at enmity with one another; probably some disagreement with regard to their estates.'

'Was that all?'

'So far as I know.'

I recollected that in a scandal the persons most interested are the last to hear it. The husband hears nothing of his wife's treachery till all the town knows every detail.

'I should like to have seen him,' I went on.

'Giorgo? Oh, he's a weak sort of creature; one of those men who commit sins and repent!'

'That is not a fault of which you will ever be guilty, Alessandro,' I said, smiling.

'I sincerely hope not. After all, if a man has a conscience he ought not to do wrong. But if he does he must be a very poor sort of a fool to repent.'

'You cannot have the rose without the thorn.'

'Why not? It only needs care. There are dregs at the bottom of every cup, but you are not obliged to drink them.'

'You have made up your mind that if you commit sins you are ready to go to hell for them?' I said.

'It is braver than going to Heaven by the back door, turning pious when you are too old to do anything you shouldn't.'

'I agree with you that one has little respect for the man who turns monk when things go wrong with him.'

I saw that Giulia was alone, and seized the opportunity to speak with her.

'Giulia,' I said, approaching.

She looked at me for a moment with an air of perplexity, as if she really could not remember whom I was.

'Ah, Messer Filippo!' she said, as if suddenly recollecting.

'It is not so long since we met that you can have forgotten me.'

'Yes. I remember last time you did me the honour to visit me you were very rude and cross.'

I looked at her silently, wondering.

'Well?' she said, steadily answering my gaze and smiling.

'Have you nothing more to say to me than that?' I asked in an undertone.

'What do you want me to say to you?'

'Are you quite heartless?'

She gave a sigh of boredom, and looked to the other end of the room, as if for someone to come and break a tedious conversation.

'How could you!' I whispered.

Notwithstanding her self-control, a faint blush came over her face. I stood looking at her for a little while and then I turned away. She was quite heartless. I left the Moratini and walked out into the town. This last interview had helped me in so far that it made certain that my love was hopeless. I stood still and stamped on the ground, vowing I would not love her. I would put her away from my thoughts entirely; she was a contemptible, vicious woman, and I was too proud to be subject to her. I wondered I did not kill her. I made up my mind to take my courage in both hands and leave Forli. Once away, I should find myself attracted to different matters, and

probably I should not live long before finding
some other woman to take Giulia's place.　She
was not the only woman in Italy; she was not
the most beautiful nor the cleverest.　Give me a
month and I could laugh at my torments. . . .

The same evening I told Matteo I meant to leave
Forli.

'Why?' he asked in astonishment.

'I have been here several weeks,' I answered;
'I don't want to outstay my welcome.'

'That is rubbish.　You know I should be only
too glad for you to stay here all your life.'

'That is very kind of you,' I replied, with a laugh,
'but the establishment is not yours.'

'That makes no difference.　Besides, Checco has
become very fond of you, and I'm sure he wishes
you to stay.'

'Of course, I know your hospitality is quite un-
limited; but I am beginning to want to get back
to Città di Castello.'

'Why?' asked Matteo, doubtfully.

'One likes to return to one's native place.'

'You have been away from Castello for ten
years; you cannot be in any particular hurry to
get back.'

I was beginning to protest when Checco came
in, and Matteo interrupted me with,—

'Listen, Checco, Filippo says he wants to leave us.'

'But he sha'n't,' said Checco, laughing.

'I really must!' I answered gravely.

'You really mustn't,' replied Checco.　'We can't
spare you, Filippo.'

'There's no great hurry about your going home,'

he added, when I had explained my reasons, 'and I fancy that soon we shall want you here. A good sword and a brave heart will probably be of good use to us.'

'Everything is as quiet as a cemetery,' I said, shrugging my shoulders.

'It is quiet above; but below there are rumblings and strange movements. I feel sure this calm only presages a storm. It is impossible for Girolamo to go on as he is now; his debts are increasing every day, and his difficulties will soon be impracticable. He must do something. There is certain to be a disturbance at any attempt to put on the taxes, and then Heaven only knows what will happen.'

I was beginning to get a little vexed at their opposition, and I answered petulantly,—

'No, I must go.'

'Stay another month; things must come to a head before then.'

A month would have been as bad as a year.

'I am out of health,' I answered; 'I feel I want to get into a different atmosphere.'

Checco thought for a moment.

'Very well,' he said, 'we can arrange matters to suit us both. I want someone to go to Florence for me to conclude a little business matter with Messer Lorenzo de' Medici. You would be away a fortnight; and if you are out of sorts the ride across country will put you right. Will you go?'

I thought for a moment. It was not a very long absence, but the new sights would distract me, and I wanted to see Florence again. On the whole, I thought it would suffice, and that I could count on the cure of my ill before the time was up.

'Very well,' I answered.

'Good! And you will have a pleasant companion. I had talked to Scipione Moratini about it; it did not occur to me that you would go. But it will be all the better to have two of you.'

'If I go,' I said, 'I shall go alone.'

Checco was rather astonished.

'Why?'

'Scipione bores me. I want to be quiet and do as I like.'

I was quite determined that neither of the Moratini should come with me. They would have reminded me too much of what I wanted to forget.

'As you like,' said Checco. 'I can easily tell Scipione that I want him to do something else for me.'

'Thanks.'

'When will you start?'

'At once.'

'Then come, and I will give you the instructions and necessary papers.'

XV

NEXT morning I mounted my horse and set out with Matteo, who was to accompany me for a little way.

But at the town gate a guard stopped us and asked where we were going.

'Out!' I answered shortly, moving on.

'Stop!' said the man, catching hold of my bridle.

'What the devil d'you mean?' said Matteo. 'D'you know whom we are?'

'I have orders to let no one go by without the permission of my captain.'

'What tyrants they are!' cried Matteo. 'Well, what the hell are you standing there for? Go and tell your captain to come out.'

The man signed to another soldier, who went into the guard-house; he was still holding my bridle. I was not very good-tempered that morning.

'Have the goodness to take your hands off,' I said.

He looked as if he were about to refuse.

'Will you do as you are told?' Then, as he hesitated, I brought down the butt-end of my whip on his

fingers, and with an oath bade him stand off. He let
go at once, cursing, and looked as if he would willingly
stab me if he dared. We waited impatiently, but the
captain did not appear.

'Why the devil doesn't this man come?' I
said; and Matteo, turning to one of the soldiers,
ordered,—

'Go and tell him to come here instantly.'

At that moment the captain appeared, and we
understood the incident, for it was Ercole Piacentini.
He had apparently seen us coming, or heard of my
intended journey, and had set himself out to insult
us. We were both furious.

'Why the devil don't you hurry up when you're
sent for?' said Matteo.

He scowled, but did not answer. Turning to me
he asked,—

'Where are you going?'

Matteo and I looked at one another in amazement
at the man's impudence, and I burst forth,—

'You insolent fellow! What do you mean by stopping me like this?'

'I have a right to refuse passage to anyone I
choose.'

'Take care!' I said. 'I swear the Count shall be
told of your behaviour, and nowadays the Count is in
the habit of doing as the Orsi tell him.'

'He shall hear of this,' growled the Piacentini.

'Tell him what you like. Do you think I care?
You can tell him that I consider his captain a very
impertinent ruffian. Now, let me go.'

'You shall not pass till I choose.'

'By God! man,' I said, absolutely beside myself,

'it seems I cannot touch you here, but if ever we meet in Città di Castello—'

'I will give you any satisfaction you wish,' he answered hotly.

'Satisfaction! I would not soil my sword by crossing it with yours. I was going to say that if ever we meet in Castello I will have you whipped by my lacqueys in the public place.'

I felt a ferocious pleasure in throwing the words of contempt in his face.

'Come on,' said Matteo; 'we cannot waste our time here.'

We put the spurs to our horses. The soldiers looked to their captain to see whether they should stop us, but he gave no order, and we passed through. When we got outside, Matteo said to me,—

'Girolamo must be planning something, or Ercole would not have dared to do that.'

'It is only the impotent anger of a foolish man,' I answered. 'The Count will probably be very angry with him when he hears of it.'

We rode a few miles, and then Matteo turned back. When I found myself alone I heaved a great sigh of relief. I was free for a while at least. . . . Another episode in my life was finished; I could forget it, and look forward to new things.

As I rode on, the March wind got into my blood and sent it whirling madly through my veins. The sun was shining brightly and covered everything with smiles; the fruit trees were all in flower— apples, pears, almonds—the dainty buds covered the branches with a snow of pink and white. The ground beneath them was bespattered with narcissi

H

and anemones, the very olive trees looked gay. All the world laughed with joy at the bright spring morning, and I laughed louder than the rest. I drew in long breaths of the keen air, and it made me drunk, so that I set the spurs to my horse and galloped wildly along the silent road.

I had made up my mind to forget Giulia, and I succeeded, for the changing scenes took me away from myself, and I was intent on the world at large. But I could not command my dreams. At night she came to me, and I dreamed that she was by my side, with her arms round my neck, sweetly caressing, trying to make me forget what I had suffered. And the waking was bitter. . . . But even that would leave me soon, I hoped, and then I should be free indeed.

I rode on, full of courage and good spirits, along endless roads, putting up at wayside inns, through the mountains, past villages and hamlets, past thriving towns, till I found myself in the heart of Tuscany, and finally I saw the roofs of Florence spread out before me.

After I had cleaned myself at the inn and had eaten, I sauntered through the town, renewing my recollections. I walked round Madonna del Fiore, and leaning against one of the houses at the back of the piazza looked at the beautiful apse, the marble all glistening in the moonlight. It was very quiet and peaceful; the exquisite church filled me with a sense of rest and purity, so that I cast far from me all vice. . . . Then I went to the baptistery and tried to make out in the dim light the details of Ghiberti's wonderful doors. It was late and the streets were

silent as I strolled to the Piazza della Signoria, and
saw before me the grim stone palace with its tower,
and I came down to the Arno and looked at the
glistening of the water, with the bridge covered with
houses ; and as I considered the beauty of it all I
thought it strange that the works of man should be
so good and pure and man himself so vile.

Next day I set about my business. I had a special
letter of introduction to Lorenzo, and was ushered in
to him by a clerk. I found two people in the room ;
one, a young man with a long, oval face, and the
bones of the face and chin very strongly marked ; he
had a very wonderful skin, like brown ivory, black
hair that fell over his forehead and ears, and, most
striking of all, large brown eyes, very soft and melancholy. I thought I had never before seen a man
quite so beautiful. Seated by him, talking with
animation, was an insignificant man, bent and
wrinkled and mean, looking like a clerk in a cloth
merchant's shop, except for the massive golden chain
about his neck and the dress of dark red velvet with
an embroidered collar. His features were ugly ; a
large, coarse nose, a heavy, sensual mouth, small eyes,
but very sharp and glittering ; the hair thin and
short, the skin muddy, yellow, wrinkled—Lorenzo
de' Medici !

As I entered the room, he interrupted himself and
spoke to me in a harsh, disagreeable voice.

'Messer Filippo Brandolini, I think. You are very
welcome.'

'I am afraid I interrupt you,' I said, looking at the
youth with the melancholy eyes.

Oh no,' answered Lorenzo, gaily. 'We were talk-

ing of Plato.   I really ought to have been attending
to very much more serious matters, but I never can
resist Pico.'

Then that was the famous Pico della Mirandola.
I looked at him again and felt envious that one
person should be possessed of such genius and such
beauty.   It was hardly fair on Nature's part.

'It is more the subject than I that is irresistible.'

'Ah, the banquet!' said Lorenzo, clasping his
hands. 'What an inexhaustible matter! I could
go on talking about it all day and all night for a
year, and then find I had left unsaid half what I had
in my mind.'

'You have so vast an experience in the subject
treated of,' said Pico, laughing ; 'you could give a
chapter of comment to every sentence of Plato.'

'You rascal, Pico!' answered Lorenzo, also laughing. 'And what is your opinion of love, Messer?'
he added, turning to me.

I answered, smiling,—

> 'Con tua promesse, et tua false parole,
> Con falsi risi, et con vago sembiante,
> Donna, menato hai il tuo fidele amante.'

.   .   .   .

> *Those promises of thine, and those false words,*
> *Those traitor smiles, and that inconstant seeming,*
> *Lady, with these thou'st led astray thy faithful lover.*

They were Lorenzo's own lines, and he was
delighted that I should quote them, but still the
pleasure was not too great, and I saw that it must
be subtle flattery indeed that should turn his
head.

'You have the spirit of a courtier, Messer Filippo,' he said in reply to my quotation. 'You are wasted on liberty!'

'It is in the air in Florence—one breathes it in through every pore.'

'What, liberty?'

'No; the spirit of the courtier.'

Lorenzo looked at me sharply, then at Pico, repressing a smile at my sarcasm.

'Well, about your business from Forli?' he said; but when I began explaining the transaction he interrupted me. 'Oh, all that you can arrange with my secretaries. Tell me what is going on in the town. There have been rumours of disturbance.'

I looked at Pico, who rose and went out, saying,—

'I will leave you. Politics are not for me.'

I told Lorenzo all that had happened, while he listened intently, occasionally interrupting me to ask a question. When I had finished, he said—

'And what will happen now?'

I shrugged my shoulders.

'Who knows?'

'The wise man knows,' he said earnestly, 'for he has made up his mind what will happen, and goes about to cause it to happen. It is only the fool who trusts to chance and waits for circumstances to develop themselves. . . .'

'Tell your master—'

'I beg your pardon?' I interrupted.

He looked at me interrogatively.

'I was wondering of whom you were speaking,' I murmured.

He understood and, smiling, said,—

'I apologise. I was thinking you were a Forlivese. Of course, I remember now that you are a citizen of Castello, and we all know how tenacious they have been of their liberty and how proud of their freedom.'

He had me on the hip; for Città di Castello had been among the first of the towns to lose its liberty, and, unlike others, had borne its servitude with more equanimity than was honourable.

'However,' he went on, 'tell Checco d'Orsi that I know Girolamo Riario. It was his father and he who were the prime movers in the conspiracy which killed my brother and nearly killed myself. Let him remember that the Riario is perfectly unscrupulous, and that he is not accustomed to forgive an injury— or forget it. You say that Girolamo has repeatedly threatened Checco. Has that had no effect on him?'

'He was somewhat alarmed.'

'Besides?'

I looked at him, trying to seize his meaning.

'Did he make up his mind to sit still and wait till Girolamo found means to carry his threats into effect?'

I was rather at a loss for an answer. Lorenzo's eyes were fixed keenly upon me; they seemed to be trying to read my brain.

'It was suggested to him that it would be unwise,' I replied slowly.

'And what did he answer to that?'

'He recalled the ill results of certain recent—events.'

'Ah!'

He took his eyes off me, as if he had suddenly

seen the meaning behind my words, and was now
quite sure of everything he wanted to know. He
walked up and down the room, thinking; then he
said to me,—

'Tell Checco that Girolamo's position is very
insecure. The Pope is against him, though he
pretends to uphold him. You remember that when
the Zampeschi seized his castle of San Marco,
Girolamo thought they had the tacit consent of the
Pope, and dared make no reprisal. Lodovico Sforza
would doubtless come to the assistance of his half-
sister, but he is occupied with the Venetians—and if
the people of Forli hate the Count!'

'Then you advise—'

'I advise nothing. But let Checco know that it is
only the fool who proposes to himself an end when
he cannot or will not attain it; but the man who
deserves the name of man, marches straight to the
goal with clearness of mind and strength of will. He
looks at things as they are and puts aside all vain
appearances; and when his intelligence has shown
him the means to his end, he is a fool if he refuses
them, and he is a wise man if he uses them steadily
and unhesitatingly. Tell that to Checco!'

He threw himself into his chair with a little cry of
relief.

'Now we can talk of other things. Pico!'

A servant came in to say that Pico had gone
away.

'The villain!' cried Lorenzo. 'But I daresay you
will want to go away too, Messer Brandolini. But
you must come to-morrow; we are going to act the
Menacchini of Plautus; and besides the wit of the

Latin you will see all the youth and beauty of Florence.'

As I took my leave, he added,—

' I need not warn you to be discreet.'

XVI

A FEW days later I found myself in sight of Forli.
As I rode along I meditated; and presently the
thought came to me that after all there was perhaps
a certain equality in the portioning out of good and
evil in this world. When fate gave one happiness
she followed it with unhappiness, but the two lasted
about an equal time, so that the balance was not
unevenly preserved. . . . In my love for Giulia I
had gone through a few days of intense happiness;
the first kiss had caused me such ecstasy that I was
rapt up to heaven; I felt myself a god. And this
was followed by a sort of passive happiness, when I
lived but to enjoy my love and cared for nothing in
the world besides. Then came the catastrophe, and
I passed through the most awful misery that man
had ever felt: even now as I thought of it the sweat
gathered on my forehead. But I noticed that
strangely as this wretchedness was equal with the
first happiness, so was it equal in length. And this
was followed by a passive unhappiness when I no
longer felt all the bitterness of my woe, but only a

certain dull misery, which was like peace. And half
smiling, half sighing, I thought that the passive
misery again was equal to the passive happiness.
Finally came the blessed state of indifference, and,
except for the remembrance, my heart was as if
nothing had been at all. So it seemed to me that
one ought not to complain ; for if the world had no
right to give one continual misery, one had no cause
to expect unmingled happiness, and the conjunction
of the two, in all things equal, seemed normal and
reasonable. And I had not noticed that I was come
to Forli.

I entered the gate with a pleasant sense of home-
coming. I passed along the grey streets I was
beginning to know so well, and felt for them something of the affection of old friends. I was glad, too,
that I should shortly see Checco and my dear Matteo.
I felt I had been unkind to Matteo: he was so fond
of me and had always been so good, but I had been
so wrapped up in my love that his very presence had
been importunate, and I had responded coldly to his
friendliness. And being then in a sentimental mood,
I thought how much better and more trustworthy a
friend is to the most lovely woman in the world.
You could neglect him and be unfaithful to him, and
yet if you were in trouble you could come back and
he would take you to his arms and comfort you, and
never once complain that you had strayed away. I
longed to be with Matteo, clasping his hand. In my
hurry I put the spurs to my horse, and clattered
along the street. In a few minutes I had reached the
Palazzo, leapt off my horse, sprung up the stairs, and
flung myself into the arms of my friend.

After the first greetings, Matteo dragged me along to Checco.

'The good cousin is most eager to hear your news. We must not keep him waiting.'

Checco seemed as pleased to see me as Matteo. He warmly pressed my hand, and said,—

'I am glad to have you back, Filippo. In your absence we have been lamenting like forsaken shepherdesses. Now, what is your news?'

I was fully impressed with my importance at the moment, and the anxiety with which I was being listened to. I resolved not to betray myself too soon, and began telling them about the kindness of Lorenzo, and the play which he had invited me to see. I described the brilliancy of the assembly, and the excellence of the acting. They listened with interest, but I could see it was not what they wanted to hear.

'But I see you want to hear about more important matters,' I said. 'Well—'

'Ah!' they cried, drawing their chairs closer to me, settling themselves to listen attentively.

With a slight smile I proceeded to give them the details of the commercial transaction which had been the ostensible purpose of my visit, and I laughed to myself as I saw their disgust. Checco could not restrain his impatience, but did not like to interrupt me. Matteo, however, saw that I was mocking, and broke in.

'Confound you, Filippo! Why do you torment us when you know we are on pins and needles?'

Checco looked up and saw me laughing, and implored,—

'Put us out of torture, for Heaven's sake!'

'Very well!' I answered.   'Lorenzo asked me about the state of Forli, and I told him.   Then, after thinking awhile, he said, "Tell this to Checco—"'

And I repeated word for word what Lorenzo had said to me, and, as far as I could, I reproduced his accent and gesture.

When I had finished they both sat still and silent. At last Matteo, glancing to his cousin, said,—

'It seems sufficiently clear.'

'It is, indeed, very clear,' answered Checco, gravely.

XVII

I MADE up my mind to amuse myself now. I was
sick of being grave and serious. When one thinks
how short a while youth lasts it is foolish not to take
the best advantage of it; the time man has at his
disposal is not long enough for tragedy and moaning;
he has only room for a little laughter, and then his
hair gets grey and his knees shaky, and he is left
repenting that he did not make more of his oppor-
tunities. So many people have told me that they
have never regretted their vices, but often their
virtues! Life is too short to take things seriously.
Let us eat, drink and be merry, for to-morrow we die.

There was really so much to do in Forli that
amusement became almost hard work. There were
hunting parties in which we scoured the country all
day and returned at night, tired and sleepy, but with
a delicious feeling of relief, stretching our limbs like
giants waking from their sleep. There were excur-
sions to villas, where we would be welcomed by some
kind lady, and repeat on a smaller scale the Decam-
eron of Boccaccio, or imitate the learned conversa-
tions of Lorenzo and his circle at Careggio; we

could platonise as well as they, and we discovered the charm of treating impropriety from a philosophic point of view. We would set ourselves some subject and all write sonnets on it, and I noticed that the productions of our ladies were always more highly spiced than our own. Sometimes we would play at being shepherds and shepherdesses, but in this I always failed lamentably, for my nymph invariably complained that I was not as enterprising as a swain should be. Then we would act pastoral plays in the shadow of the trees; Orpheus was our favourite subject, and I was always set for the title part, rather against my will, for I could never bring the proper vigour into my lament for Eurydice, since it always struck me as both unreasonable and ungallant to be so inconsolable for the loss of one love when there were all around so many to console one. . . .

And in Forli itself there was a continuous whirl of amusement, festivities of every kind crowded on one, so that one had scarcely time to sleep; from the gravity and instructive tedium of a comedy by Terence to a drinking bout or a card party. I went everywhere, and everywhere received the heartiest of welcomes. I could sing and dance, and play the lute, and act, and I was ready to compose a sonnet or an ode at a moment's notice; in a week I could produce a five-act tragedy in the Senecan manner, or an epic on Rinaldo or Launcelot; and as I had not a care in the world and was as merry as a drunken friar, they opened their arms to me and gave me the best of all they had. . . .

I was attentive to all the ladies, and scandalous tongues gave me half a dozen mistresses, with details of the siege and capture. I wondered whether the amiable Giulia heard the stories, and what she thought of them. Occasionally I saw her, but I did not trouble to speak to her; Forli was large enough for the two of us; and when people are disagreeable why should you trouble your head about them?

One afternoon I rode with Matteo a few miles out of Forli to a villa where there was to be some festivity in honour of a christening. It was a beautiful spot, with fountains and shady walks, and pleasant lawns of well-mown grass; and I set myself to the enjoyment of another day. Among the guests was Claudia Piacentini. I pretended to be very angry with her because, at a ball which she had recently given, I had not received the honour of an invitation. She came to me to ask forgiveness.

'It was my husband,' she said, which I knew perfectly well. 'He said he would not have you in his house. You've had another quarrel with him!'

'How can I help it, when I see him the possessor of the lovely Claudia!'

'He says he will never be satisfied till he has your blood.'

I was not alarmed.

'He talked of making a vow never to cut his beard or his hair till he had his revenge, but I implored him not to make himself more hideous than a merciful Providence had already made him.'

I thought of the ferocious Ercole with a long, untrimmed beard and unkempt hair falling over his face.

'He would have looked like a wild man of the woods,' I said. 'I should have had to allow myself to be massacred for the good of society. I should have been one more of the martyrs of humanity—Saint Philip Brandolini!'

I offered her my arm, suggesting a saunter through the gardens. . . . We wandered along cool paths bordered with myrtle and laurel and cypress trees; the air was filled with the song of birds, and a gentle breeze bore to us the scent of the spring flowers. By-and-by we came to a little lawn shut in by tall shrubs; in the middle a fountain was playing, and under the shadow of a chestnut-tree was a marble seat supported by griffins; in one corner stood a statue of Venus framed in green bushes. We had left the throng of guests far behind, and the place was very still; the birds, as if oppressed with its beauty, had ceased to sing, and only the fountain broke the silence. The unceasing fall of water was like a lullaby in its monotony, and the air was scented with lilac.

We sat down. The quiet was delightful; peace and beauty filled one, and I felt a great sense of happiness pass into me, like some subtle liquid permeating every corner of my soul. The smell of the lilac was beginning to intoxicate me; and from my happiness issued a sentiment of love towards all nature; I felt as though I could stretch out my arms and embrace its impalpable spirit. The Venus in the corner gained flesh-like tints of green and yellow, and seemed to be melting into life; the lilac came across to me in great waves, oppressive, overpowering.

I looked at Claudia. I thought she was affected as myself; she, too, was overwhelmed by the murmur of the water, the warmth, the scented air. And I was struck again with the wonderful voluptuousness of her beauty; her mouth sensual and moist, the lips deep red and heavy. Her neck was wonderfully massive, so white that the veins showed clear and blue; her clinging dress revealed the fulness of her form, its undulating curves. She seemed some goddess of Sensuality. As I looked at her I was filled with a sudden blind desire to possess her. I stretched out my arms, and she, with a cry of passion, like an animal, surrendered herself to my embrace. I drew her to me and kissed her beautiful mouth sensual and moist, her lips deep red and heavy. . . .

We sat side by side looking at the fountain, breathing in the scented air.

'When can I see you?' I whispered.

'To-morrow. . . . After midnight. Come into the little street behind my house, and a door will be opened to you.'

'Claudia!'

'Good-bye. You must not come back with me now, we have been away so long, people would notice us. Wait here a while after me, and then there will be no fear. Good-bye.'

She left me, and I stretched myself on the marble seat, looking at the little rings which the drops made as they fell on the water. My love for Giulia was indeed finished now—dead, buried, and a stone Venus erected over it as only sign of its existence. I tried to think of a suitable inscription. . . . Time could kill the most obstinate love, and a beautiful woman,

I

with the breezes of spring to help her, could carry away even the remembrance. I felt that my life was now complete. I had all pleasures imaginable at my beck and call: good wines to drink, good foods to eat, nice clothes; games, sports and pastimes; and, last of all, the greatest gift the gods can make, a beautiful woman to my youth and strength. I had arrived at the summit of wisdom, the point aimed at by the wise man, to take the day as it comes, seizing the pleasures, avoiding the disagreeable, enjoying the present, and giving no thought to the past or future. That, I said to myself, is the highest wisdom — never to think; for the way of happiness is to live in one's senses as the beasts, and like the ox, chewing the cud, use the mind only to consider one's superiority to the rest of mankind.

I laughed a little as I thought of my tears and cries when Giulia left me. It was not a matter worth troubling about; all I should have said to myself was that I was a fool not to abandon her before she abandoned me. Poor Giulia! I quite frightened her in the vehemence of my rage.

The following evening I would not let Matteo go to bed.

'You must keep me company,' I said, 'I am going out at one.'

'Very well,' he said, 'if you will tell me where you're going.'

'Ah, no, that is a secret; but I am willing to drink her health with you.'

'Without a name?'

'Yes!'

'To the nameless one, then; and good luck!'

Then, after a little conversation, he said,—

'I am glad you have suffered no more from Giulia dall' Aste. I was afraid—'

'Oh, these things pass off. I took your advice, and found the best way to console myself was to fall in love with somebody else.'

There was a little excitement in going to this mysterious meeting. I wondered whether it was a trap arranged by the amiable Ercole to get me in his power and rid himself of my unpleasant person. But faint heart never won fair lady; and even if he set on me with two or three others, I should be able to give a reasonable account of myself.

But there had been nothing to fear. On my way home, as the day was breaking, I smiled to myself at the matter-of-fact way in which a woman had opened the little door, and shown me into the room Claudia had told me of. She was evidently well used to her business; she did not even take the trouble to look into my face to see who was the newcomer. I wondered how many well-cloaked gallants she had let in by the same door; I did not care if they were half a hundred. I did not suppose the beautiful Claudia was more virtuous than myself. Suddenly it occurred to me that I had revenged myself on Ercole Piacentini at last; and the quaint thought, coming unexpectedly, made me stop dead and burst into a shout of laughter. The thought of that hang-dog visage, and the beautiful ornaments I had given him, was enough to make a dead man merry. Oh, it was a fairer revenge than any I could have dreamed of!

But, besides that, I was filled with a great sense
of pleasure because I was at last free. I felt that
if some slight chain still bound me to Giulia now,
even that was broken and I had recovered my liberty.
There was no love this time. There was a great
desire for the magnificent sensual creature, with the
lips deep red and heavy; but it left my mind free.
I was now again a complete man; and this time I
had no Nemesis to fear.

XVIII

AND so my life went on for a little while, filled with
pleasure and amusement. I was contented with my
lot, and had no wish for change. The time went by,
and we reached the first week in April. Girolamo
had organised a great ball to celebrate the completion of his Palace. He had started living in it as
soon as there were walls and roof, but he had spent
years on the decorations, taking into his service the
best artists he could find in Italy; and now at last
everything was finished. The Orsi had been invited
with peculiar cordiality, and on the night we betook
ourselves to the Palace.

We walked up the stately staircase, a masterpiece
of architecture, and found ourselves in the enormous
hall which Girolamo had designed especially for
gorgeous functions. It was ablaze with light. At
the further end, on a low stage, led up to by three
broad steps, under a daïs, on high-backed, golden
chairs, sat Girolamo and Caterina Sforza. Behind
them, in a semicircle, and on the steps at each side,
were the ladies of Caterina's suite, and a number of

gentlemen; at the back, standing like statues, a row of men-at-arms.

'It is almost regal!' said Checco, pursing up his lips.

'It is not so poor a thing to be the Lord of Forli,' answered Matteo.   Fuel to the fire!

We approached, and Girolamo, as he saw us, rose and came down the steps.

'Hail, my Checco!' he said, taking both his hands. 'Till you had come the assembly was not complete.'

Matteo and I went to the Countess.   She had surpassed herself this night.   Her dress was of cloth of silver, shimmering and sparkling.   In her hair were diamonds shining like fireflies in the night; her arms, her neck, her fingers glittered with costly gems.   I had never seen her look so beautiful, nor so magnificent.   Let them say what they liked, Checco and Matteo and the rest of them, but she was born to be a queen.   How strange that this off-spring of the rough Condottiere and the lewd woman should have a majesty such as one imagines of a mighty empress descended from countless kings.

She took the trouble to be particularly gracious to us.   Me she complimented on some verses she had seen, and was very flattering in reference to a pastoral play which I had arranged.   She could not congratulate my good Matteo on any intellectual achievements, but the fame of his amours gave her a subject on which she could playfully reproach him. She demanded details, and I left her listening intently to some history which Matteo was whispering in her ear; and I knew he was not particular in what he said.

I felt in peculiarly high spirits, and I looked about for somone on whom to vent my good humour. I caught sight of Giulia. I had seen her once or twice since my return to Forli, but had never spoken to her. Now I felt sure of myself; I knew I did not care two straws for her, but I thought it would please me to have a little revenge. I looked at her a moment. I made up my mind; I went to her and bowed most ceremoniously.

'Donna Giulia, behold the moth!' I had used the simile before, but not to her, so it did not matter.

She looked at me undecidedly, not quite knowing how to take me.

'May I offer you my arm,' I said as blandly as I could.

She smiled a little awkwardly and took it.

'How beautiful the Countess is to-night!' I said. 'Everyone will fall in love with her.' I knew she hated Caterina, a sentiment which the great lady returned with vigour. 'I would not dare say it to another; but I know you are never jealous: she is indeed like the moon among the stars.'

'The idea does not seem too new,' she said coldly.

'It is all the more comprehensible. I am thinking of writing a sonnet on the theme.'

'I imagined it had been done before; but the ladies of Forli will doubtless be grateful to you.'

She was getting cross; and I knew by experience that when she was cross she always wanted to cry.

'I am afraid you are angry with me,' I said.

'No, it is you who are angry with me,' she answered rather tearfully.

'I? Why should you think that?'

'You have not forgiven me for—'

I wondered whether the conscientious Giorgio had had another attack of morality and ridden off into the country.

'My dear lady,' I said, with a little laugh, 'I assure you that I have forgiven you entirely. After all, it was not such a very serious matter.'

'No?' She looked at me with a little surprise.

I shrugged my shoulders.

'You were quite right in what you did. Those things have to finish some time or other, and it really does not so much matter when.'

'I was afraid I had hurt you,' she said in a low voice.

The scene came to my mind; the dimly-lit room, the delicate form lying on the couch, cold and indifferent, while I was given over to an agony of despair. I remembered the glitter of the jewelled ring against the white hand. I would have no mercy.

'My dear Giulia—you will allow me to call you Giulia?'

She nodded.

'My dear Giulia, I was a little unhappy at first, I acknowledge, but one get's over those things so quickly—a bottle of wine, and a good sleep: they are like bleeding to a fever.'

'You were unhappy?'

'Naturally; one is always rather put out when one is dismissed. One would prefer to have done the breaking oneself.'

'It was a matter of pride?'

'I am afraid I must confess to it.'

'I did not think so at the time.'

I laughed.

'Oh, that is my excited way of putting things. I frightened you ; but it did not really mean anything.'

She did not answer. After a while I said,—

'You know, when one is young one should make the most of one's time. Fidelity is a stupid virtue, unphilosophical and extremely unfashionable.'

'What do you mean ? '

'Simply this ; you did not particularly love me, and I did not particularly love you.'

'Oh ! '

'We had a passing fancy for one another, and that satisfied there was nothing more to keep us together. We should have been very foolish not to break the chain ; if you had not done so, I should have. With your woman's intuition, you saw that and fore-stalled me ! '

Again she did not answer.

'Of course, if you had been in love with me, or I with you, it would have been different. But as it was—'

' I see my cousin Violante in the corner there; will you lead me to her ? '

I did as she asked, and as she was bowing me my dismissal I said,—

'We have had a very pleasant talk, and we are quite good friends, are we not ? '

'Quite ! ' she said.

I drew a long breath as I left her. I hoped I had hurt ; I hoped I had humiliated her. I wished I could have thought of things to say that would have cut her to the heart. I was quite indifferent to her, but when I remembered—I hated her.

I knew everyone in Forli by now, and as I turned away from Giulia I had no lack of friends with whom to talk. The rooms became more crowded every moment. The assembly was the most brilliant that Forli had ever seen; and as the evening wore on the people became more animated; a babel of talk drowned the music, and the chief topic of conversation was the wonderful beauty of Caterina. She was bubbling over with high spirits; no one knew what had happened to make her so joyful, for of late she had suffered a little from the unpopularity of her husband, and a sullen look of anger had replaced the old smiles and graces. But to-night she was herself again. Men were standing round talking to her, and one heard a shout of laughter from them as every now and then she made some witty repartee; and her conversation gained another charm from a sort of soldierly bluntness which people remembered in Francesco Sforza, and which she had inherited. People also spoke of the cordiality of Girolamo towards our Checco; he walked up and down the room with him, arm in arm, talking affectionately; it reminded the onlookers of the time when they had been as brothers together. Caterina occasionally gave them a glance and a little smile of approval; she was evidently well pleased with the reconciliation.

I was making my way through the crowd, watching the various people, giving a word here and there or a nod, and I thought that life was really a very amusing thing. I felt mightily pleased with myself, and I wondered where my good friend Claudia was; I must go and pay her my respects.

'Filippo!'

I turned and saw Scipione Moratini standing by his sister, with a number of gentlemen and ladies, most of them known to me.

'Why are you smiling so contentedly?' he said. 'You look as if you had lost a pebble and found a diamond in its place.'

'Perhaps I have; who knows?'

At that moment I saw Ercole Piacentini enter the room with his wife; I wondered why they were so late. Claudia was at once seized upon by one of her admirers, and, leaving her husband, sauntered off on the proferred arm. Ercole came up the room on his way to the Count. His grim visage was contorted into an expression of amiability, which sat on him with an ill grace.

'This is indeed a day of rejoicing,' I said; 'even the wicked ogre is trying to look pleasant.'

Giulia gave a little silvery laugh. I thought it forced.

'You have a forgiving spirit, dear friend,' she said, accenting the last word in recollection of what I had said to her. 'A truly Christian disposition!'

'Why?' I asked, smiling.

'I admire the way in which you have forgiven Ercole for the insults he has offered you; one does not often find a gentleman who so charitably turns his other cheek to the smiter!'

I laughed within myself; she was trying to be even with me. I was glad to see that my darts had taken good effect. Scipione interposed, for what his sister had said was sufficiently bitter.

'Nonsense, Giulia!' he said. 'You know Filippo

is the last man to forgive his enemies until the breath is well out of their bodies; but circumstances—'

Giulia pursed up her lips into an expression of contempt.

'Circumstances. I was surprised, because I remembered the vigour with which Messer Filippo had vowed to revenge himself.

'Oh, but Messer Filippo considers that he has revenged himself very effectively,' I said.

'How?'

'There are more ways of satisfying one's honour than by cutting a hole in a person's chest.'

'What do you mean, Filippo?' said Scipione.

'Did you not see as he passed?'

'Ercole? What?'.

'Did you not see the adornment of his noble head, the elegant pair of horns?'

They looked at me, not quite understanding; then I caught sight of Claudia, who was standing close to us.

'Ah, I see the diamond I have found in place of the pebble I have lost. I pray you excuse me.'

Then as they saw me walk towards Claudia they understood, and I heard a burst of laughter. I took my lady's hand, and bowing deeply, kissed it with the greatest fervour. I glanced at Giulia from the corner of my eyes and saw her looking down on the ground, with a deep blush of anger on her face. My heart leapt for joy to think that I had returned something of the agony she had caused me.

The evening grew late and the guests began to go. Checco, as he passed me, asked,—

'Are you ready?'

'Yes!' I said, accompanying him to Girolamo and the Countess to take our leave.

'You are very unkind, Checco,' said the Countess. 'You have not come near me the whole evening.'

'You have been so occupied,' he answered.

'But I am not now,' she replied, smiling. 'The moment I saw you free I came to you.'

'To say good-bye.'

'It is very late.'

'No, surely; sit down and talk to me.'

Checco did as he was bid, and I, seeing he meant to stay longer, sauntered off again in search of friends. The conversation between Checco and the Countess was rather hindered by the continual leave-takings, as the people began to go away rapidly, in groups. I sat myself down in a window with Matteo, and we began comparing notes of our evening; he told me of a new love to whom he had discovered his passion for the first time.

'Fair wind, foul wind?' I asked, laughing.

'She pretended to be very angry,' he said, 'but she allowed me to see that if the worst came to the worst she would not permit me to break my heart.'

I looked out into the room and found that everyone had gone, except Ercole Piacentini, who was talking to the Count in undertones.

'I am getting so sleepy,' said Matteo. We went forward to the Countess, who said, as she saw us come,—

'Go away, Matteo! I will not have you drag Checco away yet; we have been trying to talk to one another for the last half-hour, and now that we have the chance at last I refuse to be disturbed.'

'I would not for worlds rob Checco of such pleasure,' said Matteo; adding to me, as we retired to our window, 'What a nuisance having to wait for one's cousin while a pretty woman is flirting with him!'

'You have me to talk to—what more can you want!'

'I don't want to talk to you at all,' he answered, laughing.

Girolamo was still with Ercole. His mobile eyes were moving over the room, hardly ever resting on Ercole's face, but sometimes on us, more often on Checco. I wondered whether he was jealous.

At last Checco got up and said Good-night. Then Girolamo came forward.

'You are not going yet,' he said. 'I want to speak with you on the subject of those taxes.'

It was the first time he had mentioned them.

'It is getting so late,' said Checco, 'and these good gentlemen are tired.'

'They can go home. Really, it is very urgent.'

Checco hesitated, and looked at us.

'We will wait for you,' said Matteo.

Girolamo's eyes moved about here and there, never resting a moment, from Checco to me, from me to Matteo, and on to his wife, and then on again, with extraordinary rapidity—it was quite terrifying.

'One would think you were afraid of leaving Checco in our hands,' said the Countess, smiling.

'No,' returned Matteo; 'but I look forward to having some of your attention now that Checco is otherwise occupied. Will you let me languish?'

She laughed, and a rapid glance passed between her and the Count.

' I shall be only too pleased,' she said, ' come and sit by me, one on each side.'

The Count turned to Ercole.

' Well, good-night, my friend,' he said. ' Good-night ! '

Ercole left us, and Girolamo, taking Checco's arm, walked up and down the room, speaking. The Countess and Matteo commenced a gay conversation. Although I was close to them I was left alone, and I watched the Count. His eyes fascinated me, moving ceaselessly. What could be behind them ? What could be the man's thoughts that his eyes should never rest ? They enveloped the person they looked at—his head, every feature of his face, his body, his clothes ; one imagined there was no detail they had not caught ; it was as if they ate into the very soul of the man.

The two men tramped up and down, talking earnestly ; I wondered what they were saying. At last Girolamo stopped.

' Ah, well, I must have mercy on you ; I shall tire you to death. And you know I do not wish to do anything to harm you.'

Checco smiled.

' Whatever difficulty there has been between us, Checco, you know that there has never on my part been any ill-feeling towards you. I have always had for you a very sincere and affectionate friendship.'

And as he said the words an extraordinary change came over him. The eyes, the mobile eyes, stopped still at last ; for the first time I saw them perfectly steady, motionless, like glass; they looked fixedly into Checco's eyes, without winking, and their immobility was as strange as their perpetual movement, and to me it was more terrifying. It was as if Girolamo was trying to see his own image in Checco's soul.

We bade them farewell, and together issued out into the silence of the night; and I felt that behind us the motionless eyes, like glass, were following us into the darkness.

XIX

WE issued out into the silence of the night. There had been a little rain during the day, and the air in consequence was fresh and sweet; the light breeze of the spring made one expand one's lungs and draw in long breaths. One felt the trees bursting out into green leaves, and the buds on the plants opening their downy mantles and discovering the flower within. Light clouds were wandering lazily along the sky, and between them shone out a few dim stars. Checco and Matteo walked in front, while I lingered enjoying the spring night; it filled me with a sweet sadness, a reaction from the boisterous joy of the evening, and pleasant by the contrast.

When Matteo fell behind and joined me, I received him a little unwillingly, disappointed at the interruption of my reverie.

'I asked Checco what the Count had said to him of the taxes, but he would not tell me; he said he wanted to think about the conversation.'

I made no answer, and we walked on in silence. We had left the piazza, and were going through the narrow streets bordered by the tall black houses. It was very late, and there was not a soul about; there

K

was no sound but that of our own footsteps, and of
Checco walking a few yards in front. Between the
roofs of the houses only a little strip of sky could be
seen, a single star, and the clouds floating lazily.
The warm air blew in my face, and filled me with an
intoxication of melancholy. I thought how sweet it
would be to fall asleep this night, and never again
to wake. I was tired, and I wanted the rest of an
endless sleep. . . .

Suddenly I was startled by a cry.

I saw from the shadow of the houses black forms
spring out on Checco. An arm was raised, and a
glittering instrument flashed in the darkness. He
staggered forward.

'Matteo,' he cried. 'Help! Help!'

We rushed forward, drawing our swords. There
was a scuffle, three of us against four of them, a flash
of swords, a cry from one of the men as he reeled and
fell with a wound from Matteo's sword. Then another
rush, a little band of men suddenly appeared round
the corner, and Ercole Piacentini's voice, crying,—

'What is it? What is it?'

And Matteo's answer,—

'Help us, Ercole! I have killed one. Checco is
stabbed.'

'Ah!' a cry from Ercole, and with his men he
rushed into the fray.

A few more cries, still the flash of swords, the fall of
heavy bodies on the stones.

'They are done for!' said Matteo.

The shouts, the clang of metal woke up the neighbours; lights were seen at the windows, and night-
capped women appeared shrieking; doors were

thrown open, and men came out in their shirts, sword in hand.

'What is it? What is it?'

'Checco, are you hurt?' asked Matteo.

'No; my coat of mail!'

'Thank God you had it on! I saw you stagger.'

'It was the blow. At first I did not know whether I was hurt or not.'

'What is it? What is it?'

The neighbours surrounded us.

'They have tried to murder Checco! Checco d'Orsi!'

'My God! Is he safe?'

'Who has done it?'

All eyes were turned to the four men, each one lying heaped up on the ground, with the blood streaming from his wounds.'

'They are dead!'

'Footpads!' said Ercole; 'they wanted to rob you, and did not know you were accompanied.'

'Footpads! Why should footpads rob me this night?' said Checco. 'I wish they were not dead.'

'Look, look!' said a bystander, 'there is one moving.'

The words were hardly out of the man's mouth before one of Ercole's soldiers snatched up his dagger and plunged it in the man's neck, shouting,—

'Bestia!'

A tremor went through the prostrate body, and then it was quite still.

'You fool!' said Matteo, angrily. 'Why did you do that?'

'He is a murderer,' said the soldier.

'You fool, we wanted him alive, not dead. We could have found out who hired him.'

'What do you mean?' said Ercole. 'They are common robbers.'

'Here is the guard,' cried someone.

The guard came, and immediately there was a babel of explanation. The captain stepped forward, and examined the men lying on the ground.

'They are all dead,' he said.

'Take them away,' said Ercole. 'Let them be put in a church till morning.'

'Stop!' cried Checco. 'Bring a light, and let us see if we can recognise them.'

'Not now, it is late. To-morrow you can do what you like.'

'To-morrow it will be later, Ercole,' answered Checco. 'Bring a light.'

Torches were brought, and thrust into the face of each dead man. Everyone eagerly scrutinised the features, drawn up in their last agony.

'I don't know him.'

Then to another.

'No.'

And the other two also were unknown. Checco examined the face of the last, and shook his head. But a man broke out excitedly,—

'Ah! I know him.'

A cry from us all.

'Who is it?'

'I know him. It is a soldier, one of the Count's guard.'

'Ah!' said Matteo and Checco, looking at one another. 'One of the Count's guard!

'That is a lie,' said Ercole. 'I know them all, and
I have never seen that face before. It is a footpad, I
tell you.'

'It is not. I know him well. He is a member of
the guard.'

'It is a lie, I tell you.'

'Ercole is doubtless right,' said Checco. 'They are
common thieves. Let them be taken away. They
have paid a heavy price for their attempt. Good-
night, my friends. Good-night, Ercole, and thanks.'

The guard took hold of the dead men by the head
and by the feet, and one after another, in single file,
they bore them off down the dark street. We three
moved on, the crowd gradually melted away, and
everything again became dark and silent.

We walked home side by side without speaking.
We came to the Palazzo Orsi, entered, walked upstairs, one after the other, into Checco's study, lights
were brought, the door closed carefully, and Checco
turned round to us.

'Well?'

Neither I nor Matteo spoke. Checco clenched his
fist, and his eyes flashed as he hissed out,—

'The cur!'

We all knew the attempt was the Count's. . . . .

'By God! I am glad you are safe,' said Matteo.

'What a fool I was to be taken in by his protesta-
tions! I ought to have known that he would never
forget the injury I had done him.'

'He planned it well,' said Matteo.

'Except for the soldier,' I remarked. 'He should
not have chosen anyone who could be recognised.'

'Probably he was the leader. But how well he

managed everything, keeping us after the others, and nearly persuading Filippo and me to go home before you. Caterina was in the plot.'

'I wonder he did not defer the attempt when he found you would not be alone,' I said to Checco.

'He knows I am never alone, and such an opportunity would not easily occur again. Perhaps he thought they could avoid you two, or even murder you as well.'

'But Ercole and his men?' I said.

'Yes, I have been thinking about them. The only explanation I have is that he placed them there to cover their flight if they succeeded, and if they failed or could not escape, to kill them.'

'As, in fact, they did. I thought I saw Ercole make a sign to the soldier who stabbed the only living one.'

'Possibly. The idea was evidently to destroy all witnesses and all opportunity for inquiry.'

'Well,' said Matteo, 'it will show others that it is dangerous to do dirty work for the Riario.'

'It will indeed!'

'And now, what is to happen?' said Matteo.

Checco looked at him, but did not reply.

'Do you still refuse to do to Girolamo as he has tried to do to you?'

Checco answered quietly,—

'No!'

'Ah!' we both cried. 'Then you consent?'

'I see no reason now for not taking the law into my own hands.'

'Assassination?' whispered Matteo.

And Checco answered boldly,—

'Assassination!' Then, after a pause, 'It is the only way open to me. Do you remember Lorenzo's words? They have been with me every day, and I have considered them very, very deeply: "Let Checco know that it is only the fool who proposes to himself an end, when he cannot or will not attain it; but the man who deserves the name of man marches straight to the goal with clearness of mind and strength of will. He looks at things as they are, putting aside all vain appearances, and when his intelligence has shown him the means to his end, he is a fool if he refuses them, and he is a wise man if he uses them steadily and unhesitatingly." I know the end, and I will attain it. I know the means, and I will use them steadily, without hesitation.'

'I am glad to hear you speak like that at last!' said Matteo. 'We shall have plenty to help us. The Moratini will join at once. Jacopo Ronchi and Lodovico Pansecchi are so bitter against the Count they will come with us as soon as they hear you have decided to kill the enemy of us all.'

'You are blind, Matteo. Do you not see what we must do? You mistake the means for the end.'

'What do you mean?'

'The death of Girolamo is only a means. The end is further and higher.'

Matteo did not speak.

'I must keep my hands clean from any base motive. It must not seem that I am influenced by any personal incentive. Nothing must come from me. The idea of assassination must come from outside.'

'Whom do you—'

'I think Bartolomeo Moratini must propose it, and I will yield to his instances.'

'Good! then I will go to him.'

'That will not do either. Neither you nor I must be concerned in it. Afterwards it must be clear to all minds that the Orsi were influenced solely by the public welfare. Do you see? I will tell you how it must be. Filippo must help us. He must go to Bartolomeo, and from his great affection for us talk of our danger and intreat Bartolomeo to persuade me to the assassination. Do you understand, Filippo?'

'Perfectly!'

'Will you do it?'

'I will go to him to-morrow.'

'Wait till the news of the attempt has spread.'

I smiled at the completeness with which Checco had arranged everything; he had evidently thought it all out. How had his scruples disappeared?

The blackness of the night was sinking before the dawn when we bade one another good-night.

XX

I SEEMED to have slept a bare half-hour when I was awakened by a great noise downstairs. I got up, and looking out of the window saw a crowd gathered in the street below; they were talking and gesticulating furiously. Then I remembered the occurrence of the night, and I saw that the news had spread and these were citizens come to gather details. I went downstairs and found the courtyard thronged. Immediately I was surrounded by anxious people asking for news. Very contrary reports had circulated; some said that Checco had been killed outright, others that he had escaped, while most asserted that he was wounded. All asked for Checco.

'If he is unhurt, why does he not show himself?' they asked.

A servant assured them that he was dressing, and would be with them at once. . . . Suddenly there was a shout. Checco had appeared at the top of the stairs. They rushed towards him, surrounding him with cries of joy; they seized his hand, they clung to his legs, some of them touched him all over to see that he was indeed un-

wounded, others kissed the lappets of his coat. . . .
Bartolomeo Moratini entered the court with his
sons, and the people shrunk back as he came
forward and embraced Checco.

'Thank God you are saved!' he said. 'It will
be an evil day for Forli when anything happens to
you.'

The people answered in shouts. But at that
moment another sound was heard without—a long
and heavy murmur. The people surrounding the
doorway looked out and turned in astonishment
to their neighbours, pointing to the street; the
murmur spread. What was it?

'Make way! Make way!'

A strident voice called out the words, and ushers
pushed the people aside. A little troop of men
appeared in the entrance, and as they sank back
there stepped forward the Count. The Count!
Checco started, but immediately recovering himself advanced to meet his visitor. Girolomo walked
up to him, and taking him in his arms kissed him
on the cheeks, and said,—

'My Checco! My Checco!'

We who knew and the others who suspected
looked on with astonishment.

'As soon as I heard the terrible news I rushed to
find you,' said the Count. 'Are you safe—quite
safe?'

He embraced him again.

'You cannot think what agony I suffered when I
heard you were wounded. How glad I am it was
not true. Oh, God in Heaven, I thank Thee for
my Checco!'

'You are very kind, my lord,' answered our friend.

'But it is some consolation that the miscreants have met the end which they deserved. We must take steps to free the town of all such dangerous persons. What will men say of my rule when it is known that the peaceful citizen cannot walk home at night without danger to his life? Oh, Checco, I blame myself bitterly.'

'You have no cause, my lord, but—would it not be well to examine the men to see if they are known in Forli? Perhaps they have associates.'

'Certainly; the idea was in my mind. Let them be laid out in the market-place so that all may see them.'

'Pardon, sir,' said one of his suite, 'but they were laid in the Church of San Spirito last night, and this morning they have disappeared.'

Matteo and I looked at one another. Checco kept his eyes fixed on the Count.

'Disappeared!' cried the latter, displaying every sign of impatience. 'Who is responsible for this? Offer a reward for the discovery of their bodies and of any accomplices. I insist on their being discovered!'

Shortly afterwards he took his leave, after repeatedly kissing Checco, and warmly congratulating Matteo and myself on the assistance we had given to our friend. To me he said,—

'I regret, Messer Filippo, that you are not a Forlivese. I should be proud to have such a citizen.'

Bartolomeo Moratini was still at the Palazzo Orsi, so, seizing my opportunity, I took him by the arm and walked with him to the statue gallery, where we could talk in peace.

'What do you think of all this?' I said.

He shook his head.

'It is the beginning of the end. Of course it is clear to all of us that the assassination was ordered by the Count; he will persuade nobody of his innocence by his pretended concern. All the town is whispering his name.

'Having made a first attempt and failed, he will not hesitate to make a second, for if he could forgive the injury which he has received from Checco, he can never forgive the injury which he himself has done him. And next time he will not fail.'

'I am terribly concerned,' I said. 'You know the great affection I have for both the Orsi.'

He stopped and warmly shook my hand.

'I cannot let Checco throw away his life in this way,' I said.

'What can be done?'

'Only one thing, and you suggested it. . . . Girolamo must be killed.'

'Ah, but Checco will never consent to that.'

'I am afraid not,' I said gravely. 'You know the delicacy of his conscience.'

'Yes; and though I think it excessive, I admire him for it. In these days it is rare to find a man so honest and upright and conscientious as Checco. But, Messer Filippo, one must yield to the ideas of the age one lives in.'

'I, too, am convinced of his noble-mindedness, but it will ruin him.'

'I am afraid so,' sighed the old man, stroking his beard.

'But he must be saved in spite of himself. He must be brought to see the necessity of killing the Count.' I spoke as emphatically as I could.

'He will never consent.'

'He must consent; and you are the man to make him do so. He would not listen to anything that Matteo or I said, but for you he has the greatest respect. I am sure if anyone can influence him it is you.'

'I have some power over him, I believe.'

'Will you try? Don't let him suspect that Matteo or I have had anything to do with it, or he will not listen. It must come solely from you.'

'I will do my best.'

'Ah, that is good of you. But don't be discouraged by his refusals; be insistent, for our sake. And one thing more, you know his unselfishness; he would not move his hand to save himself, but if you showed him that it is for the good of others, he could not refuse. Let him think the safety of us all depends on him. He is a man you can only move by his feeling for others.'

'I believe you,' he answered. 'But I will go to him, and I will leave no argument unused.'

'I am sure that your efforts will be rewarded.'

Here I showed myself a perfectly wise man, for I only prophesied because I knew.

XXI

In the evening Bartolomeo returned to the Palace and asked for Checco. At his request Matteo and I joined him in Checco's study, and besides there were his two sons, Scipione and Alessandro. Bartolomeo was graver than ever.

'I have come to you now, Checco, impelled by a very strong sense of duty, and I wish to talk with you on a matter of the greatest importance.'

He cleared his throat.

'Firstly, are you convinced that the attempt on your life was plotted by Girolamo Riario?'

'I am sorry for his sake, but—I am.'

'So are we all, absolutely. And what do you intend to do now?'

'What can I do? Nothing!'

'The answer is not nothing. You have something to do.'

'And that is?'

'To kill Girolamo before he has time to kill you.'

Checco started to his feet.

'They have been talking to you—Matteo and Filippo. It is they who have put this in your head. I knew it would be suggested again.'

158

' Nothing has given me the idea but the irresistible force of circumstances.'

' Never! I will never consent to that.'

' But he will kill you.'

' I can die!'

' It will be the ruin of your family. What will happen to your wife and children if you are dead?'

' If need be they can die too. No one who bears the name of Orsi fears death.'

' You cannot sacrifice their lives in cold blood.'

' I cannot kill a fellow-man in cold blood. Ah, my friend, you don't know what is in me. I am not religious; I have never meddled with priests; but something in my heart tells me not to do this thing. I don't know what it is—conscience or honour—but it is speaking clearly within me.'

He had his hand on his heart, and was speaking very earnestly. We followed his eyes and saw them resting on a crucifix.

' No, Bartolomeo,' he said, ' one cannot forget God. He is above us always, always watching us; and what should I say to Him with the blood of that man on my hands? You may say what you like, but, believe me, it is best to be honest and straightforward, and to the utmost of one's ability to carry out the doctrines which Christ has left us, and upon which he set the seal with the blood of His hands and feet and the wound in His side.'

Bartolomeo looked at me as if it were hopeless to attempt anything against such sentiments. But I signed him energetically to go on; he hesitated. It would be almost tragic if he gave the matter up before Checco had time to surrender. However, he proceeded,—

'You are a good man, Checco, and I respect you deeply for what you have said. But if you will not stir to save yourself, think of the others.'

'What do you mean?' said Checco, starting as if from a dream.

'Have you the right to sacrifice your fellow-men? The citizens of Forli depend on you.'

'Ah, they will easily find another leader. Why, you yourself will be of greater assistance to them than I have ever been. How much better will they be in your strong hands than with me!'

'No, no! You are the only man who has power here. You could not be replaced.'

'But what can I do more than I am doing. I do not seek to leave Forli; I will stay here and protect myself as much as I can. I cannot do more.'

'Oh, Checco, look at their state. It cannot continue. They are ground down now; the Count must impose these taxes, and what will be their condition then? The people are dying in their misery, and the survivors hold happy those who die. How can you look on and see all this? And you, you know Girolamo will kill you; it is a matter of time, and who can tell how short a time? Perhaps even now he is forging the weapon of your death.'

'My death! My death!' cried Checco. 'All that is nothing!'

'But what will be the lot of the people when you are gone? You are the only curb on Riario's tyranny. When you are dead, nothing will keep him back. And when once he has eased his path by murder he

will not fail to do so again. We shall live under
perpetual terror of the knife. Oh, have mercy on
your fellow-citizens.'

'My country!' said Checco. 'My country!'

'You cannot resist this. For the good of your
country you must lead us on.'

'And if my soul—'

'It is for your country. Ah! Checco, think of us
all. Not for ourselves only, but for our wives, our
innocent children, we beg you, we implore. Shall we
go down on our knees to you?'

'Oh, my God, what shall I do?' said Checco,
extremely agitated.

'Listen to my father, Checco!' said Scipione. 'He
has right on his side.'

'Oh, not you, too! Do not overwhelm me. I feel
you are all against me. God help me! I know it is
wrong, but I feel myself wavering.'

'Do not think of yourself, Checco ; it is for others,
for our liberty, our lives, our all, that we implore you.'

'You move me terribly. You know how I love my
country, and how can I resist you, appealing on her
behalf!'

'Be brave, Checco!' said Matteo.

'It is the highest thing of all that we ask you,'
added Bartolomeo. 'Man can do nothing greater.
We ask you to sacrifice yourself, even your soul,
may be, for the good of us all.'

Checco buried his face in his hands and groaned,—

'Oh, God! Oh, God!'

Then, with a great sigh, he rose and said,—

'Be it as you will. . . .   For the good of my
country!'

L

'Ah, thanks, thanks!'

Bartolomeo took him in his arms and kissed him on both cheeks. Then suddenly Checco tore himself away.

'But listen to this, all of you. I have consented, and now you must let me speak. I swear that in this thing I have no thought of myself. If I alone were concerned I would not move; I would wait for the assassin's knife calmly. I would even sacrifice my wife and children, and God knows how dearly I love them! I would not stir a finger to save myself. And I swear, by all that is most holy to me, that I am actuated by no base motive, no ambition, no thought of self, no petty revenge. I would willingly forgive Girolamo everything. Believe me, my friends, I am honest. I swear to you that I am only doing this for the welfare of the men I love, for the sake of you all, and—for Liberty.'

They warmly pressed his hands.

'We know it, Checco, we believe it. You are a great and a good man.'

A little later we began to discuss the ways and means. Everyone had his plan, and to it the others had the most conclusive objections. We all talked together, each one rather annoyed at the unwillingness of the others to listen to him, and thinking how contemptible their ideas were beside his own. Checco sat silent. After a while Checco spoke,—

'Will you listen to me?'

We held our tongues.

'First of all,' he said, 'we must find out who is with us and who is against us.'

'Well,' interrupted Scipione, 'there are the two

soldiers, Jacopo Ronchi and Lodovico Pansecchi; they are furious with the Count, and said to me a long while since that they would willingly kill him.'

'Our six selves and those two make eight.'

'Then there are Pietro Albanese, and Paglianino, and Marco Scorsacana.'

They were devoted adherents of the house of Orsi, and could be trusted to follow the head of the family to the bottomless pit.

'Eleven,' counted Bartolomeo.

'And then—'

Each mentioned a name till the total was brought to seventeen.

'Who else?' asked Matteo.

'That is enough,' said Checco. 'It is as foolish to have more than necessary as to have less. Now, once more, who are they?'

The names were repeated. They were all known enemies of the Count, and most of them related to the Orsi.

'We had better go to them separately and talk to them.'

'It will want care!' said Bartolomeo.

'Oh, they will not be backward. The first word will bring their adhesion.'

'Before that,' said Checco, 'we must make all arrangements. Every point of the execution must be arranged, and to them nothing left but the performance.'

'Well, my idea is—'

'Have the goodness to listen to me,' said Checco. 'You have been talking of committing the deed in

church, or when he is out walking. Both of those
ways are dangerous, for he is always well surrounded, and in the former, one has to remember
the feeling of horror which the people have for
sacrilege.   Witness Galeazzo in Milan and the
Medici in Florence. One is always wise to respect
the prejudices of the mob. . . .'

'What do you propose?'

'After the mid-day meal the—our friend is in
the habit of retiring to a private room while his
servants dine. He is then almost alone. I have
often thought it would be an excellent opportunity
for an assassin; I did not know it would be myself
to take the opportunity.'

He paused and smiled at the pleasantness of the
irony.

'Afterwards we shall raise the town, and it is well
that as many of our partisans as possible be present.
The best day for that is a market-day, when they
will come in, and we shall have no need of specially
summoning them, and thus giving rise to suspicion.'

Checco looked at us to see what we thought of his
idea; then, as if from an after thought, he added,—

'Of course, this is all on the spur of the moment.'

It was well he said that, for I was thinking how
elaborately everything was planned. I wondered
how long he had the scheme in his head.

We found nothing to say against it.

'And who will do the actual deed?'

'I will!' answered Checco, quietly.

'You!'

'Yes, alone. I will tell you your parts later.'

'And when?'

' Next Saturday. That is the first market-day.'

' So soon.' We were all surprised ; it was only
five days off, it gave us very little time to think. It
was terribly near. Alessandro voiced our feelings.

' Does that give us enough time ? Why not Saturday week ? There are many needful preparations.'

' There are no needful preparations. You have
your swords ready ; the others can be warned in a
few hours. I wish it were to-morrow.'

' It is—it is very soon.'

' There is less danger of our courage failing meanwhile. We have our goal before us, and we must go
to it straight, with clearness of mind and strength of
will.'

There was nothing more to be said. As we
separated, one of the Moratini asked,—

' About the others, shall we—'

' You can leave everything to me. I take all on
my hands. Will you three come here to play a
game of chess on Friday night at ten ? Our affairs
will occupy us so that we shall not meet in the
interval. I recommend you to go about as much as
possible, and let yourselves be seen in all assemblies
and parties. . . .'

Checco was taking his captaincy in earnest. He
would allow no contradiction, and no swerving from
the path he had marked out—on the spur of the
moment.

We had four days in which to make merry and
gather the roses ; after that, who knows ? We might
be dangling from the Palace windows in an even line,
suspended by elegant hempen ropes ; or our heads
might be decorating spear heads and our bodies

God knows where. I suggested these thoughts to
Matteo, but I found him singularly ungrateful. Still,
he agreed with me that we had better make the most
of our time, and as it accorded with Checco's wishes,
we were able to go to the devil from a sense of duty.
I am sure Claudia never had a lover more ardent
than myself during these four days; but, added to
my duties towards that beautiful creature, were routs
and banquets, drinking-parties, gaming-parties, where
I plunged heavily in my uncertainty of the future,
and consequently won a fortune. Checco had taken
on his own shoulders all preparations, so that Matteo
and I had nothing to do but to enjoy ourselves; and
that we did. The only sign I had that Checco had
been working was a look of intelligence given me by
one or two of those whose names had been mentioned
in Checco's study. Jacopo Ronchi, taking leave of
me on the Thursday night, said,—

'We shall meet to-morrow.'

'You are coming to play chess, I think,' I said,
smiling.

When, at the appointed hour, Matteo and I found
ourselves again in Checco's study, we were both
rather anxious and nervous. My heart was beating
quite painfully, and I could not restrain my impatience. I wished the others would come. Gradually they made their way in, and we shook hands
quietly, rather mysteriously, with an air of school-
boys meeting together in the dark to eat stolen
fruit. It might have been comic if our mind's eye
had not presented us with so vivid a picture of a
halter.

Checco began to speak in a low voice, slightly

trembling; his emotion was real enough this time, and he did all he could to conceal it.

'My very dear and faithful fellow-citizens,' he began, 'it appears that to be born in Forli, and to live in it in our times, is the very greatest misfortune with which one can be born or with which one can live.'

I never heard such silence as that among the listeners. It was awful. Checco's voice sank lower and lower, but yet every word could be distinctly heard. The tremor was increasing.

'Is it necessary that birth and life here should be the birth and life of slaves? Our glorious ancestors never submitted to this terrible misfortune. They were free, and in their freedom they found life. But this is a living death. . . .'

He recounted the various acts of tyranny which had made the Count hateful to his subjects, and he insisted on the insecurity in which they lived.

'You all know the grievous wrongs I have suffered at the hands of the man whom I helped to place on the throne. But these wrongs I freely forgive. I am filled only with devotion to my country and love to my fellowmen. If you others have private grievances, I implore you to put them aside, and think only that you are the liberators from oppression of all those you love and cherish. Gather up to your hearts the spirit of Brutus, when, for the sake of Freedom, he killed the man whom above all others he loved.'

He gave them the details of the plot; told them what he would do himself, and what they should do, and finally dismissed them.

' Pray to God to-night,' he said earnestly, ' that He will look with favour upon the work which we have set ourselves, and implore Him to judge us by the purity of our intentions rather than by the actions which, in the imperfection of our knowledge, seem to us the only means to our end.'

We made the sign of the cross, and retired as silently as we had come.

XXII

My sleep was troubled, and when I woke the next morning the sun had only just risen.

It was Saturday, the 14th of April 1488.

I went to my window and saw a cloudless sky, brilliantly yellow over in the east, and elsewhere liquid and white, hardening gradually into blue. The rays came dancing into my room, and in them incessantly whirled countless atoms of dust. Through the open window blew the spring wind, laden with the scents of the country, the blossoms of the fruit trees, the primroses and violets. I had never felt so young and strong and healthy. What could one not do on such a day as this! I went into Matteo's room, and found him sleeping as calmly as if this were an ordinary day like any other.

'Rise, thou sluggard!' I cried.

In a few minutes we were both ready, and we went to Checco. We found him seated at a table polishing a dagger.

'Do you remember in Tacitus,' he said, smiling pleasantly, 'how the plot against Nero was discovered by one of the conspirators giving his dagger to his freedman to sharpen? Whereupon the freedman became suspicious, and warned the Emperor.'

'The philosophers tell us to rise on the mistakes of others,' I remarked in the same tone.

'One reason for my affection towards you, Filippo,' he answered, 'is that you have nice moral sentiments, and a pleasant moral way of looking at things.'

He held out his dagger and looked at it. The blade was beautifully damaskeened, the hilt bejewelled.

'Look,' he said, showing me the excellence of the steel, and pointing out the maker's name. Then, meditatively, 'I have been wondering what sort of blow would be most effective if one wanted to kill a man.'

'You can get most force,' said Matteo, 'by bringing the dagger down from above your head—thus.'

'Yes; but then you may strike the ribs, in which case you would not seriously injure your friend.'

'You can hit him in the neck.'

'The space is too small, and the chin may get in the way. On the other hand, a wound in the large vessels of that region is almost immediately fatal.'

'It is an interesting subject,' I said. 'My opinion is that the best of all blows is an underhand one, ripping up the stomach.'

I took the dagger and showed him what I meant.

'There are no hindrances in the way of bones; it is simple and certainly fatal.'

'Yes,' said Checco, 'but not immediately! My impression is that the best way is between the shoulders. Then you strike from the back, and your

victim can see no uplifted hand to warn him, and, if
he is very quick, enable him to ward the blow.'

'It is largely a matter of taste,' I answered, shrugging my shoulders. 'In these things a man has to
judge for himself according to his own idiosyncrasies.'

After a little more conversation I proposed to
Matteo that we should go out to the market-place
and see the people.

'Yes, do!' said Checco, 'and I will go and see my
father.'

As we walked along, Matteo told me that Checco
had tried to persuade his father to go away for a
while, but that he had refused, as also had his wife.
I had seen old Orso d'Orsi once or twice; he was
very weak and decrepit; he never came downstairs, but
stayed in his own rooms all day by the fireside, playing
with his grand-children. Checco was in the habit of
going to see him every day, morning and evening,
but to the rest of us it was as if he did not exist.
Checco was complete master of everything.

The market-place was full of people. Booths were
erected in rows, and on the tables the peasant women
had displayed their wares: vegetables and flowers,
chickens, ducks and all kinds of domestic fowls,
milk, butter, eggs; and other booths with meat and
oil and candles. And the sellers were a joyful crew,
decked out with red and yellow handkerchiefs, great
chains of gold around their necks, and spotless head-
dresses; they were standing behind their tables, with
a scale on one hand and a little basin full of coppers
on the other, crying out to one another, bargaining,
shouting and joking, laughing, quarrelling. Then
there were the purchasers, who walked along looking

at the goods, picking up things and pinching them, smelling them, tasting them, examining them from every point of view. And the sellers of tokens and amulets and charms passed through the crowd crying out their wares, elbowing, cursing when someone knocked against them. Gliding in and out, between people's legs, under the barrow wheels, behind the booths, were countless urchins, chasing one another through the crowd unmindful of kicks and cuffs, pouncing on any booth of which the proprietor had turned his back, seizing the first thing they could lay hands on, and scampering off with all their might. And there was a conjurer with a gaping crowd, a quack extracting teeth, a ballad singer. Everywhere was noise, and bustle, and life.

'One would not say on the first glance that these people were miserably oppressed slaves,' I said maliciously.

'You must look beneath the surface,' replied Matteo, who had begun to take a very serious view of things in general. I used to tell him that he would have a call some day and end up as a shaven monk.

'Let us amuse ourselves,' I said, taking Matteo by the arm, and dragging him along in search of prey. We fixed on a seller of cheap jewellery—a huge woman, with a treble chin and a red face dripping with perspiration. We felt quite sorry for her, and went to console her.

'It is a very cold day,' I remarked to her, whereupon she bulged out her cheeks and blew a blast that nearly carried me away.

She took up a necklace of beads and offered it to Matteo for his lady love. We began to bargain, offering her just a little lower than she asked, and then, as she showed signs of coming down, made her a final offer a little lower still. At last she seized a broom and attacked us, so that we had to fly precipitately.

I had never felt in such high spirits. I offered to race Matteo in every way he liked—riding, running and walking—but he refused, brutally telling me that I was frivolous. Then we went home. I found that Checco had just been hearing mass, and he was as solemn and silent as a hangman. I went about lamenting that I could get no one to talk to me, and at last took refuge with the children, who permitted me to join in their games, so that, at 'hide-and-seek and 'blind man's buff,' I thoroughly amused myself till dinner-time. We ate together, and I tried not to be silenced, talking the greatest nonsense I could think of; but the others sat like owls and did not listen, so that I too began to feel depressed. . . .

The frowns of the others infected me, and the dark pictures that were before their eyes appeared to mine; my words failed me and we all three sat gloomily. I had started with an excellent appetite, but again the others influenced me, and I could not eat. We toyed with our food, wishing the dinner over. I moved about restlessly, but Checco was quite still, leaning his face on his hand, occasionally raising his eyes and fixing them on Matteo or me. One of the servants dropped some plates; we all started at the sound, and Checco uttered an oath; I had never heard him swear before. He was so pale I wondered if he were nervous. I asked the time: still two hours before we could start. How long would

they take to pass! I had been longing to finish
dinner, so that I might get up and go away. I felt
an urgent need for walking, but when the meal was
over a heaviness came to my legs and I could do
nothing but sit and look at the other two. Matteo
filled his tankard and emptied it several times, but
after awhile, as he reached over for the wine, he saw
Checco's eyes fixed on the flagon, with a frown on his
forehead, and the curious raising of one corner of the
mouth, which was a sign he was displeased. Matteo
withdrew his hand and pushed his mug away; it
rolled over and fell on the floor. We heard the
church bell strike the hour; it was three o'clock.
Would it never be time! We sat on and on. At
last Checco rose and began walking up and down the
room. He called for his children. They came, and
he began talking to them in a husky voice, so that
they could scarcely understand him. Then, as if
frightened of himself, he took them in his arms, one
after the other, and kissed them convulsively, passionately, as one kisses a woman; and he told them to
go. He stifled a sob. We sat on and on. I counted
the minutes. I had never lived so long before. It
was awful. . . .

At last!

It was half-past three; we got up and took our
hats.

'Now, my friends!' said Checco, drawing a breath
of relief, 'our worst troubles are over.'

We followed him out of the house. I noticed the
jewelled hilt of his dagger, and every now and then I
saw him put his hand to it to see that it was really
there. We passed along the streets, saluted by the

people.   A beggar stopped us, and Checco threw him
a piece of gold.

'God bless you ! ' said the man.

And Checco thanked him fervently.

We walked along the narrow streets in the shade,
but as we turned a corner the sun came full on our
faces.   Checco stopped a moment and opened his
arms, as if to receive the sunbeams in his embrace,
and, turning to us, with a smile, he said,—

' A good omen ! '

A few more steps brought us to the piazza.

XXIII

AMONG the members of the Count's household was
Fabrizio Tornielli, a cousin of the Orsi on the
mother's side. Checco had told him that he wished
to talk with Girolamo about the money he owed
him, and thought the best opportunity would be
when the Count was alone after the meal which
he was in the habit of taking at three. But as he
was very anxious to find the Count entirely by
himself, he begged his cousin to make him a sign
when the time came. . . . Fabrizio had agreed,
and we had arranged to stroll about the piazza
till we saw him. We came across our friends;
to me they looked different from everyone else.
I wondered that people as they passed did not
stop them and ask what was disturbing them.

At last, one of the Palace windows was opened,
and we saw Fabrizio Tornielli standing in it, looking down on the piazza. Our opportunity has
come. My heart beat so violently against my chest
that I had to put my hand to it. Besides Matteo
and myself, Marco Scorsacana, Lodovico Pansecchi
and Scipione Moratini were to accompany Checco

into the Palace. Checco took my arm and we walked
slowly up the steps while the others followed on
our heels. The head of the Orsi had a key of gold,
that is to say he was admitted to the ruler's presence
whenever he presented himself, and without formality.
The guard at the door saluted as we passed, making
no question. We ascended to Girolamo's private
apartments, and were admitted by a servant. We
found ourselves in an ante-room, in one wall of which
was a large doorway, closed by curtains. . . .

'Wait for me here,' said Checco. 'I will go in to
the Count.'

The servant raised the curtain; Checco entered,
and the curtain fell back behind him.

Girolamo was alone, leaning against the sill of
an open window. He stretched out his hand kindly.

'Ah, Checco, how goes it?'

'Well; and you?'

'Oh, I am always well when I get among my
nymphs.'

He waved his hand to the frescoes on the walls.
They were the work of a celebrated artist, and re-
presented nymphs sporting, bathing, weaving garlands
and offering sacrifice to Pan; the room had been
christened the Chamber of the Nymphs.

Girolamo looked round with a contented smile.

'I am glad everything is finished at last,' he said.
'Eight years ago the stones with which the house
is built had not been hewn out of the rock, and
now every wall is painted, everything is carved
and decorated, and I can sit down and say, "It is
finished."'

'It is indeed a work to be proud of,' said Checco.

M

'You don't know how I have looked forward to this, Checco. Until now I have always lived in houses which others had built, and decorated, and lived in ; but this one has grown up out of my own head; I have watched every detail of its construction, and I feel it mine as I have never felt anything mine before.'

He paused a minute, looking at the room.

'Sometimes I think I have lost in its completion, for it gave me many pleasant hours to watch the progress. The hammer of the carpenter, the click of the trowel on the brick were music to my ears. There is always a melancholy in everything that is finished; with a house, the moment of its completion is the commencement of its decay. Who knows how long it will be before these pictures have mouldered off the walls, and the very walls themselves are crumbling to dust?'

'As long as your family reigns in Forli your palace will preserve its splendour.'

'Yes, and it seems to me that as the family will preserve the house, so the house will preserve the family. I feel myself firmer and more settled in Forli; this seems like a rock to which my fortunes can cling. But I am full of hope. I am still young and strong. I have a good thirty years of life before me, and what can one not do in thirty years? And then, Checco, my children! What a proud day it will be for me when I can take my son by the hand and say to him, "You are a full-grown man, and you are capable of taking up the sceptre when death takes it from my hand." And it will be a good present I shall leave him. My head is full of plans.

Forli shall be rich and strong, and its prince shall
not need to fear his neighbours, and the Pope and
Florence shall be glad of his friendship.'

He looked into space, as if he saw the future.

'But, meanwhile, I am going to enjoy life. I have
a wife whom I love, a house to be proud of, two
faithful cities. What more can I want?'

'You are a fortunate man,' said Checco.

There was a short silence. Checco looked at him
steadily. The Count turned away, and Checco put
his hand to his dagger. He followed him. As he
was approaching, the Count turned again with a jewel
that he had just taken from the window sill.

'I was looking at this stone when you came,' he
said. 'Bonifazio has brought it me from Milan,
but I am afraid I cannot afford it. It is very
tempting.'

He handed it to Checco to look at.

'I don't think it is better than the one you have
on your neck,' he said, pointing to the jewel which
was set in a medallion of gold hanging from a heavy
chain.

'Oh yes,' said Girolamo. 'It is much finer. Look
at the two together.'

Checco approached the stone he held in his hand
to the other, and, as he did so, with his other fingers
pressed against the Count's chest. He wanted to see
whether by any chance he wore a coat of mail; he
did not mean to make the same mistake as the
Count. . . . He thought there was nothing; but he
wished to make quite sure.

'I think you are right,' he said, 'but the setting
shows off the other, so that at first sight it seems

more brilliant. And no wonder, for the chain is a masterpiece.'

He took it up as if to look at it, and as he did so put his hand on the Count's shoulder. He was certain now.

'Yes,' said Girolamo, 'that was made for me by the best goldsmith in Rome. It is really a work of art.'

'Here is your stone,' said Checco, handing it to him, but awkwardly, so that when Girolamo wanted to take it, it fell between their hands. Instinctively he bent down to catch it. In a moment Checco drew his dagger and buried it in the Count's back. He staggered forward and fell in a heap on his face.

'Oh God!' he cried, 'I am killed.'

It was the first thing we had heard outside. We heard the cry, the heavy fall. The servant rushed to the curtain.

'They are killing my master,' he cried.

'Be quiet, you fool!' I said, seizing his head from behind and with my hands on his mouth dragging him backwards. At the same moment Matteo drew his dagger and pierced the man's heart. He gave a convulsive leap into the air, and then as he fell I pushed him so that he rolled to one side.

Immediately afterwards the curtain was lifted and Checco appeared, leaning against the door-post. He was as pale as death, and trembling violently. He stood silent for a moment, open-mouthed, so that I thought he was about to faint ; then with an effort he said in a hoarse, broken voice,—

'Gentlemen, we are free!'

A cry burst from us,—

' Liberty ! '

Lodovico Pansecchi asked,—

' Is he dead ? '

A visible shudder passed through Checco, as if he had been struck by an icy wind. He staggered to a chair and groaned,—

' Oh God ! '

' I will go and see,' said Pansecchi, lifting the curtain and entering.

We stood still, waiting for him. We heard a heavy sound, and as he appeared, he said,—

' There is no doubt now.'

There was blood on his hands. Going up to Checco, he handed him the jewelled dagger.

' Take this. It will be more use to you than where you left it.'

Checco turned away in disgust.

' Here, take mine,' said Matteo. ' I will take yours. It will bring me good luck.'

The words were hardly out of his mouth when a step was heard outside. Scipione looked out cautiously.

' Andrea Framonti,' he whispered.

' Good luck, indeed ! ' said Matteo.

It was the captain of the guard. He was in the habit of coming every day about this hour to receive the password from the Count. We had forgotten him. He entered.

' Good-day to you, gentlemen ! Are you waiting to see the Count ? '

He caught sight of the corpse lying against the wall.

' Good God ! what is this ? What is—? '

He looked at us, and stopped suddenly. We had surrounded him.

'Treason!' he cried.   'Where is the Count?'

He looked behind him; Scipione and Matteo barred the door.

'Treason!' he shouted, drawing his sword.

At the same moment we drew ours and rushed for him. He parried a few of our blows, but we were too many, and he fell pierced with a dozen wounds.

The sight of the fray had a magical effect on Checco. We saw him standing up, drawn to his full height, his cheeks aflame, his eyes flashing.

'Good, my friends, good!   Luck is on our side,' he said. 'Now we must look alive and work. Give me my dagger, Matteo; it is sacred now. It has been christened in blood with the name of Liberty. Liberty, my friends, Liberty!'

We flourished our swords and shouted,—

'Liberty!'

'Now, you, Filippo, take Lodovico Pansecchi and Marco, and go to the apartment of the Countess; tell her that she and her children are prisoners, and let no one enter or leave. Do this at any cost. . . . The rest of us will go out and rouse the people. I have twenty servants armed whom I told to wait in the piazza; they will come and guard the Palace and give you any help you need. Come!'

I did not know the way to the Countess's chamber, but Marco had been a special favourite and knew well the inns and outs of the Palace. He guided me to the door, where we waited. In a few minutes we heard cries in the piazza, and shouts of 'Liberty.' There came a tramp of feet up the stairs. It was

Checco's armed servants. Some of them appeared
where we were. I sent Marco to lead the others.

'Clear the Palace of all the servants. Drive them
out into the piazza, and if anyone resists, kill him.'

Marco nodded and went off. The door off the
Countess's apartments was opened, and a lady said,—

'What is this noise?'

But immediately she saw us, she gave a shriek and
ran back. Then, leaving two men to guard the door,
I entered with Pansecchi and the rest. The Countess
came forward.

'What is the meaning of this?' she said angrily.
'Who are you? What are these men?'

'Madam,' I said, 'the Count, your husband, is
dead, and I have been sent to take you prisoner.'

The women began to weep and wail, but the
Countess did not move a muscle. She appeared
indifferent to my intelligence.

'You,' I said, pointing to the ladies and women
servants, 'you are to leave the Palace at once. The
Countess will be so good as to remain here with her
children.'

Then I asked where the children were. The
women looked at their mistress, who said shortly,—

'Bring them!'

I signed to Pansecchi, who accompanied one of the
ladies out of the room, and reappeared with the three
little children.

'Now, madam,' I said, 'will you dismiss these
ladies?'

She looked at me a moment, hesitating. The cries
from the piazza were growing greater; it was becoming a roar that mounted to the Palace windows.

· 'You can leave me,' she said.

They broke again into shrieks and cries, and seemed disinclined to obey the order.   I had no time to waste.

'If you do not go at once, I shall have you thrown out!'

The Countess stamped her foot.

'Go when I tell you!   Go!' she said.   'I want no crying and screaming.'

They moved to the door like a flock of sheep, trampling on one another, bemoaning their fate.   At last I had the room free.

'Madam,' I said, 'you must allow two soldiers to remain in the room.'

I locked the two doors of the chamber, mounted a guard outside each, and left her.

XXIV

I WENT out into the piazza. It was full of men, but where was the enthuiasm we had expected, the tumult, the shouts of joy? Was not the tyrant dead? But they stood there dismayed, confounded, like sheep. . . . And was not the tyrant dead? I saw partisans of Checco rushing through the crowd with cries of 'Death to all tyrants,' and 'Liberty, liberty!' but the people did not move. Here and there were men mounted on barrows, haranguing the people, throwing out words of fire, but the wind was still and they did not spread. . . . Some of the younger ones were talking excitedly, but the merchants kept calm, seeming afraid. They asked what was to happen now—what Checco would do? Some suggested that the town should be offered to the Pope; others talked of Lodovico Sforza and the vengeance he would bring from Milan.

I caught sight of Alessandra Moratini.

'What news? What news?'

'Oh God, I don't know!' he said with an expression of agony. 'They won't move. I thought they would rise up and take the work out of our hands. But they are as dull as stones.'

'And the others?' I asked.

'They are going through the town trying to rouse the people. God knows what success they will have!'

At that moment there was a stir at one end of the square, and a crowd of mechanics surged in, headed by a gigantic butcher, flourishing a great meat-axe. They were crying 'Liberty!' Matteo went towards them and began to address them, but the butcher interrupted him and shouted coarse words of enthusiasm, at which they all yelled with applause.

Checco came on the scene, accompanied by his servants. A small crowd followed, crying,—

'Bravo, Checco! bravo!'

As soon as the mechanics saw him, they rushed towards him, surrounding him with cries and cheers. . . . The square was growing fuller every moment; the shops had been closed, and from all quarters came swarming artisans and apprentices. I made my way to Checco and whispered to him,—

'The people! Fire them, and the rest will follow.'

'A leader of rabble!'

'Never mind,' I said. 'Make use of them. Give way to them now, and they will do your will. Give them the body of the Count!'

He looked at me, then nodded and whispered,—

'Quickly!'

I ran to the Palace and told Marco Scorsacana what I had come for. We went into the Hall of the

Nymphs; the body was lying on its face, almost doubled up, and the floor was stained with a horrible stream of blood; in the back were two wounds. Lodovico had indeed made sure that the Count was safe. . . . We caught hold of the body; it was not yet cold, and dragged it to the window. With difficulty we lifted it on to the sill.

'Here is your enemy!' I cried.

Then hoisting him, we pushed him out, and he fell on the stones with a great, dull thud. A mighty shout burst from the mob as they rushed at the body. One man tore the chain off his neck, but as he was running away with it another snatched at it. In the struggle it broke, and one got away with the chain, the other with the jewel. Then, with cries of hate, they set on the corpse. They kicked him and slapped his face and spat on him. The rings were wrenched off his fingers, his coat was torn away; they took his shoes, his hose; in less than a minute everything had been robbed, and he was lying naked, naked as when he was born. They had no mercy those people; they began to laugh and jeer, and make foul jokes about his nakedness.

The piazza was thronged, and every moment people entered; the women of the lower classes had come, joining their shrill cries to the shouts of the men. The noise was stupendous, and above all rang the cries of Liberty and Death.

'The Countess! The Countess!'

It became the general cry, drowning the others, and from all quarters.

'Where is the Countess? Bring her out. Death to the Countess!'

A cry went up that she was in the Palace, and the shout became,—

'To the Palace! To the Palace!'

Checco said to us,—

'We must save her. If they get hold of her she will be torn to pieces. Let her be taken to my house.'

Matteo and Pansecchi took all the soldiers they could and entered the Palace. In a few minutes they appeared with Caterina and her children; they had surrounded her and were walking with drawn swords.

A yell broke from these thousands of throats, and they surged towards the little band. Checco shouted out to them to let her go in peace, and they held back a little; but as she passed they hissed and cursed and called her foul names. Caterina walked proudly, neither turning to the right nor to the left, no sign of terror on her face, not even a pallid cheek. She might have been traversing the piazza amidst the homage of her people. Suddenly it occurred to a man that she had jewels concealed on her. He pushed through the guards and put his hand to her bosom. She lifted her hand and hit him in the face. A cry of rage broke from the populace, and they made a rush. Matteo and his men stopped, closing together, and he said,—

'By God! I swear I will kill any man who comes within my reach.'

They shrank back frightened, and taking advantage of this, the little band hurried out of the piazza.

Then the people looked at one another, waiting for something to do, not knowing where to begin. Their

eyes were beginning to flame, and their hands to itch
for destruction. Checco saw their feeling, and at once
pointed to the Palace.

'There are the fruits of your labours, your money,
your jewels, your taxes. Go and take back your own.
There is the Palace. We give you the Palace.'

They broke into a cheer, a rush was made, and they
struggled in by the great doors, fighting their way up
the stairs in search of plunder, dispersing through the
splendid rooms. . . .

Checco looked at them disappearing through the
gateway.

'Now, we have them at last.'

In a few minutes the stream at the Palace gates
became double, for it consisted of those coming out
as well as of those going in. The confusion became
greater and greater, and the rival bands elbowed and
struggled and fought. The windows were burst open
and things thrown out — coverlets, linen, curtains,
gorgeous silks, Oriental brocades, satins—and the
women stood below to catch them. Sometimes there
was a struggle for possession, but the objects were
poured out so fast that everyone could be satisfied.
Through the doors men could be seen coming with
their arms full, their pockets bulging, and handing
their plunder to their wives to take home, while they
themselves rushed in again. All the little things were
taken first, and then it was the turn of the furniture.
People came out with chairs or coffers on their heads,
bearing them away quickly lest their claim should be
disputed. Sometimes the entrance was stopped by
two or three men coming out with a heavy chest or
with the pieces of a bedstead. Then the shouting

and pushing and confusion were worse than ever. . . .
Even the furniture gave out under the keen hands,
and looking round they saw that the walls and floors
were bare.   But there was still something for them.
They made for the doors and wrenched them away.
From the piazza we saw men tear out the window
frames, even the hinges were taken, and they
streamed out of the Palace heavily laden, their
hands bloody from the work of destruction.

All over the town the bells were ringing, and still
people surged into the piazza.   Thousands had got
nothing from the Palace, and they cried out in anger
against their companions, envious at their good luck.
Bands had formed themselves with chiefs, and they
were going about exciting the others.   Checco stood
among them, unable to restrain them.   Suddenly
another cry rose from a thousand throats,—

'The Treasury!'

And irresistible as the sea, they rushed to the
Gabella.   In a few minutes the same ruin had
overtaken it, and it was lying bare and empty.

Scarcely one of them remained in the piazza.   The
corpse was lying on the cold stones, naked, the face
close to the house in which the living man had taken
such pride; and the house itself, with the gaping
apertures from the stolen windows, looked like a
building which had been burnt with fire, so that
only the walls remained.   And it was empty but
for a few rapacious men, who were wandering about
like scavengers to see whether anything had been left
unfound.

The body had done its work and it could rest in
peace.   Checco sent for friars, who placed it on a

stretcher, covering its nakedness, and bore it to their church.

Night came, and with it a little peace. The tumult with which the town was filled quietened down; one by one the sounds ceased, and over the city fell a troubled sleep. . . .

XXV

WE were up betimes. The town was ours, except the citadel. Checco had gone to the fortress, which stood above the town, to one side, and had summoned the Castellan to surrender. He had refused, as we expected; but we were not much troubled, for we had Caterina and her children in our power, and by their means thought we could get hold of the castle.

Checco had called a meeting of the Council to decide what should be done with the town. It was purely a measure of politeness, for he had already made up his mind and taken steps in accordance. With the town so troubled, the citadel still in our opponent's hands, and the armies of Lodovico Moro at Milan, it was hopeless to suggest standing alone; and Checco had decided to offer Forli to the Pope. This would give a protection against external enemies and would not greatly interfere with the internal relations. The real power would belong to the chief citizen, and Checco knew well enough whom that was. Further, the lax grasp of the Pope would soon be loosed by death, and in the confusion of a long conclave and a change of rulers, it would not be impossible to change the state of dependence into real liberty, and for Checco to add the rights and titles of lordship to the power. On the previous night he had sent a messenger to the Protonotary Savello, the papal governor of Cesena, with an account of what had happened and the offer of the town. Checco had requested an immediate reply, and was expecting it every minute.

The Council was called for ten o'clock. At nine Checco received Savello's secret consent.

The President of the Council was Niccolo Tornielli, and he opened the sitting by reminding his hearers of their object, and calling for their opinions. At first no one would speak. They did not know what was in Checco's mind, and they had no wish to say anything that might be offensive to him. The Forlivesi are a cautious race! After a while an old man got up and timidly expressed the thanks of the citizens for the freedom which Checco had bestowed upon them, suggesting also that he should speak first. The lead thus given, the worthies rose, one after another, and said the same things with an air of profound originality.

Then Antonio Sassi stood up. It was he who had advised Girolamo to impose the taxes on the town; and he was known to be a deadly enemy of Checco. The others had been sufficiently astonished when they saw him enter the Council chamber, for it was thought that he had left the town, as Ercole Piacentini and others of the Count's favourites had done. When he prepared to speak, the surprise was universal.

'Our good friend, Niccolo,' he said, 'has called

N

upon us to decide what shall be done with the town.

'Your thoughts seem to be inclining to one foreign master or another. But my thoughts are inclining to the Liberty, in whose name the town has been won.

'Let us maintain the Liberty which these men have conquered at the risk of their lives. . . .

'Why should we doubt our ability to preserve the Liberty of our ancestors? Why should we think that we, who are descended from such fathers, born from their blood, bred in their houses, should have degenerated so far as to be incapable of seizing the opportunity which is presented to us?

'Let us not fear that the Mighty Monarch, who defends and protects him who walks the path of the Just, will fail to give us spirit and strength to introduce and firmly to implant in this city the blessed state of Liberty.'

At the end of the sentence Antonio Sassi paused to see the effect on his auditors.

He went on,—

'But as the example of Our Master has shown us that the shepherd is necessary for the preservation of the flock; and as He seems to point out our guardian by the success which He has granted to his arms in the extermination of the Wolf, I propose that we surrender our Liberty to the hands of him who is best able to preserve it—Checco d'Orsi.'

A cry of astonishment burst from the Councillors. Was this Antonio Sassi? They looked at Checco, but he was impassive; not even the shadow of a thought could be read on his face. They asked themselves whether this was pre-arranged, whether

Checco had bought his enemy, or whether it was a sudden device of Antonio to make his peace with the victor. One could see the agitation of their minds. They were tortured: they did not know what Checco thought. Should they speak or be silent? There was a look of supplication in their faces which was quite pitiful. Finally, one of them made up his mind, and rose to second Antonio Sassi's motion. Then others took their courage in both hands and made speeches full of praise for Checco, begging him to accept the sovereignty.

A grave smile appeared on Checco's face, but it disappeared at once. When he thought there had been sufficient talking he rose to his feet, and, after thanking his predecessors for their eulogies, said,—

'It is true that we have conquered the city at the risk of our lives; but it was for the city, not for ourselves. . . . No thought of our own profit entered our minds, but we were possessed by a grave sense of our duty towards our fellowmen. Our watchwords were Liberty and the Commonweal! From the bottom of my heart I thank Antonio Sassi and all of you who have such confidence in me that you are willing to surrender the town to my keeping. In their good opinion I find a sufficient reward for all I have done. But, God knows, I have no desire to rule. I want the love of my fellow-citizens, not the fear of subjects; I look with dismay upon the toils of a ruler. And who would believe in my disinterestedness when he saw me take up the sceptre which the lifeless hand has dropped?

'Forgive me; I cannot accept your gift.

'But there is one who can and will. The Church

is not wont to close her breast to him who seeks refuge beneath her sacred cloak, and she will pardon us for having shaken from our necks the hard yoke of Tyranny. Let us give ourselves to the Holy Father—'

He was interrupted by the applause of the councillors: they did not want to hear further, but agreed unanimously; and it was forthwith arranged that an embassy should be sent to the Governor of Cesena to make the offer. The meeting was broken up amidst shouts of praise for Checco. If he had been strong before, he was ten times stronger now, for the better classes had been afraid of the mob and angry that he should depend on them; now they were won too.

The people knew that the Council was assembled to consult on the destinies of the town, and they had come together in thousands outside the Council House. The news was made known to them at once, and when Checco appeared at the top of the stairs a mighty shout burst from them, and they closed round him with cries and cheers.

'Bravo! Bravo!'

He began to walk homewards, and the crowd followed, making the old grey streets ring with their shouts. On each side people were thronging and stood on tiptoe to see him, the men waving their caps and throwing them in the air, the women madly flourishing handkerchiefs; children were hoisted up that they might see the great man pass, and joined their shrill cries to the tumult. Then it occurred to someone to spread his cloak for Checco to walk on, and at once everyone followed his example, and the people pressed and struggled to lay their garments before his feet. And baskets of flowers were obtained and scattered before him, and the heavy scent of the narcissi filled the air. The shouts were of all kinds; but at last one arose, and gathered strength, and replaced the others, till ten thousand throats were shouting,—

'*Pater Patriæ! Pater Patriæ!*'

Checco walked along with bare head, his eyes cast down, his face quite white. His triumph was so great—that he was afraid!

The great procession entered the street in which stood the Palazzo Orsi, and at the same moment, from the gates of the palace issued Checco's wife and his children. They came towards us, followed by a troop of noble ladies. They met and Checco, opening his arms, clasped his wife to his breast and kissed her tenderly; then, with his arm round her waist, the children on each side, he proceeded towards his house. If the enthusiasm had been great before, now it was ten times greater. The people did not know what to do to show their joy; no words could express their emotion; they could only give a huge deafening shout,—

'*Pater Patriæ! Pater Patriæ!*'

XXVI

AFTER a while the formal embassy sent to Cesena came back with the message that the Protonotary Savello had been filled with doubts as to whether he should accept the town or no; but seeing the Forlivesi firm in their desire to come under the papal rule, and being convinced that their pious wish had been inspired by the most High Ruler of Kings, he had not ventured to contradict the manifest will of Heaven, and therefore would come and take possession of the city in person.

Checco smiled a little as he heard of the worthy man's doubts and the arguments used by the ambassadors to persuade him; but he fully agreed with Monsignor Savello's decision, thinking the reasons very cogent. . . .

The protonotary was received with all due honour. Savello was a middle-sized, stout man, with a great round belly and a fat red face, double-chinned and bull-necked. He had huge ears and tiny eyes, like pig's eyes, but they were very sharp and shrewd. His eyebrows were pale and thin, so that with the

enormous expanse of shaven cheek his face had a
look of almost indecent nakedness. His hair was
scanty and his crown quite bald and shiny. He was
gorgeously dressed in violet. After the greetings and
necessary courtesies, he was informed of the state of
things in Forli. He was vexed to find the citadel
still in the hands of the Castellan, who had been
summoned with great courtesy to surrender to the
papal envoy, but without any courtesy at all had very
stoutly declined. Savello said he would speak to the
Countess and make her order the Castellan to open
his gates. I was sent forward to inform Caterina
of the last occurrences and of the protonotary's
desire for an interview.

The Countess had received apartments in the Orsi
Palace, and it was in one of these rooms that the
good Savello was ushered.

He stopped on the threshold, and lifting up his
arm stretched out two fingers, and in his thick, fat
voice, said,—

'The peace of God be upon you!'

Caterina bowed and crossed herself. He went up to
her and took her hand in his.

'Madam, it has always been my hope that I
should some day meet the lady whose fame has
reached me as the most talented, most beautiful,
and most virtuous of her time. But I did not think
that the day of our meeting would be one of such
bitterness and woe!'

He expressed himself in measured tones, grave and
slow, and very fit to the occasion.

'Ah, lady, you do not know the grief I felt when
I was made acquainted with your terrible loss. I

knew your dear husband in Rome, and I always felt for him a most profound affection and esteem.

'You are very kind!' she said.

'I can understand that you should be overwhelmed with grief, and I trust you do not think my visit importunate. I have come to offer you such consolation as is in my power; for is it not the most blessed work that our Divine Master has imposed upon us, to comfort the afflicted?'

'I was under the impression that you had come to take over the city on behalf of the Pope.'

'Ah, lady, I see that you are angry with me for taking the city from you; but do not think I do it of myself. Ah, no; I am a slave, I am but a servant of his Holiness. For my part, I would have acted far otherwise, not only for your own merits, great as they are, but also for the merits of the Duke, your brother.'

His unction was most devout. He clasped his hand to his heart and looked up to Heaven so earnestly that the pupils of his eyes disappeared beneath the lids, and one could only see the whites. In this attitude he was an impressive picture of morality.

'I beseech you, madam, bravely to bear your evil fortunes. Do we not know that fortune is uncertain? If the city has been taken from you it is the will of God, and as a Christian you must, with resignation, submit yourself to His decrees. Remember that the ways of the Almighty are inscrutable. The soul of the sinner is purified by suffering. We must all pass through the fire. Perhaps these misfortunes will be the means of saving your soul alive. And now that this city has returned to the fold of the Master—for is not the Holy Father the Vicar of Christ—be assured that the loss you have suffered will be made good to you in the love of his Holiness, and that eventually you will receive the reward of the sinner who has repented, and sit amongst the elect singing hymns of praise to the glory of the Master of all things.'

He paused to take breath. I saw Caterina's fingers convulsively close round the arm of her chair; she was restraining herself with difficulty.

'But the greatest grief of all is the loss of your husband, Girolamo. Ah, how beautiful is the grief of a widow! But it was the will of God. And what has he to complain of now? Let us think of him clad in robes of light, with a golden harp in his hands. Ah, lady, he is an angel in heaven, and we are miserable sinners upon earth. How greatly to be envied is his lot! He was a humble, pious man, and he has his reward. Ah—'

But she could hold back no longer. She burst forth like a fury.

'Oh, how can you stand before me, uttering these hypocrisies? How dare you say these things to me, when you are enjoying the fruits of his death and my misfortune? Hypocrite! You are the vulture feeding with the crows, and you come and whine and pray and talk to me of the will of God!'

She clasped her hands and lifted them passionately towards heaven.

'Oh, I hope that my turn will come, and then I will show you what is the will of God. Let them take care!'

'You are incensed, dear lady, and you know not

what you say. You will regret that you have accepted my consolations with disdain. But I forgive you with a Christian spirit.'

'I do not want your forgiveness. I despise you.'

She uttered the words like the hiss of a serpent. Savello's eyes sparkled a little, and his thin lips were drawn rather thinner than before, but he only sighed, and said gently,—

'You are beside yourself. You should turn to the Consoler of Sorrow. Watch and pray!'

'What is it you want with me?' she said, taking no notice of his remark.

Savello hesitated, looking at her. She beat her foot impatiently.

'Quick!' she said. 'Tell me, and let me remain in peace. I am sick of you.'

'I came to offer you consolation, and to bid you be of good faith.'

'Do you think I am a fool? If you have no further business with me—go!'

The priest now had some difficulty in containing himself; his eyes betrayed him.

'I am a man of peace, and I desire to spill no blood. Therefore I wished to propose that you should come with me and summon the Castellan to give up the citadel, which may be the means of avoiding much bloodshed, and also of gaining the thanks of the Holy Father.'

'I will not help you. Shall I aid you to conquer my own town?'

'You must remember that you are in our hands, fair lady,' he answered meekly.

'Well?'

'I am a man of peace, but I might not be able to prevent the people from revenging themselves on you for your refusal. It will be impossible to hide from them that you are the cause of the holding back of the citadel.'

'I can well understand that you would hesitate at nothing.'

'It is not I, dear lady—'

'Ah, no; you are the servant of the Pope! It is the will of God!'

'You would be wise to do as we request.'

There was a look of such ferocity in his face that one saw he would indeed hesitate at nothing. Caterina thought a little. . . .

'Very well,' she said, to my intense surprise, 'I will do my best.'

'You will gain the gratitude of the Holy Father and my own thanks.'

'I put an equal value upon both.'

'And now, madam, I will leave you. Take comfort, and apply yourself to pious exercises. In prayer you will find a consolation for all your woes.'

He raised his hand as before, and, with the outstretched fingers, repeated the blessing.

XXVII

WE went to the fortress in solemn procession, the people, as we passed, mingling shouts of praise for Checco with yells of derision for Caterina. She walked on with her stately indifference, and when the protonotary addressed her, repelled him with disdain.

The Castellan was summoned, and the Countess addressed him in the words which Savello had suggested,—

'As Heaven has taken the Count from me, and also the city, I beg you, by the confidence I showed in choosing you as Castellan, to surrender this fortress to the ministers of His Holiness the Pope.'

There was a light tinge of irony in her voice, and her lips showed the shadow of a smile.

The Castellan replied gravely,—

'By the confidence you showed in choosing me as Castellan, I refuse to surrender this fortress to the ministers of his Holiness the Pope. And as Heaven has taken the Count from you, and also the city, it may take the citadel too, but, by God! madam, no power on earth shall.'

Caterina turned to Savello,—

'What shall I do?'

'Insist.'

She solemnly repeated her request, and he solemnly made his reply.

'It is no good,' she said, 'I know him too well. He thinks I am speaking under compulsion. He does not know that I am acting of my own will, for the great love I bear the Pope and the Church.'

'We must have the citadel,' said Savello, emphatically. 'If we do not get it, I cannot answer for your safety.'

She looked at him ; then an idea seemed to occur to her.

'Perhaps if I went in and spoke to him he would consent to surrender.'

'We cannot allow you out of our power,' said Checco.

'You would have my children as hostages.'

'That is true,' mused Savello ; I think we can let her go.'

Checco disapproved, but the priest overruled him, and the Castellan was summoned again, and ordered to admit the Countess. Savello warned her,—

'Remember that we hold your children, and shall not hesitate to hang them before your eyes if—'

'I know your Christian spirit, Monsignor,' she interrupted.

But when she was inside she turned to us, and from the ramparts addressed us with mocking laughter. The fury which had been boiling within her burst out. She hurled at us words of foul abuse, so that one might have thought her a fishwife; she threatened us with death, and every kind of torture, in revenge for the murder of her husband. . . .

We stood looking up at her with open mouths, dumbfoundered. A cry of rage broke from the people; Matteo uttered an oath. Checco looked angrily at Savello, but said nothing. The priest was furious; his big red face grew purple, and his eyes glistened like a serpent's.

'Bastard!' he hissed. 'Bastard!'

Trembling with anger, he ordered the children to be sent for, and he cried out to the Countess,—

'Do not think that we shall hesitate. Your sons shall be hanged before your very eyes.'

'I have the means of making more,' she replied scornfully.

She was lion-hearted. I could not help feeling admiration for the extraordinary woman. Surely she could not sacrifice her children! And I wondered if a man would have had the courage to give that bold answer to Savello's threats.

Savello's expression had become fiendish. He turned to his assistants.

'Let a double scaffold be erected here, at once and quickly.'

The chiefs of the conspiracy retired to a sheltered place, while the mob gathered in the piazza; and soon the buzz of many voices mingled with hammering and the cries of workmen. The Countess stood above looking at the people, watching the gradual erection of the scaffold.

In a little while its completion was announced. Savello and the others came forward, and the priest

once more asked her whether she would surrender.
She did not deign to answer. The two boys were
brought forward—one was nine, the other seven.
As the people looked upon their youth a murmur
of pity passed through them. My own heart began
to beat a little. They looked at the scaffold and
could not understand; but Cesare, the younger,
seeing the strange folk round him and the angry
faces, began to cry. Ottaviano was feeling rather
tearful too; but his superior age made him ashamed,
and he was making mighty efforts to restrain himself.
All at once Cesare caught sight of his mother, and
he called to her. Ottaviano joined him, and they
both cried out,—

'Mother! Mother!'

She looked at them, but made not the slightest
motion, she might have been of stone. . . . Oh,
it was horrible; she was too hard!

'Once more, I ask you,' said Savello, 'will you
surrender the castle?'

'No—no!'

Her voice was quite steady, ringing clear as a
silver bell.

Savello made a sign, and two men approached
the boys. Then suddenly they seemed to understand; with a shriek they ran to Checco, and,
falling at his feet, clasped his knees. Ottaviano
could hold out no longer; he burst into tears, and
his brother, at the elder's weakness, redoubled his
own cries.

'Oh, Checco, don't let them touch us!'

Checco took no notice of them; he looked straight
in front of him. And even when the Count had just

fallen under his dagger he had not been so ghastly
pale. . . . The children were sobbing desperately
at his knees. The men hesitated; but there was no
pity in the man of God; he repeated his sign more
decisively than before, and the men advanced. The
children clung to Checco's legs, crying,—

'Checco, don't let them touch us!'

He made no sign. He held his eyes straight in
front of him, as if he saw nothing, heard nothing.
But his face! Never have I seen such agony. . . .

The children were torn from him, their hands
bound behind their backs. How could they! My
heart was bursting within me, but I dared say
nothing. They were led to the scaffold. A
sobbing cry came from the people and wailed
through the heavy air.

The Countess stood still, looking at her children.
She made not the slightest motion; she might have
been of stone.

The children cried out,—

'Checco! Checco!'

It was heartbreaking.

'Go on!' said Savello.

A groan burst from Checco, and he swayed to and
fro, as if he were going to fall.

'Go on!' said Savello.

But Checco could not bear it.

'Oh, God! Stop!—stop!'

'What do you mean?' said Savello, angrily.
'Go on!'

'I cannot! Untie them!'

'You fool! I threatened to hang them, and I
will. Go on!'

'You shall not! Untie them, I tell you!'

'I am master here. Go on!'

Checco strode towards him with clenched fists.

'By God, Master Priest, you shall go the way you came, if you thwart me. Untie them!'

In a moment Matteo and I had pushed aside the men who held them, and cut their cords. Checco staggered towards the children, and they with a bound threw themselves into his arms. He clasped them to him passionately, and covered them with kisses. A shout of joy broke from the people, and many burst into tears.

Suddenly we saw a commotion on the castle walls. The Countess had fallen back, and men were pressing round her.

She had fainted.

O

XXVIII

WE went home rather troubled. Savello was walking alone, very angry, with a heavy frown between his eyes, refusing to speak. . . . Checco was silent and angry too, half blaming himself for what he had done, half glad, and Bartolomeo Moratini was by his side, talking to him. Matteo and I were behind with the children. Bartolomeo fell back and joined us.

'I have been trying to persuade Checco to apologise to Savello, but he will not.'

'Neither would I,' said Matteo.

'If they quarrel, it will be the worse for the town.'

'If I were Checco, I would say that the town might go to the devil, but I would not apologise to that damned priest.'

When we reached the Palazzo Orsi a servant came out to meet us, and told Checco that a messenger was waiting with important news. Checco turned to Savello, and said gloomily,—

'Will you come? It may need some consultation.'

The protonotary did not answer, but walked

sulkily into the house. After a few minutes, Checco came to us, and said,—

'The Duke of Milan is marching against Forli with five thousand men.'

No one spoke, but the expression on the proto-notary's face grew darker.

'It is fortunate we have preserved the children,' said Bartolomeo. 'They will be more useful to us alive than dead.'

Savello looked at him; and then, as if trying to mend the breach, but rather against his will, said ungraciously,—

'Perhaps you were right, Checco, in what you did. I did not see at the moment the political wisdom of your act.'

He could not help the sneer. Checco flushed a little, but on a look from Bartolomeo answered,—

'I am sorry if I was too quick of tongue. The excitement of the moment and my temper made me scarcely responsible.'

Checco looked as if it were a very bitter pill he had been forced to swallow; but the words had a reasonable effect, and the clouds began to clear away. An earnest discussion was commenced on the future movements. The first thing was to send for help against the Duke Lodovico. Savello said he would apply to Rome. Checco counted on Lorenzo de' Medici, and messengers were forthwith despatched to both. Then it was decided to gather as much victuals as possible into the town, and fortify the walls, so that they might be prepared for a siege. As to the citadel, we knew it was impossible to take it by storm; but it would not be difficult to starve it into surrender, for on the news of the Count's death the gates had been shut with such precipitation that the garrison could not have food for more than two or three days.

Then Checco sent away his wife and children; he tried to persuade his father to go too, but the Orso said he was too old and would rather die in his own town and palace than rush about the country in search of safety. In the troubled days of his youth he had been exiled many times, and now his only desire was to remain at home in his beloved Forli.

The news of Lodovico's advance threw consternation into the town, and when cartloads of provisions were brought in, and the fortifications worked at day and night, the brave citizens began to quake and tremble. They were going to have a siege and would have to fight, and it was possible that if they did not sufficiently hide themselves behind the walls, they might be killed. As I walked through the streets, I noticed that the whole populace was distinctly paler. . . . It was as if a cold wind had blown between their shoulders, and bleached and pinched their faces. I smiled, and said to them, in myself,—

'You have had the plunder of the Palace and the custom-houses, my friends, and you liked that very well; now you will have to pay for your pleasure.'

I admired Checco's wisdom in giving them good reasons for being faithful to him. I imagined that, if the beneficent rule of the Countess returned, it would fare ill with those who had taken part in the looting. . . .

Checco had caused his family to leave the town as

secretly as possible; the preparations had been made
with the greatest care, and the departure effected
under cover of night. But it leaked out, and then
the care he had taken in concealing the affair made
it more talked of. They asked why Checco had
sent away his wife and children. Was he afraid of
the siege? Did he intend to leave them himself?
At the idea of a betrayal, anger mixed itself with
their fear, and they cried out against him! And
why did he want to do it so secretly? Why should
he try to conceal it? A thousand answers were
given, and all more or less discreditable to Checco.
His wonderful popularity had taken long enough to
reach the point when he had walked through the
streets amidst showers of narcissi; but it looked as
if less days would destroy it than years had built
it up. Already he could walk out without being
surrounded by the mob and carried about in triumph.
The shouts of joy had ceased to be a burden to
him; and no one cried 'Pater Patriæ' as he passed.
Checco pretended to notice no change, but in his
heart it tormented him terribly. The change had
begun on the day of the fiasco at the fortress; people
blamed the leaders for letting the Countess out of
their hands, and it was a perpetual terror to them
to have the enemy in their very midst. It would
have been bearable to stand an ordinary siege, but
when they had their own citadel against them, what
could they do?

The townspeople knew that help was coming from
Rome and Florence, and the general hope was that
the friendly armies would arrive before the terrible
Duke. Strange stories were circulated about Lodo-

vico. People who had seen him at Milan described his sallow face with the large, hooked nose and the broad, heavy chin. Others told of his cruelty. It was notorious that he had murdered his nephew after keeping him a prisoner for years. They remembered how he had crushed the revolt of a subject town, hanging in the market-place the whole council, young and old, and afterwards hunting up everyone suspected of complicity, and ruthlessly putting them to death, so that a third of the population had perished. The Forlivesi shuddered, and looked anxiously along the roads by which the friendly armies were expected.

Lorenzo de' Medici refused to help.

There was almost a tumult in the town when the news was told. He said that the position of Florence made it impossible for him to send troops at the present moment, but later he would be able to do whatever we wished. It meant that he intended to wait and see how things turned out, without coming to open war with the Duke unless it was certain that victory would be on our side. Checco was furious, and the people were furious with Checco. He had depended entirely on the help from Florence, and when it failed the citizens murmured openly against him, saying that he had entered into this thing without preparation, without thought of the future. We begged Checco not to show himself in the town that day, but he insisted. The people looked at him as he passed, keeping perfect silence. As yet they neither praised nor blamed, but how long would it be before they refrained from cursing him they had blessed? Checco walked through with set face, very pale. We asked him to turn back, but he refused, slackening his pace to prolong the walk, as if it gave him a certain painful pleasure to drain the cup of bitterness to the dregs. In the piazza we saw two councillors talking together; they crossed over to the other side, pretending not to see us.

Now our only hope was in Rome. The Pope had sent a messenger to say that he was preparing an army, and bidding us keep steadfast and firm. Savello posted the notice up in the market-place, and the crowd that read broke out into praises of the Pope and Savello. And as Checco's influence diminished Savello's increased; the protonotary began to take greater authority in the councils, and often he seemed to contradict Checco for the mere pleasure of overbearing and humiliating him. Checco became more taciturn and gloomy every day.

But the high spirits of the townsmen sank when it was announced that Lodovico's army was within a day's march, and nothing had been heard from Rome. Messengers were sent urging the Pope to hasten his army, or at least to send a few troops to divert the enemy and encourage the people. The citizens mounted the ramparts and watched the two roads— the road that led from Milan and the road that led to Rome. The Duke was coming nearer and nearer; the peasants began to flock into the town, with their families, their cattle, and such property as they had been able to carry with them. They said the Duke was approaching with a mighty army, and that he had vowed to put all the inhabitants to the sword to revenge the death of his brother. The fear of the fugitives spread to the citizens, and there was a general panic. The gates were closed, and all grown men summoned to arms. Then they began to lament, asking what inexperienced townsmen could do against the trained army of the Duke, and the women wept and implored their husbands not to risk their precious lives; and above all rose the murmur against Checco.

When would the army come from Rome? They asked the country folk, but they had heard of nothing; they looked and looked, but the road was empty.

And suddenly over the hills was seen appearing the vanguard of the Duke's army. The troops wound down into the plain, and others appeared on the brow of the hills; slowly they marched down and others again appeared, and others and others, and still they appeared on the summit and wound down into the plain. They wondered, horror-stricken, how large the army was—five, ten, twenty thousand men! Would it never end? They were panic-stricken. At last the whole army descended and halted; there was a confusion of commands, a rushing hither and thither, a bustling, a troubling; it looked like a colony of ants furnishing their winter home. The camp was marked out, entrenchments were made, tents erected, and Forli was in a state of siege.

XXIX

THE night fell and was passed without sleep or rest. The citizens were gathered together on the walls, talking anxiously, trying to pierce the darkness to see the rescuing army from Rome. Now and then someone thought he heard the tramp of cavalry or saw a gleam of armour, and then they stood still, holding their breaths, listening. But they heard nothing, saw nothing. . . . Others were assembled in the piazza, and with them a crowd of women and children ; the churches were full of women praying and weeping. The night seemed endless. At last a greater chilliness of the air told them that the dawn was at hand ; gradually the darkness seemed to thin away into a cold pallor, and above a bank of cloud in the east appeared a sickly light. More anxiously than ever our eyes turned towards Rome ; the mist hid the country from us, but some of the watchers thought they saw a black mass, far away. They pointed it out to the others, and all watched eagerly ; but the black mass grew neither larger nor clearer nor nearer ; and as great yellow rays shot up above the clouds, and the sun rose slowly, we saw the road stretched out before us, and it was empty, empty, empty.

It was almost a sob that burst from them, and moaningly they asked when help was coming. At that moment a man ascended the ramparts and told us that the protonotary had received a letter from the Pope, in which he informed him that relief was on the way. A cheer broke from us. At last!

The siege began in earnest with a simultaneous attack on the four gates of the town, but they were well defended, and the enemy easily beaten off. But all at once we heard a great sound of firing, and shouts, and shrieks, and we saw flames burst from the roof of a house. In our thought of Lodovico we had forgotten the enemy in our midst, and a terrible panic broke out when it was found that the citadel had opened fire. The castellan had turned his cannon on the houses surrounding the fortress, and the damage was terrible. The inhabitants hurried out for their lives, taking with them their chattels and fled to safer parts of the town. One house had been set on fire and for a while we feared that others would catch and a general conflagration be added to our woes. People said it was a visitation of God; they talked of Divine vengeance for the murder of the Count, and when Checco hurried to the scene of the fire they did not care to restrain themselves any longer, but broke out into yells and hisses. Afterwards, when the flames had been extinguished and Checco was passing through the piazza, they surrounded him, hooting, and would not let him pass.

'Curs!' he hissed, looking at them furiously, with clenched fists. Then, as if unable to contain himself he drew his sword, shouting,—

'Let me pass!'

They shank back and he went his way. But immediately he had gone the storm redoubled, and the place rang with their cries.

'By God,' said Checco, 'how willingly I would turn the cannon on them and mow them down like grass !'

They were the first words he had said of the change of feeling . . .

It was the same with us, when we walked through the streets—Matteo and I and the Moratini—they hissed and groaned at us. And a week before they would have licked our boots and kissed the ground we trod on !

The bombardment continued, outside and in, and it was reported through the town that Lodovico had vowed to sack the place and hang every third citizen. They knew he was the man to keep his word. The murmurs began to grow even louder, and voices were heard suggesting a surrender. . . . It had occurred to all of them, and when the most timid, driven to boldness by their fear, spoke the word, they looked at one another guiltily. They gathered together in little knots, talking in undertones, suspicious, stopping suddenly if they saw near anyone who was known to be in favour of the party of Liberty. They discussed how to make terms for themselves ; some suggested giving up the town unconditionally, others proposed an agreement. At last they spoke of appeasing the Duke by handing over to him the seventeen conspirators who had planned the murder of Girolamo. The thought frightened them at first, but they soon became used to it. They said the Orsi had really had no thought of the common good, but it was for their private ends that they had killed the Count and brought this evil on the town. They railed against Checco for making them suffer for his own ambition ; they had lauded him to the skies for refusing the sovereignty, but now they said he had only feigned, and that he intended to seize the city at the first good opportunity. And as to the others, they had helped for greed and petty malice. As they talked they grew more excited, and soon they said it would only be justice to hand over to the Duke the authors of their troubles.

The day passed, and the second night, but there were no signs of the help from Rome.

Another night passed by and still nothing came ; the dawn, and the road was as empty as before.

And the fourth night came and went and still there was nothing. Then a great discouragement fell upon the people ; the army was on the way, but why did it not arrive? Suddenly here and there people were heard asking about the letter from the Pope. No one had seen the messenger. How had it come? And a horrible suspicion seized the people, so that they rushed to the Palazzo Orsi, asking for Savello. As soon as he appeared they broke out clamorously.

'Show us the letter !'

Savello refused ! They insisted ; they asked for the messenger who had brought it. Savello said he had been sent back. None of us had seen letter or messenger ; the suspicion seized us too, and Checco asked,—

'Is there a letter?'

Savello looked at him for a moment, and answered,—

'No!'

'Oh God, why did you say there was?'

'I felt sure the army was on the way. I wanted to give them confidence.'

'You fool! Now they will believe nothing. You fool, you have muddled everything!'

'It is you! You told me that the city was firm for the Pope.'

'So it was till you came with your lies and your treacheries.'

Savello closed his fist, and I thought he was going to strike Checco. A yell burst from the people.

'The letter! the messenger!'

Checco sprang to the window.

'There is no letter! The protonotary has lied to you. No help is coming from Rome nor from Florence!'

The people yelled again, and another cry arose,—

'Surrender! Surrender!'

'Surrender at your pleasure,' shouted Checco, 'but do not think that the Duke will forgive you for stripping the Count and insulting his body and sacking his Palace.'

Savello was standing alone, struck dumb in his rage. Checco turned to him and smiled mockingly.

XXX

NEXT day there was a secret meeting of the council, of which neither Checco nor his friends knew anything. But it leaked out that they had been discussing terms which Lodovico had offered. And the Duke's proposal was that Riario's children should be surrendered to him and the town ruled by a commission, appointed partly by him, partly by the Forlivesi. About mid-day a servant came and told us that Niccolo Tornielli and the other members of the council were below, seeking admission. Checco went down, and as soon as he saw him Niccolo said,—

'Checco, we have decided that it will be better for us to have charge of the children of Count Girolamo; and therefore we have come to summon you to give them into our hands.'

Checco's answer was short and pointed.

'If that is all you came for, Niccolo, you can go.' . . .

At this Antonio Sassi broke in,—

'We shall not go without the children.'

'I imagine that depends on me; and I intend to keep the children.'

'Take care, Checco; remember that you are not our master.'

'And who are you, Antonio, I should like to know?'

'I am a member of the council of Forli, just as you are; no more, no less.'

'No,' said Checco, furiously; 'I will tell you whom you are. You are the miserable cur who pandered to the tyrant and helped him to oppress the people which I liberated; and the people spat upon you! You are the miserable cur who fawned upon me when I had killed the tyrant, and in your slavish adulation you proposed to make me ruler in his stead; and I spat upon you! And now you are afraid again and you are trying to make peace with the Duke by betraying me, and it is from you that come the propositions to give me up to Lodovico. That is what you are! Look at yourself and be proud!'

Antonio was about to give a heated answer, but Niccolo interrupted him.

'Be quiet, Antonio! Now, Checco, let us have the children.'

'I will not, I tell you! I saved their lives, and they are mine by right. They are mine because I killed the Count; because I took them prisoners; because I hold them; and because they are necessary for my safety.'

'They are necessary for our safety, too, and we, the council of Forli, summon you, Checco d'Orsi, to surrender them.'

'And I, Checco d'Orsi refuse!'

'Then we shall take them by force.'

Niccolo and Antonio stepped forward. Checco whipped out his sword.

'By God, I swear I will kill the first man who crosses this threshold!'

Gradually the people had collected, till behind the councillors there was a formidable crowd. They watched with eagerness the dispute, hailing with joy the opportunity of humiliating their old hero. They had broken out in mocking laughter while Checco was railing at Antonio, now they shouted,—

'The children! Surrender the children!'

'I will not, I tell you!'

They began to hoot and hiss, calling Checco foul names, accusing him of causing all their troubles, naming him tyrant and usurper. Checco stood looking at them, trembling with rage. Niccolo stepped forward once more.

'Give them up, Checco, or it will be the worse for you.'

'Advance one step further and I will kill you!'

The people grew suddenly exasperated; a shower of stones fell on us, and one, striking Checco, caused a long streak of blood to flow down his forehead.

'Give us the children! Give us the children!'

'We will call the guard,' said Antonio.

'The children!' shouted the mob. 'He will kill them. Take them from him.'

There was a rush from behind; the councillors and their supporters were driven forward; they were met by our drawn swords; in another moment it would have been too late, and against two hundred we should have been helpless. Suddenly Bartolomeo

appeared at the head of the great staircase with the
boys.

'Stop!' he cried. 'Here are the children. Stop!'
Checco turned round to him.

'I will not have them given up. Take them
away!'

'I have never asked you anything before, Checco,'
said Bartolomeo; 'I have always done as you com-
manded; but this time I implore you to give way.'

I joined my words to his.

'You must give way. We shall all be massacred.'

Checco stood for a moment undecided, then, without speaking, he turned into a room looking on the
court. We took it for consent, and Bartolomeo
handed the frightened children to the councillors.
A shout of joy broke from the people and they
marched off with their prize in triumph. . . .

I sought Checco and found him alone. As he
heard the shouts of the people, a sob came from him
in the misery of his humiliation.

But Jacopo Ronchi and the two sons of Bartolomeo
were sent out to discover what was going on. We
could not think what had driven the council to their
step; but we felt sure they must have good reasons
for acting so courageously. We felt also that we had
lost all power, all hope. The wheel had turned, and
now we were at the bottom. After several hours,
Alessandro Moratini came back and said,—

'The council has been meeting again, and it has
been receiving messengers; but that is all I know.
Everyone looks upon me with an evil eye and becomes
silent at my approach. I ask questions and they

P

say they know nothing, have seen nothing, heard nothing.'

'Brutes!' said Matteo.

'And for these people we risked our lives and fortunes!' said Bartolomeo.

Checco looked at him curiously; and, like him, I thought of our disinterestedness! Alessandro, having given his news, filled a glass with wine and sat down. We all kept silence. The time went on, and the afternoon began to close; the hours seemed interminable. At last Jacopo Ronchi came panting.

'I have discovered everything,' he said. 'The council has resolved to surrender the town to the Duke, who promises, in return for the children, to forgive everything and allow them to rule themselves, with half the council appointed by him.'

We sprang up with a cry.

'I will not allow it,' said Checco.

'If the conspirators make any disturbance, they are to be outlawed and a price set upon their heads.'

'How far have the negotiations gone?' I asked.

'The messengers have been sent to the Duke now.'

'In that case there is no time to lose,' I said.

'What do you mean?' said Checco.

'We must escape.'

'Escape!'

'Or we shall be taken alive; and you know what to expect from Caterina and Lodovico. Do not think of their promises of pardon.'

'I put no trust in their promises,' said Checco, bitterly.

'Filippo is right,' said Bartolomeo. 'We must escape.'

' And quickly ! ' I said.

' I cannot throw up the game,' said Checco. ' And without me, what will happen to my supporters ? '

' They may find forgiveness in submission. But you can do no good here. If you are in safety, you may be of some assistance. Anyhow, you will have life.'

Checco buried his face in his hands.

' I cannot, I cannot.'

The Moratini and I insisted. We adduced every argument. Finally he consented.

' We must go together,' I said ; ' we may have to fight our way through.'

' Yes,' said Scipione. ' Let us meet at the gate by the river—at two.'

' But go there separately. If the people find we are attempting to escape, they will set upon us.'

' I wish they would,' said Matteo. ' It would give me such satisfaction to put my sword into half a score of their fat bellies ! '

' There is no moon.'

' Very well ; at two ! '

The night was cloudy, and if there had been a moon, it would have been covered. A thin, cold rain was falling, and it was pitch dark. When I got to the river gate, four or five of them were already there. We felt too cold and miserable to speak ; we sat on our horses, waiting. As new arrivals came, we peered into their faces, and then, on recognising them, bent back and sat on silently. We were all there but Checco. We waited for a time. At last Barto- lomeo Moratini whispered to Matteo,—

'Where did you leave Checco?'

'In the house. He told me to go on, saying he would follow shortly. Two horses were saddled besides mine.'

'Whom was the second for?'

'I don't know!'

We waited on. The rain fell thin and cold. It struck half-past two. Immediately afterwards, we heard the sound of hoofs, and through the mist saw a black form coming towards us.

'Is it you, Checco?' we whispered, for the guard of the gate might have heard us. We were standing in a little plot of waste ground, ten yards from the walls.

'I cannot go with you,' said Checco.

'Why?' we cried.

'Ssh!' said Checco. 'I intended to bring my father, but he will not come.'

None of us had thought of old Orso Orsi.

'He says he is too old, and will not leave his native town. I did all I could to persuade him, but he bade me go, and said they would not dare to touch him. I cannot leave him; therefore go, all of you, and I will remain.'

'You must come, Checco; without you we are helpless.'

'And what of your wife and children?'

'Your presence will exasperate the tyrants. You can do no good, only harm.'

'I cannot leave my father unprotected.'

'I will stay, Checco,' I said. 'I am not well known as you are. I will take care of your father, and you can watch over your family and your interests in safety.'

'No, you must go. It is too dangerous for you.'

'Not half so dangerous as for you. I will do my best to preserve him. Let me stay.'

'Yes,' said the others, 'let Filippo stay. He may escape detection, but you would have no chance.'

The clock struck three.

'Come, come; it is getting late. We must be thirty miles away before daybreak.'

We had already arranged to go to Citta di Castello, which was my native place, and in case of accident I had given them letters, so that they might be housed and protected for the present.

'We must have you, Checco, or we will all stay.'

'You will take care of him?' said Checco to me at last.

'I swear it!'

'Very well! Good-bye, Filippo, and God bless you!'

They advanced to the gate, and Checco summoned the captain.

'Open the gate,' he said shortly.

The captain looked at them undecisively. I stood behind in the shade, so that I could not be seen.

'If you make a sound, we will kill you,' said Checco.

They drew their swords. He hesitated, and Checco repeated,—

'Open the gate!'

Then he brought out the heavy keys; the locks were turned, the gate growled on its hinges, and one by one they filed out. Then the gate swung back behind them. I heard a short word of command,

and the clatter of horses' hoofs. I put the spurs to my own, and galloped back into the town.

In half an hour the bells were ringing furiously; and it was announced from house to house that the conspirators had fled and the town was free.

XXXI

IN the morning the council met again and resolved
that the town should return to its old obedience,
and by surrendering without conditions hoped to
receive pardon for its offences. Lodovico Moro
entered in triumph, and going to the fortress was
received by Caterina, who came forth from the
citadel and with him proceeded to the cathedral
to hear mass. The good Forlivesi were getting used
to ovations; as the Countess passed through the
streets they received her with acclamation, thronging
the road on each side, blessing her, and her mother,
and all her ancestors. She went her way as indifferent as when she had crossed the same streets
a few days back amid the execrations of her faithful
subjects. The keen observers noticed the firm
closing of her mouth, which boded no particular
good to the Forlivesi, and consequently redoubled
their shouts of joy.

The protonotary Savello had mysteriously disappeared when the news of Checco's flight had been
brought him ; but Caterina was soon informed that

he had taken refuge in a Dominican monastery. A light smile broke over her lips as she remarked,—

'One would rather have expected him to take refuge in a convent.'

Then she sent people to him to assure him of her good will and beg him to join her. The good man turned pale at the invitation, but he dared not refuse it. So, comforting himself with the thought that she dared not harm the legate of the Pope, he clothed himself in all his courage and his most gorgeous robes, and proceeded to the cathedral.

When she saw him she lifted up two fingers and said solemnly,—

'The peace of God be upon you!'

Then, before he could recover himself, she went on,—

'Sir, it has always been my hope that I should some day meet the gentleman whose fame has reached me as the most talented, most beautiful and most virtuous of his day.'

'Madam—' he interrupted.

'Sir, I beseech you bravely to bear your evil fortunes. Do you not know that fortune is uncertain? If the city has been taken from you, it is the will of God, and as a Christian you must with resignation submit yourself to His decrees.'

It was the beginning of her revenge, and one could see how sweet it was. The courtiers were sniggering at Caterina's speech, and Savello was the picture of discomfort.

'Messer Savello,' she proceeded, 'on a previous meeting you made me some very excellent admonitions on the will of God; now, notwithstanding your order, I am going to be so bold as to-give you some equally excellent lessons on the same subject. If you will take your place by my side, you will have every opportunity of examining the ways of the Almighty, which, as you may remember you re-marked, are inscrutable.'

Savello bowed and advanced to the place pointed out to him.

XXXII

THE first thing I had done on returning to the
Palazzo Orsi was to strip myself of my purple and
fine linen, shave my beard and moustache, cut my
hair short, put on the clothes of a serving-man, and
look at myself in a mirror. If I had met in the street
the image I saw I should have passed on without
recognising it. Still I was not dissatisfied with myself, and I smiled as I thought that it would not be
too extraordinary if a lady's wench lost her heart to
such a serving-man.

I went to the old Orso's apartments, and found
everything quiet; I lay down on a couch outside the
doors and tried to sleep; but my thoughts troubled
me. My mind was with the sad horsemen galloping
through the night, and I wondered what the morrow
had in store for them and me. I knew a price would
be set upon my head, and I had to remain here in
the midst of my enemies as the only protection of
an old man of eighty-five.

In a little while I heard the bells which told the
town that the conspirators had fled, and at last I fell

into a restless sleep. At six I was awakened by a hurry and bustle in the house. . . . The servants told one another that Checco had gone, and the Countess would come out of the fortress in a little while; and then God only knew what would happen. They cowered about, whispering, taking no notice of the new serving-man who had appeared in the night. They said that the Palace would be given over to the vengeance of the people, that the servants would suffer instead of the master; and soon one of them gave the signal; he said he would not stay, and since his wages had not been paid he would take them with him. He filled his pockets with such valuables as he could find, and going down a back staircase slid out of a little side door and was lost in the labyrinth of streets. The others were quick to follow his example, and the Palace was subjected to a looting in miniature; the old steward stood by, wringing his hands, but they paid no attention to him, thinking only of their safety and their pockets. Before the sun had had time to clear away the early mists, they had all fled; and besides the old man, the house contained only the white-haired steward, a boy of twenty, his nephew, and myself; and Checco had been such a sweet and gentle master!

We went in to the old Orso. He was seated in a large arm-chair by the fireside, huddled up in a heavy dressing-gown. He had sunk his head down in his collar to keep warm, so that one could only see the dead eyes, the nose, and the sunken, wrinkled cheeks; a velvet cap covered his hair and forehead. He was holding his long, shrivelled hands to the fire, and the flames almost shone through them; they trembled incessantly.   He looked up at the sound of our entrance.

'Ah, Pietro!' he said to the steward.   Then, after a pause, 'Where is Fabrizio?'

Fabrizio was the servant in whose particular charge the Orso had been put, and the old man had become so fond of him that he would take food only from his hand, and insisted on having him near at every moment of the day.   He had been among the first to fill his pockets and decamp.

'Why does not Fabrizio come?' he asked querulously.   'Tell him I want him.   I will not be neglected in this way.'

Pietro did not know what to answer.   He looked about him in embarrassment.

'Why does not Fabrizio come?   Now that Checco is master here, they neglect me.   It is scandalous.   I shall talk to Checco about it.   Where is Fabrizio? Tell him to come immediately on pain of my displeasure.'

His voice was so thin and weak and trembling it was like that of a little child ill with some fever.   I saw that Pietro had nothing to say, and Orso was beginning to moan feebly.

'Fabrizio has been sent away,' I said, 'and I have been put in his place.'

Pietro and his nephew looked at me.   They noticed for the first time that my face was new, and they glanced at one another with upraised brows.

'Fabrizio sent away!   Who sent him away?   I won't have him sent away.'

'Checco sent him away.'

'Checco had no right to send him away.   I am

master here. They treat me as if I were a child. It is shameful! Where is Fabrizio? I will not have it, I tell you. It is shameful! I shall speak to Checco about it. Where is Checco?'

None of us answered.

'Why don't you answer when I speak to you? Where is Checco?'

He raised himself in his chair and bent forward to look at us, then he fell back.

'Ah, I remember now,' he murmured. 'Checco has gone. He wanted me to go too. But I am too old, too old, too old. I told Checco what it would be. I know the Forlivesi; I have known them for eighty years. They are more fickle and cowardly than any other people in this cesspool which they call God's earth. I have been an exile fourteen times. Fourteen times I have fled from the city, and fourteen times I have returned. Ah yes, I have lived the life in my time, but I am tired now. I don't want to go out again; and besides, I am so old. I might die before I returned, and I want to die in my own house.'

He looked at the fire, murmuring his confidences to the smouldering ashes. Then he seemed to repeat his talk with Checco.

'No, Checco, I will not come. Go alone. They will not touch me. I am Orso Orsi. They will not touch me; they dare not. Go alone, and give my love to Clarice.'

Clarice was Checco's wife. He kept silence for a while, then he broke out again,—

'I want Fabrizio.'

'Will I not do instead?' I asked.

'Who are you?'

I repeated patiently,—

'I am the servant placed here to serve you instead of Fabrizio. My name is Fabio.'

'Your name is Fabio?' he asked, looking at me.

'Yes.'

'No, it is not! Why do you tell me your name is Fabio? I know your face. You are not a serving-man.'

'You are mistaken,' I said.

'No, no. You are not Fabio. I know your face. Who are you?'

'I am Fabio.'

'Who are you?' he asked again querulously. 'I cannot remember whom you are. Why don't you tell me? Can't you see that I am an old man? Why don't you tell me?'

His voice broke into the moan, and I thought he would cry. He had only seen me twice, but among his few visitors the faces of those he saw remained with him, and he recognised me partly.

'I am Filippo Brandolini,' I said. 'I have remained here to look after you and see that no harm happens. Checco wished to stay himself, but we insisted on his going.'

'Oh, you are a gentleman,' he answered. 'I am glad of that.'

Then, as if the talk had tired him, he sank deeper down in his chair and fell into a doze.

I sent Andrea, the steward's nephew, to see what was happening in the town, and Pietro and I sat in the large window talking in undertones. Suddenly Pietro stopped and said,—

'What is that?'

We both listened. A confused roar in the distance;
it resembled the raging of the sea very far away. I
opened the window and looked out. The roar became
louder, louder, and at last we discovered that it was
the sound of many voices.

'What is it?' asked Pietro again.

There was a scrambling up the stairs, the noise of
running feet. The door was burst violently open,
and Andrea rushed in.

'Save yourselves!' he cried. 'Save yourselves!'

'What is it?'

'They are coming to sack the Palace. The Countess
has given them leave, and the whole populace is up.'

The roar increased, and we could distinctly hear the
shouting.

'Be quick!' cried Andrea. 'For God's sake be
quick! They will be here in a moment!'

I looked to the door, and Pietro, seeing my
thoughts, said,—

'Not that way! Here is another door which leads
along a passage into a side street.'

He lifted the tapestry and showed a tiny door,
which he opened. I ran to old Orso and shook him.

'Wake up!' I said; 'wake up and come with me!'

'What is it?' he asked.

'Never mind; come with me!'

I took his arm and tried to lift him out of his chair,
but he caught hold of the handles and would not stir.

'I will not move,' he said. 'What is it?'

'The mob is coming to sack the Palace, and if they
find you here they will kill you.'

'I will not move. I am Orso Orsi. They dare
not touch me.'

'Be quick! be quick!' screamed Andrea from the window. 'The first of them have appeared in the street. In a moment they will be here.'

'Quick! quick!' cried Pietro.

Now the roar had got so loud that it buzzed in one's ears, and every instant it grew louder.

'Be quick! be quick!'

'You must come,' I said, and Pietro joined his prayers to my commands, but nothing would move the old man.

'I tell you I will not fly. I am the head of my house. I am Orso Orsi. I will not fly like a dog before the rabble.'

'For your son's sake—for our sake,' I implored. 'We shall be killed with you.'

'You may go. The door is open for you. I will stay alone.'

He seemed to have regained his old spirit. It was as if a last flame were flickering up.

'We will not leave you,' I said. 'I have been put by Checco to protect you, and if you are killed I must be killed too. Our only chance is to fly.'

'Quick! quick!' cried Andrea. 'They are nearly here!'

'Oh, master, master,' cried Pietro, 'accept the means he offers you!'

'Be quick! be quick!'

'Would you have me slink down a back passage, like a thief, in my own house? Never!'

'They have reached the doors,' cried Andrea.

The noise was deafening below. The gates had been closed, and we heard a thunder of blows; stones were thrown, sticks beaten against the iron; then

they seemed to take some great instrument and
pound against the locks. Again and again the blows
were repeated, but at last there was a crash. A
mighty shout broke from the people, and we heard a
rush. I sprang to the door of the Orso's room and
locked and bolted it, then, calling the others to help
me, I dragged a heavy chest against it. We placed
another chest on the first, and dragged the bedstead
up, pushing it against the chests.

We were only just in time, for, like water rushing
at once through every crevice, the mob surged up
and filled every corner of the house. They came to
our door and pushed it. To their surprise it did not
open. Outside someone cried,—

'It's locked!'

The hindrance excited them, and the crowd gathered
greater outside.

'Break it open,' they cried.

Immediately heavy blows thundered down on the
lock and handle.

'For God's sake, come,' I said, turning to Orso.

He did not answer. There was no time to lose,
and I could not conquer his obstinacy.

'Then I shall force you,' I cried, catching hold of
both his arms and dragging him from the chair. He
held on as tight as he could, but his strength was
nothing against mine. I caught hold of him, and
was lifting him in my arms when the door was burst
open. The rush of people threw down the barricade,
and the crowd surged into the room. It was too late.
I made a rush for the little door with Orso, but I
could not get to it. They crowded round me with
a shout.

Q

'Take him,' I cried to Pietro, 'while I defend you.'

I drew my sword, but immediately a bludgeon fell on it and it smashed in two. I gave a shout and rushed at my assailants, but it was hopeless. I felt a crushing blow on my head. I sank down insensible.

XXXIII

WHEN I opened my eyes I found myself on a bed in a darkened room. By my side was sitting a woman. I looked at her, and wondered who she was.

'Who the devil are you?' I asked, somewhat impolitely.

At the words someone else stepped forward and bent over me. I recognised Andrea; then I recollected what had occurred.

'Where is the Orso?' I asked. 'Is he safe?'

'Do you feel better?' he said.

'I am all right. Where is the Orso?' I tried to sit up, but my head swam. I felt horribly sick and sank back.

'What is the matter?' I moaned.

'Only a broken head,' said Andrea, with a little smile. 'If you had been a real serving-man, instead of a fine gentleman masquerading, you wouldn't think twice about it.'

'Have pity on my infirmities, dear boy,' I murmured faintly. 'I don't pretend that my head is as wooden as yours.'

243

Then he explained.

'When you were beaten down they made a rush for the old master and bore him off.'

'Oh!' I cried. 'I promised Checco to look after him. What will he think!'

'It was not your fault.' At the same time he renewed the bandages round my head and put cooling lotions on.

'Good boy!' I said, as I enjoyed the cold water on my throbbing head.

'When I saw the blows come down on your head, and you fall like a stone, I thought you were killed. With you soft-headed people one never knows!'

'It appears to amuse you,' I said. 'But what happened afterwards?'

'In the excitement of their capture they paid no attention to us, and my uncle and I dragged you through the little door, and eventually carried you here. You are a weight!'

'And where am I?'

'In my mother's house, where you are requested to stay as long as it suits your convenience.'

'And Orso?'

'My uncle went out to see, and reports that they have put him in prison. As yet no harm has been done him. The palace has been sacked; nothing but the bare walls remain.'

At that moment Pietro came in panting.

'Two of the conspirators have been taken.'

'My God, not Checco or Matteo!'

'No; Pietro Albanese and Marco Scorsacana.'

'How did the others escape?'

'I don't know. All I heard was that the horse of

Marco broke down, and Pietro refused to leave him.
At a village close to the frontier Pietro was recognised,
and they were both arrested and sent here for the sake
of the reward.'

'My God!'

'They were brought into the town on asses, with
their hands tied behind their backs, and the mob
yelled with derision, and threw stones and refuse at
them.'

'And now?'

'They have been taken to the prison, and—'

'Well?'

'The execution is to take place to-morrow.'

I groaned. Pietro Albanese and Marco had been
like Damon and Pythias. I shuddered as I thought
of the fate in store for them. They had been conspicuous in their hatred of the Count, and it was they
who had helped to throw the body into the piazza.
I knew there would be no forgiveness in Caterina's
heart, and all the night I wondered what vengeance
she was meditating.

XXXIV

NEXT day I insisted on getting up. Andrea helped me to dress, and we went out together.

'No one would mistake you for a gentleman to-day,' he laughed.

My clothes were shabby enough in the first instance, and in the scuffle of the previous day they had received usage which did not improve them; moreover, I had a two days' beard, and my head muffled up in bandages, so that I could well imagine that my appearance was not attractive. But I was too sore at heart to smile at his remark, or make retort. I could not help thinking of the terrible scene which awaited us.

We found the piazza crowded. Opposite the Riario Palace was erected a stage on which were seats, but these were empty. The sky was blue, the sun shone merrily on the people, and the air was soft and warm. Nature was full of peace and goodwill; but in men's hearts was lust of blood. . . . A flourish of trumpets announced the approach of Caterina and her suite. Amid ringing cheers she entered the square, accompanied by her half-brother, the Duke of Milan, and by the Protonotary Savello. They took their seats on the platform, the Duke on her right, Savello on her left. She turned to the priest and talked most amiably to him; he smiled and bowed, but his agitation was shown by the twitching of his hands fidgetting with the lappet of his cloak.

A beating of drums was heard, followed by a sudden silence. A guard of soldiers entered the piazza, tramping steadily with heavy footsteps; then two steps behind them a single figure, without a doublet, hatless, his shirt all torn, his hands tied behind his back. It was Marco Scorsacana. The foul mob broke out into a yell at the sight of him; he walked slowly, but with his head proudly erect, paying no heed to the hooting and hissing which rang in his ears. On each side walked a barefooted monk, bearing a crucifix. . . . He was followed by another troop of soldiers, and after them came another bare-headed figure, his hands also tied behind his back; but he kept his head bent over his chest and his eyes fixed on the ground, shrinking at the yells of derision. Poor Pietro! He, too, was accompanied by the solemn monks; the procession was finished by the drummers, beating their drums incessantly, maddeningly.

They advanced to the platform, and there, the soldiers falling back, the prisoners were left standing before their judges.

'Marco Scorsacana and Pietro Albanese,' said the Countess, in a clear, calm voice, 'you have been found guilty of murder and treason; and as it was

you who cast the body of my dear husband out of
the Palace window on to the hard stones of the
piazza, so you are sentenced to be hanged from that
same window, and your bodies cast down on to the
hard stones of the piazza.'

A murmur of approval came from the populace.
Pietro winced, but Marco turned to him and said
something which I could not hear; but I saw the
glance of deep affection, and the answering smile
of Pietro as he seemed to take courage.

The Countess turned to Savello.

'Do you not agree that the judgment is just?'

'Most just!' he whispered.

'The protonotary says, "Most just!"' she called
aloud, so that all should hear. The man winced.

Marco looked at him scornfully, and said, 'I would
ten times rather be in my place than in yours.'

The Countess smiled at the priest and said, 'You
see, I carry out the will of God in doing unto others
as they themselves have done.'

She made a sign, and the two men were led to the
Palace and up the stairs. The window of the Hall
of Nymphs was thrown open, and a beam thrust
out, to which was attached a rope. Pietro appeared
at the window, with one end of the rope round his
neck.

'Good-bye, sweet friend,' he said to Marco.

'Good-bye, Pietrino,' and Marco kissed him.

Then two men hurled him from the sill, and he
swung in mid-air; a horrible movement passed
through his body, and it swayed from side to side.
There was a pause; a man stretched out with a
sword and cut the rope. From the people came a

huge shout,,and they caught the body as it fell and tore it to pieces. In a few minutes Marco appeared at the window, but he boldly sprang out into space, needing no help. In a little while he was a hanging corpse, and in a little while more the mob had fallen on him like wolves. I hid my face in my hands. It was awful! Oh, God! Oh, God!

Then another beating of drums broke through the tumult. I looked up, wondering what was coming. A troop of soldiers entered the square, and after them an ass led by a fool with bells and bauble; on the ass was a miserable old man, Orso Orsi.

'Oh,' I groaned. 'What are they going to do to him?'

A shout of laughter burst from the mob, and the clown flourished his bauble and bowed acknowledgments from side to side. A halt was made before the stage, and Caterina spoke again.

, 'Orso Orsi. You have been sentenced to see your palace destroyed before your eyes—stone by stone.'

The people shouted, and a rush was made for the Orsi Palace. The old man said nothing and showed no sign of hearing or feeling. I hoped that all sensation had left him. The procession moved on until it came to the old house, which stood already like a wreck, for the pillagers had left nothing which could be moved. Then the work began, and stone by stone the mighty building was torn to pieces. Orso looked on indifferently at the terrible work, for no greater humiliation can be offered to the Italian nobleman than this. The Orso Palace had stood three hundred years, and the most famous architects, craftsmen and artists had worked on it. And now it was gone.

The old man was brought back into the piazza, and once more the cruel woman spoke.

'You have received punishment for yourself, Orso, and now you are to receive punishment for your son. Make room!'

And the soldiers, repeating her words, cried,—

'Make room!'

The people were pushed and hustled back till they were crammed against the house walls, leaving in the centre an enormous empty space. Then a flourish of trumpets, and the people made an opening at the end of the square to allow the passage of a horse and man, the horse—a huge black stallion—prancing and plunging, and on each side a man was holding the bridle. On his back sat a big man, dressed all in flaming red, and a red hood covered his head and face, leaving two apertures for the eyes. A horrified whisper ran round the square.

'The hangman!'

In the centre of the piazza he stopped. Caterina addressed the Orso.

'Have you anything to say, Orso Orsi?'

At last he seemed to hear, he looked at her and then, with all the strength he had, hurled the word at her,—

'Bastard!'

She flushed angrily and made a sign. Two men seized the old man and dragged him off the mule; they caught hold of his legs, throwing him to the ground, and with a thick rope tied his ankles together.

At this I understood. I was seized with sudden horror, and I cried out. Obeying a sudden impulse, I started forward; I don't know what I was going to do; I felt I must protect him or die with him. I started forward, but Andrea threw his arms round me and held me back.

'Let me go,' I said, struggling.

'Don't be a fool!' he whispered. 'What can you do against all these?'

It was no use; I gave way. Oh, God! that I should stand by and see this awful thing and be utterly powerless. I wondered the people could suffer this last atrocity; I thought they must scream and rush to save the wretched man. But they watched—they watched eagerly. . . .

By his feet they dragged him to the horse, and the end of the rope round his ankles they tied to the horse's tail and about the rider's waist.

'Ready?' cried the hangman.

'Yes!' answered the soldiers.

They all sprang back; the hangman dug the spurs into his horse. The people gave a huge shout, and the fiery beast went careering round the square at full tilt. The awful burden dragging behind terrified him, and with head strained forward and starting eyes he galloped madly. The mob urged him on with cries, and his rider dug the spurs in deeply; the pavement was scattered with blood.

God knows how long the wretched man lived. I hope he died at once. At last the brute's furious career was stopped, the ropes were cut, the corpse fell back, and, the people again making passage, horse and rider disappeared. In the middle of the piazza, in a pool of blood, lay a shapeless mass. It was ordered that it should be left there till nightfall as an example to evildoers.

Andrea wanted to come away, but I insisted on staying to see what happened more. But it was the end, for Caterina turned to Savello and said,—

'I do not forget that all power comes from God, Monsignor, and I wish solemnly to render thanks to the Divine Majesty, who has saved me, my children and the State. Therefore, I shall order a grand procession which shall march round the town and afterwards hear mass at the cathedral.'

It shows, madam,' replied Savello, 'that you are a pious and truly Christian woman.'

XXXV

WHEN it was night and the piazza deserted, Andrea and I and the old steward went out and made our way to the place where the horrible corpse was lying. We wrapped it in a long black cloth and took it up silently, bearing it to the church where for generations the Orsi had been buried. A dark-robed monk met us in the nave and led the way to a door, which he opened; then, as if frightened, left us. We found ourselves in the cloisters. We laid the body down under an arch and advanced into the centre, where was a plot of green scattered over with little crosses. We took spades and began to dig; a thin rain drizzled down and the ground was stiff and clayey. It was hard work and I sweated; I took off my coat and allowed the rain to fall on me unprotected; I was soon wet to the skin. Silently Andrea and I turned up the soil, while Pietro, beneath the cloisters, watched by the body and prayed. We were knee deep now, and still we threw up heavy spadefuls of clay. At last I said,—

'It is enough.'

We climbed out and went to the body. We took it up and bore it to the grave, and reverently we laid it in. Pietro placed a crucifix on the old master's breast, and then we began to pile in the earth.

And so without priests, without mourning, in the dead of night, and by the drizzling rain, was buried Orso Orsi, the great head of the family. In his time he had been excellent in war and in all the arts of peace. He had been noted for his skill in commerce; in politics he had been the first of his city, and, besides, he had been a great and generous patron of the arts. But he lived too long, and died thus miserably.

Next day I set about thinking what I should do. I could be of no more use to anyone in Forli; indeed, I had never been of use, for I had only stood by and watched while those I loved and honoured were being put to cruel deaths. And now I must see that my presence did not harm my kind hosts. Caterina had thrown into prison some fifty of those who had taken part in the rebellion, notwithstanding her solemn promise of amnesty, and I knew well enough that if I were discovered Pietro and Andrea would suffer as severe a punishment as myself. They gave no sign that my presence was a menace to them, but in the woman's eyes, Andrea's mother, I saw an anxious look, and at any unexpected sound she would start and look fearfully at me. I made up my mind to go immediately. When I told Andrea, he insisted on coming with me, and although I painted the danger in lively colours he would not be dissuaded. The next day was market-day, and we resolved to slip out in a cart as soon as the gates were opened. We would be taken for tradesmen, and no one would pay attention to us.

I was anxious to see what was happening in the town and what people were talking of; but I thought it prudent not to venture out, for my disguise might be seen through, and if I were discovered I knew well what to expect. So I sat at home twiddling my thumbs and chattering with Andrea. At last, getting tired of doing nothing, and seeing the good woman about to scrub out her courtyard, I volunteered to do it for her. I got a broom and a pail of water and began sweeping away vigorously, while Andrea stood in the doorway scoffing. For a little while I forgot the terrible scene in the piazza.

There was a knock at the door. We stopped and listened; the knock was repeated, and as no answer was given, the latch was raised and the door opened. A servant-maid walked in and carefully closed it behind her. I recognised her at once; it was Giulia's maid. I shrank back, and Andrea stood in front of me. His mother went forward.

'And pray, madam, what can I do for you?'

The maid did not answer, but stepped past her.

'There is a serving-man here for whom I have a message.'

She came straight towards me, and handed me a piece of paper; then, without another word, slid back to the door and slipped out.

The note contained four words, 'Come to me to-night,' and the handwriting was Giulia's. A strange feeling came over me as I looked at it, and my hand trembled a little. . . . Then I began pondering. Why did she want me? I could not think, and it occurred to me that perhaps she wished to give me up to the Countess. I knew she hated me, but I could not think her as vile as that; after all, she was her father's daughter, and Bartolomeo was a .gentleman. Andrea looked at me questioningly.

'It is an invitation from my greatest enemy to put myself in her hands.'

'But you will not?'

'Yes,' I said, 'I will.'

'Why?'

'Because it is a woman.'

'But do you think she would betray you?'

'She might.'

'And you are going to take the risk?'

'I think I should be glad to prove her so utterly worthless.'

Andrea looked at me open-mouthed; he could not understand. An idea struck him.

'Are you in love with her?'

'No; I was.'

'And now?'

'Now, I do not even hate her.'

XXXVI

THE night came, and when everyone had gone to bed and the town was quiet, I said to Andrea, 'Wait for me here, and if I do not come back in two hours you will know—'

He interrupted me.

'I am coming with you.'

'Nonsense!' I said. 'I don't know what danger there may be, and there is no object in your exposing yourself to it.'

'Where you go I will go too.'

I argued with him, but he was an obstinate youth.

We walked along the dark streets, running like thieves round corners when we heard the heavy footsteps of the watch. The Palazzo Aste was all dark ; we waited outside a little while, but no one came, and I dared not knock. Then I remembered the side door. I still had the key, and I took it from my pocket.

'Wait outside,' I said to Andrea.

No, I am coming with you.'

'Perhaps there is an ambush.'

'Two are more likely to escape than one.'

R

I put the key in the lock, and as I did so my heart
beat and my hand trembled, but not with fear.   The
key turned, and I pushed the door open.   We entered
and walked up the stairs.   Sensations which I had
forgotten crowded upon me, and my heart turned
sick. . . .   We came to an ante-room dimly lit.   I
signed Andrea to wait, and myself passed into the
room I knew too well.   It was that in which I had
last seen Giulia—the Giulia I had loved—and nothing
was altered in it.   The same couch stood in the
centre, and on it lay Giulia, sleeping.   She started
up.

'Filippo!'

'At your service, madam.'

'Lucia recognised you in the street yesterday,
and she followed you to the house in which you
are staying.'

'Yes.'

'My father sent me a message that you were still
here, and if I wanted help would give it me.'

'I will do whatever I can for you.'

What a fool I was to come.   My head was in a
whirl, my heart was bursting.   My God! she was
beautiful!   I looked at her, and suddenly I knew
that all the dreary indifference I had built up had
melted away at the first look into her eyes.   And I
was terrified. . . .   My love was not dead; it was
alive, alive!   Oh, how I adored that woman!   I
burned to take her in my arms and cover her soft
mouth with kisses.

Oh, why had I come?   I was mad.   I cursed my
weakness. . . .   And, when I saw her standing there,
cold and indifferent as ever, I felt so furious a rage

within me that I could have killed her. And I felt
sick with love. . . .

'Messer Filippo,' she said, 'will you help me now?
I have been warned by one of the Countess's women
that the guard have orders to arrest me to-morrow;
and I know what the daughter of Bartolomeo
Moratini may expect. I must fly to-night—at
once.'

'I will help you,' I answered.

'What shall I do?'

'I can disguise you as a common woman. The
mother of my friend Andrea will lend you clothes;
and Andrea and I will accompany you. Or, if you
prefer, after we have safely passed the gates, he shall
accompany you alone wherever you wish to go.'

'Why will you not come?'

'I feared my presence would make the journey
more tedious to you.'

'And to you?'

'To me it would be a matter of complete indifference.'

She looked at me a moment, then she cried,—

'No, I will not come!'

'Why not?'

'Because you hate me.'

I shrugged my shoulders.

'I should have thought my sentiments were of no
consequence.'

'I will not be helped by you. You hate me too
much. I will stay in Forli.'

'You are your own mistress . . . Why do you mind?'

'Why do I mind? Shall I tell you?' She came
close up to me. 'Because—because I love you.'

My head swam, and I felt myself stagger. . . . . I did not know what was happening.

'Filippo!'

'Giulia!'

I opened my arms, and she fell into them, and I held her close to my heart, and I covered her with kisses . . . I covered her mouth and eyes and neck with kisses.

'Giulia! Giulia!'

But I wrenched myself away, and taking hold of her shoulders, said almost savagely.

'But this time I must have you altogether. Swear that you will—'

She lifted her sweet face and smiled, and nestling close up to me, whispered,—

'Will you marry me?'

I kissed her.

'I loved you always,' I said. 'I tried to hate you, but I could not.'

'Do you remember that night at the Palace? You said you had never cared for me.'

'Ah, yes! but you did not believe me.'

'I felt it was not true, but I did not know; and it pained me. And then Claudia—'

'I was so angry with you, I would have done anything to revenge myself; but still I loved you.'

'But, Claudia—you loved her too?'

'No,' I protested, 'I hated her and despised her; but I tried to forget you; and I wanted you to feel certain that I no longer cared for you.'

'I hate her.'

'Forgive me,' I said.

'I forgive you everything,' she answered.

I kissed her passionately; and I did not remember that I too had something to forgive.

The time flew on, and when a ray of light pierced through the windows I started up in surprise.

'We must make haste,' I said. I went into the ante-room and found Andrea fast asleep. I shook him.

'At what time do the gates open?' I asked.

He rubbed his eyes, and, on a repetition of the question, answered, 'Five!'

It was half-past four; we had no time to lose. I thought for a minute. Andrea would have to go to his mother's and find the needful clothes, then come back; it would all take time, and time meant life and death. Then, the sight of a young and beautiful woman might arouse the guard's attention, and Giulia might be recognised.

An idea struck me.

'Undress!' I said to Andrea.

'What?'

'Undress! Quickly.'

He looked at me blankly, I signed to him, and as he was not rapid enough I tore off his coat; then he understood and in a minute he was standing in his shirt while I had walked off with his clothes. I handed them to Giulia and came back. Andrea was standing in the middle of the room, the very picture of misery. He looked very ridiculous.

'Look here, Andrea,' I said. 'I have given your clothes to a lady, who is going to accompany me instead of you. Do you see?'

'Yes, and what am I to do?'

'You can stay with your mother for the present,

and then, if you like, you can join me at my house
in Citta di Castello.'

'And now?'

'Oh, now you can go home.'

He did not answer, but looked at me dubiously,
then at his bare legs and his shirt, then again at me.
I pretended not to understand.

'You seem troubled, my dear Andrea. What is
the matter?'

He pointed to his shirt.

'Well?' I said.

'It is usual to go about in clothes.'

'A broad-minded youth like you should be free
from such prejudice,' I answered gravely. 'On such
a morning you will find life much pleasanter without
hose and doublet.'

'Common decency—'

'My dear boy, are you not aware that our first
parents were content with fig-leaves, and are you not
satisfied with a whole shirt? Besides, have you not a
fine pair of legs and a handsome body; what are you
ashamed of?

'Everyone will follow me.'

'All the more reason to have something to show
them.'

'The guard will lock me up.'

'How will the jailor's daughter be able to resist
you in that costume!'

Then another idea struck me, and I said,—

'Well, Andrea, I am grieved to find you of so
unpoetical a turn of mind; but I will deny you
nothing. I went to Giulia, and taking the clothes
she had just cast off brought them to Andrea.

' There ! '

He gave a cry of delight, but on seizing them, and discovering petticoats and flounces, his face fell. I leant against the wall and laughed till my sides ached.

Then Giulia appeared, a most fascinating serving-boy. . . .

' Good-bye,' I cried, and hurried down the stairs. We marched boldly to the city gate, and with beating hearts and innocent countenances, passed through and found ourselves in the open country.

XXXVII

THE Orsi and the Moratini had taken my advice and gone to Citta di Castello; so it was to that city we directed our way, and eventually reached it in safety. I did not know where Bartolomeo Moratini was, and I did not wish to take Giulia to my own house, so I placed her in a Benedictine convent, the superior of which, on hearing my name, promised to give her guest every care.

Then I went to the old palace which I had not seen for so many years. I had been too excited to get really home to notice anything of the streets as I passed through them; but as I came in view of the well-remembered walls, I stopped, overcome with strange emotions. . . . I remembered the day when news had been brought me that the old Vitelli, who was then ruler of Castello, had murmured certain things about me which caused my neck to itch uncomfortably—and upon this I had entrusted my little brother to a relative, who was one of the canons of the cathedral, and the palace to my steward, and mounting my horse, ridden off with all possible haste. I had supposed that a few months would calm the

angry Vitelli, but the months had lengthened out
into years, and his death had come before his forgiveness. But now I really was back, and I did not
mean to go away; my travels had taught me caution,
and my intrigues at Forli given me enough excitement for some time. Besides, I was going to marry
and rear a family; for, as if Fortune could not give
scantily, I had gained a love as well as a home,
and everything I wished was granted.

My meditations were interrupted.

' *Corpo di Bacco !* '

It was Matteo, and in a moment I was in his arms.

' I was just asking myself what that fool was
staring at this house for, and thinking of telling him
it was impolite to stare, when I recognised the ~~horse~~'s *house's*
owner.'

I laughed, and shook his hand again.

' Well Filippo, I am sure we shall be very pleased
to offer you hospitality.'

' You are most kind.'

' We have annexed the whole place, but I daresay
you will be able to find room somewhere. But
come in.'

' Thanks,' I said, ' if you do not mind.'

I found Checco, Bartolomeo and his two sons
sitting together. They jumped up when they saw
me.

' What news? What news? ' they asked.

Then suddenly I remembered the terrible story
I had to tell, for in my own happiness I had
forgotten everything that went before. I suddenly
became grave.

' Bad news,' I said. ' Bad news.'

'Oh, God! I have been foreboding it. Every night I have dreamed awful things.'

'Checco,' I answered. 'I have done all I could; but, alas! it has been of no avail. You left me as a protector and I have been able to protect no one.'

'Go on!'

Then I began my story. I told them how the Council had opened the gates, surrendering unconditionally, and how the Countess had sallied forth in triumph. That was nothing. If there had been no worse news for them than that! But Checco clenched his hands as I related the sacking of his palace. And I told him how old Orso had refused to fly and had been seized, while I had lain senseless on the floor.

'You did your best, Filippo,' said Checco. 'You could do nothing more. But afterwards?'

I told them how Marco Scorsacana and Pietro had been taken prisoners, and led into the town like thieves caught in the act; how the crowd had gathered together, and how they had been brought to the square and hanged from the Palace window, and their bodies torn to pieces by the people.

'Oh, God!' uttered Checco. 'And all this is my fault.'

I told them that the old Orso was brought forward and taken to his palace, and before his eyes it was torn down, stone after stone, till only a heap of ruins marked the site.

Checco gave a sob.

'My palace, my home!'

And then, as if the blow was too great, he bent his head and burst into tears.

'Do not weep yet, Checco,' I said. 'You will have cause for tears presently.'

He looked up.

'What more?

'Your father.'

'Filippo!'

He started up, and stepping back, stood against the wall, his arms against it, outstretched, with white and haggard face and staring eyes, like a hunted beast at bay.

I told him how they had taken his father and bound him, and thrown him down, and tied him to the savage beast, and how he had been dragged along till his blood spattered on the pavement and his soul left him.

Checco uttered a most awful groan, and, looking up to heaven, as if to call it in witness, cried,—

'Oh, God!'

Then, sinking into a chair, he buried his face in his hands, and in his agony swayed from side to side. Matteo went up to him and put his hand on his shoulder, trying to comfort him; but he motioned him aside.

'Let me be.'

He rose from his seat, and we saw that his eyes were tearless, for his grief was too great for weeping. Then, with his hands before him like a blind man, he staggered to the door and left us.

Scipione, the weak man, was crying.

XXXVIII

ONE does not really feel much grief at other people's
sorrows; one tries, and puts on a melancholy face
—thinking oneself brutal for not caring more, but
one cannot; and it is better, for if one grieved too
deeply at other people's tears life would be un-
endurable; and every man has sufficient sorrows
of his own without taking to heart his neighbour's.
The explanation of all this is that three days after
my return to Citta di Castello I was married to
Giulia.

Now I remember nothing more. I have a confused idea of great happiness; I lived in an intoxication, half fearing it was all a dream, enchanted when
anything occurred to assure me it was true. But
the details of our life I have forgotten; I remember
I was happy. Is it not a curious irony that we
should recall our miseries with such plainness, and
that our happiness should pass over us so indistinctly,
that when it has gone we can scarcely realise that
it ever existed? It is as though Fortune were
jealous of the little happiness she has given us,
and to revenge herself blots it out of the memory,
filling the mind with miseries past.

But some things I recollect about others. I came across Ercole Piacentini and his wife Claudia. Castello being his native place, he had gone there on the death of the Count; and now, although the Riarii were restored to power, he remained, presumably to watch our movements and report them at Forli. I inquired whom he was, and after some difficulty discovered that he was the bastard of a Castello nobleman and the daughter of a trades-man. I saw that he did not lie when he said he had in his veins as good blood as I. Still I did not think him a very desirable acquisition to the town, and as I was in some favour with the new Lord I determined to procure his expulsion. Matteo pro-posed picking a quarrel with him and killing him, but that was difficult, because the bold man had become singularly retiring, and it was almost impos-sible to meet him. The change was so noticeable that we could not help thinking he had received special instructions from Forli; and we determined to take care.

I invited the Moratini to live with me; but they preferred to take a house of their own. The old man, when I asked him for his daughter's hand, told me he wished no better son-in-law, and was very contented to see his daughter again settled under a man's protection. Scipione and Alessandro were both most pleased, and they redoubled the affection they had felt for me before. It all made me ex-tremely happy; for after my long years of wandering I yearned very much for the love of others, and the various affections that surrounded me soothed and comforted me. From Giulia I could ask for nothing more, and I thought she really loved me—of course, not as I loved her, for that would have been impossible; but I was happy. Sometimes I wondered perplexedly at the incident which had separated us, for I could understand nothing of it; but I put it away from me, I did not want to understand, I wanted only to forget.

Then there were Checco and Matteo. The Orsi family had bought a palace in Castello, and there they could have settled themselves happily enough had they not been driven on by an unextinguishable desire to regain what they had lost. Checco was rich even now, able to live as luxuriously as before, and in a little while he might have gained in Castello as much power as he had lost in Forli, for the young Vitelli had been singularly attracted by him, and was already inclined to give trust to his counsels; but the wretched man was filled with sadness. All day his thoughts were in the town he loved so well, and now his love was increased tenfold. . . . Sometimes he would think of Forli before the troubles, when he was living a peaceful life surrounded by his friends; and in mind, he wandered through the quiet streets, every house of which he knew. He would go from room to room in his palace, looking at the pictures, the statues, the armour; from the window at night he gazed upon the dark, silent town, with the houses rising like tall phantoms; in the morning a silver mist covered the earth, and as it rose left the air cool and fresh. But when his house appeared before him, a bare heap of ruins, with the rain beating down on the roofless stones, he would bury his face in his hands, and so remain during long hours of

misery. Sometimes he would review the stirring
events, which began with the attempted assassination
of himself and ended with the ride out of the gate
by the river in the cold open country beyond; and
as they passed before him, he would wonder what he
had done wrong, what he might have done differenly.
But he could alter nothing; he saw no mistake other
than of trusting the populace who vowed to follow
him to death, and of trusting the friends who promised
to send him help. He had done his part, and what
had followed was impossible to foresee. Fortune was
against him and that was all. . . .

But he did not entirely give himself over to vain
regrets; he had opened up communication with
Forli, and through his spies had learnt that the
Countess had imprisoned and put to death all
those who had been in any way connected with
the rebellion, and that the town lay cowed, submissive
as a whipped dog. And there was no hope for
Checco from within, for his open partisans had
suffered terrible punishments, and the others were
few and timid. Then Checco turned his attention
to the rival states; but everywhere he received rebuffs,
for the power of Milan overshadowed them all, and
they dared nothing while the Duke Lodovico was
almighty. 'Wait,' they said, 'till he has roused
the jealousy of the greater states of Florence and
Venice, then will be your opportunity, and then
will we willingly give you our help.' But Checco
could not wait, every lost day seemed to him a
year. He grew thin and haggard. Matteo tried
to comfort him, but gradually Checco's troubles
weighed on him too; he lost his mirth and became

as moody and silent as his cousin. So passed a
year, full of anxiety and heartburning for them,
full of the sweetest happiness for me.

One day Checco came to me and said,—

'Filippo, you have been very good to me; now
I want you to do me one more favour, and that
shall be the last I will ask you.'

'What is it?'

Then he expounded to me a scheme for interesting
the Pope in his affairs. He knew how angry his
Holiness had been, not only at the loss of the town,
but also at the humiliation he had received through
his lieutenant. There was a difficulty at the time
between the Duke of Milan and Rome respecting
certain rights of the former, and he did not think it
unlikely that the Pope would be willing to break off
negotiations and recover his advantage by making
a sudden attack on Forli. Caterina's tyranny had
become insupportable, and there was no doubt that
at the sight of Checco leading the papal army they
would open their gates and welcome him as the
Pope's representative.

I did not see of what use I could be, and I was
very unwilling to leave my young wife. But Checco
was so anxious that I should come, seeming to think
I should be of such assistance, that I felt it would be
cruel to refuse. Moreover, I reckoned a month would
bring me back to Castello, and if the parting was
bitter, how sweet would be the return! And I had
certain business of my own in Rome, which I had
delayed for months because I could not bear the
thought of separation from Giulia. So I decided
to go.

A few days later we were riding towards Rome. I was sad, for it was the first time I had left my wife since our marriage, and the parting had been even more painful than I expected. A thousand times I had been on the verge of changing my mind and saying I would not go; but I could not, for Checco's sake. I was also a little sad because I thought Giulia was not so pained as I was, but then I chid myself for my folly. I expected too much. After all, it was only four short weeks, and she was still too great a child to feel very deeply. It is only when one is old or has greatly suffered that one's emotions are really powerful.

We reached Rome and set about soliciting an audience from the Pope. I cannot remember the countless interviews we had with minor officials, how we were driven from cardinal to cardinal, the hours we spent in ante-rooms waiting for a few words from some great man. I used to get so tired that I could have dropped off to sleep standing, but Checco was so full of eagerness that I had to accompany him from place to place. The month passed, and we had done nothing. I suggested going home, but Checco implored me to stay, assuring me that the business would be finished in a fortnight. I remained, and the negotiations dragged their weary length through weeks and weeks. Now a ray of hope lightened our struggles, and Checco would become excited and cheerful; now the hope would be dashed to the ground, and Checco begin to despair. The month had drawn itself out into three, and I saw clearly enough that nothing would come of our endeavours. The conferences with the Duke

S

were still going on, each party watching the other, trying by means of untruth and deceit and bribery to gain the advantage. The King of Naples was brought in; Florence and Venice began to send ambassadors to and fro, and no one knew what would be the result of it all.

At last one day Checco came to me and threw himself on my bed.

'It's no good,' he said, in a tone of despair. 'It is all up.'

'I'm very sorry, Checco.'

'You had better go home now. You can do nothing here. Why should I drag you after me in my unhappiness?'

'But you, Checco, if you can do no good, why will not you come too?'

'I am better here than at Castello. Here I am at the centre of things, and I will take heart. War may break out any day, and then the Pope will be more ready to listen to me.'

I saw it was no use that I should stay, and I saw I could not persuade him to come with me, so I packed up my things, and bidding him good-bye, started on the homeward journey.

XXXIX

WHAT shall I say of the eagerness with which I looked forward to seeing my dear wife, the rapture with which, at last, I clasped her in my arms?

A little later I walked out to find Matteo. He was quite astonished to see me.

'We did not expect you so soon.'

'No,' I answered; 'I thought I should not arrive till after to-morrow, but I was so impatient to get home that I hurried on without stopping, and here I am.'

I shook his hand heartily, I was so pleased and happy.

'Er—have you been home?'

'Of course,' I answered, smiling; 'it was the first thing I thought of.'

I was not sure; I thought a look of relief came over Matteo's face. But why? I could not understand, but I thought it of no consequence, and it passed from my memory. I told Matteo the news

I had, and left him. I wished to get back to my wife.

On my way I happened to see Claudia Piacentini coming out of a house. I was very surprised, for I knew that my efforts had succeeded, and Ercole's banishment decreed. I supposed the order had not yet been issued. I was going to pass the lady without acknowledgment, for since my marriage she had never spoken to me, and I could well understand why she did not want to. To my astonishment she stopped me.

'Ah, Messer Filippo!'

I bowed profoundly.

'How is it that now you never speak to me? Are you so angry with me?'

'No one can be angry with so beautiful a woman.'

She flushed, and I felt I had said a stupid thing, for I had made remarks too similar on another occasion. I added, 'But I have been away.'

'I know. Will you not come in?' She pointed to the house from which she had just issued.

'But I shall be disturbing you, for you were going out.'

She smiled as she replied. 'I saw you pass my house a little while ago; I guessed you were going to Matteo d'Orsi, and I waited for you on your return.'

'You are most kind.'

I wondered why she was so anxious to see me. Perhaps she knew of her husband's approaching banishment, and the cause of it.

We went in and sat down.

'Have you been home?' she asked.

It was the same question as Matteo had asked. I gave the same answer.

'It was the first thing I thought of.'

'Your wife must have been—surprised to see you.'

'And delighted.'

'Ah!' She crossed her hands and smiled.

I wondered what she meant.

'You were not expected for two days, I think.'

'You know my movements very well. I am pleased to find you take such interest in me.'

'Oh, it is not I alone. The whole town takes interest in you. You have been a most pleasant topic of conversation.'

'Really!' I was getting a little angry. 'And what has the town to say of me?'

'Oh, I do not want to trouble your peace of mind.'

'Will you have the goodness to tell me what you mean?'

She shrugged her shoulders and smiled enigmatically.

'Well?' I said.

'If you insist, I will tell you. They say that you are a complaisant husband.'

'That is a lie!'

'You are not polite,' she answered calmly.

'How dare you say such things, you impudent woman!'

'My good sir, it is true, perfectly true. Ask Matteo.'

Suddenly I remembered Matteo's question, and his look of relief. A sudden fear ran through me. I took hold of Claudia's wrists and said,—

'What do you mean? What do you mean?'

'Leave go; you hurt me!'

'Answer, I tell you. I know you are dying to tell me. Is this why you lay in wait for me, and brought me here? Tell me.'

A sudden transformation took place in Claudia; rage and hate broke out and contorted her face, so that one would not have recognised it.

'Do you suppose you can escape the ordinary fate of husbands?' She broke into a savage laugh.

'It is a lie. You slander Giulia because you are yourself impure.'

'You were willing enough to take advantage of that impurity. Do you suppose Giulia's character has altered because you have married her? She made her first husband a cuckold, and do you suppose that she has suddenly turned virtuous? You fool!'

'It is a lie. I will not believe a word of it.'

'The whole town has been ringing with her love for Giorgio dall' Aste.'

I gave a cry; it was for him that she abandoned me before. . . .

'Ah, you believe me now!'

'Listen!' I said. 'If this is not true, I swear by all the saints that I will kill you.'

'Good; if it is not true, kill me. But, by all the saints, I swear it is true, true, true!' She repeated the words in triumph, and each one fell like the stab of a dagger in my heart.

I left her. As I walked home, I fancied the people were looking at me, and smiling. Once I was on the verge of going up to a man, and asking him why he laughed, but I contained myself. How I was suffer-

ing! I remembered that Giulia had not seemed so
pleased to see me; at the time I chid myself, and
called myself exacting, but was it true? I fancied
she turned away her lips when I was imprinting my
passionate kisses on them. I told myself I was a
fool, but was it true? I remembered a slight movement of withdrawal when I clasped her in my arms.
Was it true? Oh God! was it true?

I thought of going to Matteo, but I could not.
He knew her before her marriage; he would be willing to accept the worst that was said of her. How
could I be so disturbed at the slanders of a wicked,
jealous woman? I wished I had never known
Claudia, never given her reason to take this revenge
on me. Oh, it was cruel! But I would not believe
it; I had such trust in Giulia, such love. She could
not betray me, when she knew what passionate love
was poured down upon her. It would be too ungrateful. And I had done so much for her, but I
did not wish to think of that. . . . All that I had
done had been for pure love and pleasure, and I re-
quired no thanks. But surely if she had no love, she
had at least some tender feeling for me; she would
not give her honour to another. Ah no, I would not
believe it. But was it true, oh God! was it true?

I found myself at home, and suddenly I remembered the old steward, whom I had left in charge of
my house. His name was Fabio; it was from him
that I got the name when I presented myself as a
serving-man to old Orso. If anything had taken
place in the house he must know it; and she, Claudia,
said the whole town knew it.

'Fabio!'

'My master!'

He came into my room, and I looked at him steadily.

'Fabio, have you well looked after all I left in your hands when I went to Rome?'

'Your rents are paid, your harvests taken in, the olives all gathered.'

'I left in your charge something more precious than cornfields and vineyards.'

'My lord!'

'I made you guardian of my honour. What of that?'

He hesitated, and his voice as he answered trembled.

'Your honour is—intact.'

I took him by the shoulders.

'Fabio, what is it? I beseech you by your master, my father, to tell me.'

I knew he loved my father's memory with more than human love. He looked up to heaven and clasped his hands; he could hardly speak.

'By my dear master, your father, nothing—nothing!'

'Fabio, you are lying.' I pressed his wrists which I was holding clenched in my hands.

He sank down on his knees.

'Oh, master, have mercy on me!' He buried his face in his hands. 'I cannot tell you.'

'Speak, man, speak!'

At last, with laments and groans, he uttered the words,—

'She has—oh God, she has betrayed you!'

'Oh!' I staggered back.

'Forgive me!'

'Why did you not tell me before?'

'Ah, how could I? You loved her as I have never seen man love woman.'

'Did you not think of my honour?'

'I thought of your happiness. It is better to have happiness without honour, than honour without happiness.'

'For you,' I groaned, 'but not for me.'

'You are of the same flesh and blood, and you suffer as we do. I could not destroy your happiness.'

'Oh, Giulia! Giulia!' Then, after a while, I asked again, 'But are you sure?'

'Alas, there is no doubt!'

'I cannot believe it Oh God, help me! You don't know how I loved her! She could not! Let me see it with my own eyes, Fabio.'

We both stood silent; then a horrible thought struck me.

'Do you know—when they meet?' I whispered.

He groaned. I asked again.

'God help me!'

'You know? I command you to tell me.'

'They did not know you were coming back till after to-morrow.'

'He is coming?'

'To-day.'

'Oh!' I seized him by the hand. 'Take me, and let me see them.'

'What will you do?' he asked, horror-stricken.

'Never mind, take me!'

Trembling, he led me through ante-rooms and passages, till he brought me to a staircase. We

mounted the steps and came to a little door. He
opened it very quietly, and we found ourselves behind
the arras of Giulia's chamber. I had forgotten the
existence of door and steps, and she knew nothing
of them. There was an opening in the tapestry to
give exit.

No one was in the room. We waited, holding
our breath. At last Giulia entered. She walked to
the window and looked out, and went back to the
door. She sat down, but sprang up restlessly, and
again looked out of window. Whom was she
expecting?

She walked up and down the room, and her face
was full of anxiety. I watched intently. At last a
light knock was heard; she opened the door and
a man came in. A small, slight, thin man, with
a quantity of corn-coloured hair falling over his
shoulders, and a pale, fair skin. He had blue eyes,
and a little golden moustache. He looked hardly
twenty, but I knew he was older.

He sprang forward, seizing her in his arms, and
he pressed her to his heart, but she pushed him
back.

'Oh, Giorgio, you must go,' she cried. 'He has
come back.'

'Your husband?'

'I hoped you would not come. Go quickly. If he
found you he would kill us both.'

'Tell me you love me, Giulia.'

'Oh yes, I love you with all my heart and soul.'

For a moment they stood still in one another's
arms, then she tore herself away.

'But go, for God's sake!'

'I go, my love. Good-bye!'

'Good-bye, beloved!'

He took her in his arms again, and she placed hers around his neck. They kissed one another passionately on the lips; she kissed him as she had never kissed me.

'Oh!' I gave a cry of rage, and leaped out of my concealment. In a bound I had reached him. They hardly knew I was there; and I had plunged my dagger in his neck. Giulia gave a piercing shriek as he fell with a groan. The blood spattered over my hand. Then I looked at her. She ran from me with terror-stricken face, her eyes starting from her head. I rushed to her and she shrieked again, but Fabio caught hold of my arm.

'Not her, not her too!'

I wrenched my hand away from him, and then— then as I saw her pallid face and the look of deathly terror—I stopped. I could not kill her.

'Lock that door,' I said to Fabio, pointing to the one from which we had come. Then, looking at her, I screamed,—

'Harlot!'

I called to Fabio, and we left the room. I locked the door, and she remained shut in with her lover. . . .

I called my servants and bade them follow me, and went out. I walked proudly, surrounded by my retainers, and I came to the house of Bartolomeo Moratini. He had just finished dinner, and was sitting with his sons. They rose as they saw me.

'Ah, Filippo, you have returned.' Then, seeing my pale face, they cried, 'But what is it? What has happened?'

And Bartolomeo broke in.

'What is that on your hand, Filippo?'

I stretched it out, so that he might see.

'That—that is the blood of your daughter's lover.'

'Oh!'

'I found them together, and I killed the adulterer.'

Bartolomeo kept silence a moment, then he said,—

'You have done well, Filippo.' He turned to his sons. 'Scipione, give me my sword.'

He girded it on, and then he spoke to me.

'Sir,' he said, 'I beg you to wait here till I come.'

I bowed.

'Sir, I am your servant.'

'Scipione, Alessandro, follow me!'

And accompanied by his sons, he left the room, and I remained alone.

The servants peeped in at the door, looking at me as if I were some strange beast, and fled when I turned round. I walked up and down, up and down; I looked out of window. In the street the people were going to and fro, singing, and talking as if nothing had happened. They did not know that death was flying through the air; they did not know that the happiness of living men had gone for ever.

At last I heard the steps again, and Bartolomeo Moratini entered the room, followed by his sons; and all three were very grave.

'Sir,' he said, 'the stain on your honour and mine has been effaced.'

I bowed more deeply than before.

'Sir, I am your very humble servant.'

'I thank you that you allowed me to do my duty

as a father; and I regret that a member of my family should have shown herself unworthy of my name and yours. I will detain you no longer.'

I bowed again, and left them.

X L

I WALKED back to my house. It was very silent, and as I passed up the stairs the servants shrunk back with averted faces, as if they were afraid to look at me.

'Where is Fabio?' I asked.

A page whispered timidly,—

'In the chapel.'

I turned on my heel, and passed through the rooms, one after another, till I came to the chapel door. I pushed it open and entered. A dim light came through the painted windows, and I could hardly see. In the centre were two bodies covered with a cloth, and their heads were lighted by the yellow gleam of candles. At their feet knelt an old man, praying. It was Fabio.

I advanced and drew back the cloth; and I fell on my knees. Giulia looked as if she were sleeping. I had so often leant over her, watching the regular heaving of the breast, and sometimes I had thought her features as calm and relaxed as if she were dead. But now the breast would no more rise and fall,

286

and its wonderful soft whiteness was disfigured by a gaping wound. Her eyes were closed and her lips half parted, and the only difference from life was the fallen jaw. Her face was very pale; the rich waving hair encircled it as with an aureole.

I looked at him, and he, too, was pale, and his fair hair contrasted wonderfully with hers. He looked so young!

Then, as I knelt there, and the hours passed slowly, I thought of all that had happened, and I tried to understand. The dim light from the window gradually failed, and the candles in the darkness burnt out more brightly; each was surrounded by a halo of light, and lit up the dead faces, throwing into deeper night the rest of the chapel.

Little by little I seemed to see into the love of these two which had been so strong, that no ties of honour, faith, or truth had been able to influence it. And this is what I imagined, trying to console myself.

When she was sixteen, I thought, they married her to an old man she had never seen, and she met her husband's cousin, a boy no older than herself. And the love started and worked its way. But the boy lived on his rich cousin's charity; from him he had received a home and protection and a thousand kindnesses; he loved against his will, but he loved all the same. And she, I thought, had loved like a woman, passionately, thoughtless of honour and truth. In the sensual violence of her love she had carried him away, and he had yielded. Then with enjoyment had come remorse, and he had torn himself away from the temptress and fled.

I hardly knew what had happened when she was left alone, pining for her lover. Scandal said evil things. . . . Had she, too, felt remorse and tried to kill her love, and had the attempt failed? And was it then she flung herself into dissipation to drown her trouble? Perhaps he told her he did not love her, and she in despair may have thrown herself in the arms of other lovers. But he loved her too strongly to forget her; at last he could not bear the absence and came back. And again with enjoyment came remorse, and, ashamed, he fled, hating himself, despising her.

The years passed by, and her husband died. Why did he not come back to her? Had he lost his love and was he afraid? I could not understand. . . .

Then she met me. Ah, I wondered what she felt. Did she love me? Perhaps his long absence had made her partly forget him, and she thought he had forgotten her. She fell in love with me, and I—I loved her with all my heart. I knew she loved me then; she must have loved me! But he came back. He may have thought himself cured, he may have said that he could meet her coldly and indifferently. Had I not said the same? But as they saw one another the old love burst out, again it burnt them with consuming fire, and Giulia hated me because I had made her faithless to the lover of her heart.

The candles were burning low, throwing strange lights and shadows on the faces of the dead.

Poor fool! His love was as powerful as ever, but he fought against it with all the strength of his weak

will. She was the Evil One to him; she took his
youth from him, his manhood, his honour, his strength;
he felt that her kisses degraded him, and as he rose
from her embrace he felt vile and mean. He vowed
never to touch her again, and every time be broke the
vow. But her love was the same as ever—passionate,
even heartless. She cared not if she consumed him
as long as she loved him. For her he might ruin his
life, he might lose his soul. She cared for nothing ;
it was all and all for love.

He fled again, and she turned her eyes on me once
more. Perhaps she felt sorry for my pain, perhaps
she fancied my love would efface the remembrance of
him. And we were married. Ah! now that she was
dead I could allow her good intentions. She may
have intended to be faithful to me; she may have
thought she could truly love and honour me. Perhaps
she tried ; who knows? But love—love cares not for
vows. It was too strong for her, too strong for him.
I do not know whether she sent for him, or whether
he, in the extremity of his passion, came to her ; but
what had happened so often happened again. They
threw everything to the winds, and gave themselves
over to the love that kills. . . .

The long hours passed as I thought of these things,
and the candles were burnt to their sockets.

At last I felt a touch on my shoulder, and heard
Fabio's voice.

'Master, it is nearly morning.'

I stood up, and he added,—

'They put him in the chapel without asking me.
You are not angry?'

'They did well!'

T

He hesitated a moment and then asked,—

'What shall I do?'

I looked at him, not understanding.

'He cannot remain here, and she—she must be buried.'

'Take them to the church, and lay them in the tomb my father built—together.'

'The man too?' he asked. 'In your own tomb?'

I sighed and answered sadly,—

'Perhaps he loved her better than I.'

As I spoke I heard a sob at my feet. A man I had not seen took hold of my hand and kissed it, and I felt it wet with tears.

'Who are you?' I asked.

'He has been here all the night,' said Fabio.

'He was my master and I loved him,' replied the kneeling figure in a broken voice. 'I thank you that you do not cast him out like a dog.'

I looked at him and felt deep pity for his grief.

'What will you do now?' I asked.

'Alas! now I am a wreck that tosses on the billows without a guide.'

I did not know what to say to him.

'Will you take me as your servant? I will be very faithful.'

'Do you ask me that?' I said. 'Do you not know—'

· 'Ah, yes! you took the life that he was glad to lose. It was almost a kindness; and now you bury him peacefully, and for that I love you. You owe it to me; you have robbed me of a master, give me another.'

'No, poor friend! I want no servants now. I too

am like a wreck that drifts aimlessly across the seas.
With me, too, it is finished.'

I looked once more at Giulia, and then I replaced
the white cloth, and the faces were covered.

'Bring me my horse, Fabio.'

In a few minutes it was waiting for me.

'Will you have no one to accompany you?' he
asked.

'No one!'

Then, as I mounted and arranged the reins in my
hand, he said,—

'Where are you going?'

And I despairingly answered,—

'God knows!'

XLI

AND I rode away out of the town into the open country. The day was breaking, and everything was cold and grey. I paid no heed to my course ; I rode along, taking the roads as they came, through broad plains, eastwards towards the mountains. In the increasing day I saw the little river wind sinuously through the fields, and the country stretched flat before me, with slender trees marked out against the sky. Now and then a tiny hill was surmounted by a village, and once, as I passed, I heard the tinkling of a bell. I stopped at an inn to water the horse, and then, hating the sight of men, I hurried on. The hours of coolness had passed, and as we tramped along the shapeless roads the horse began to sweat, and the thick white dust rose in clouds behind us.

At last I came to a roadside inn, and it was nearly mid-day. I dismounted, and giving the horse to the ostler's care, I went inside and sat at a table. The landlord came to me and offered food. I could not eat, I felt it would make me sick ; I ordered wine.

It was brought; I poured some out and tasted it
Then I put my elbows on the table and held my
head with both hands, for it was aching so as almost
to drive me mad.

'Sir!'

I looked up and saw a Franciscan friar standing
by my side. On his back he bore a sack; I supposed
he was collecting food.

'Sir, I pray you for alms for the sick and needy.'

I drew out a piece of gold and threw it to him.

'The roads are hard to-day,' he said.

I made no answer.

'You are going far, sir?'

'When one gives alms to a beggar, it is so that he
may not importune one,' I said.

'Ah, no; it is for the love of God and charity. But
I do not wish to importune you, I thought I might
help you.'

'I want no help,'

'You look unhappy.'

'I beg you to leave me me in peace.'

'As you will, my son.'

He left me, and I returned to my old position. I
felt as if a sheet of lead were pressing upon my
head. A moment later a gruff voice broke in upon
me.

'Ah, Messer Filippo Brandolini!'

I looked up. At the first glance I did not recognise the speaker; but then as I cleared my mind I
saw it was Ercole Piacentini. What was he doing
here? Then I remembered that it was on the road
to Forli. I supposed he had received orders to leave
Castello and was on his way to his old haunts. How-

ever, I did not want to speak to him; I bent down,
and again clasped my head in my hands.

'That is a civil way of answering,' he said. 'Messer
Filippo!'

I looked up, rather bored.

'If I do not answer, it is evidently because I do
not wish to speak to you.'

'And if I wish to speak to you?'

'Then I must take the liberty of begging you to
hold your tongue.'

'You insolent fellow!'

I felt too miserable to be angry.

'Have the goodness to leave me,' I said. 'You
bore me intensely.'

'I tell you that you are an insolent fellow, and I
shall do as I please.'

'Are you a beggar, that you are so importunate?
What do you want?'

'Do you remember saying in Forli that you would
fight me when the opportunity presented itself. It
has! And I am ready, for I have to thank you for
my banishment from Castello.'

'When I offered to fight you, sir, I thought you
were a gentleman. Now that I know your condition,
I must decline.'

'You coward!'

'Surely it is not cowardice to refuse a duel with a
person like yourself?'

By this time he was wild with rage; but I was cool
and collected.

'Have you so much to boast?' he asked
furiously.

'Happily I am not a bastard!'

' Cuckold ! '

' Oh ! '

I sprang up and looked at him with a look of horror. He laughed scornfully and repeated,—

' Cuckold ! '

Now it was my turn. The blood rushed to my head and a terrible rage seized me. I picked up the tankard of wine which was on the table and flung it at him with all my might. The wine splashed over his face, and the cup hit him on the forehead and cut him so that the blood trickled down. In a moment he had drawn his sword, and at the same time I wrenched mine from its sheath.

He could fight well.

He could fight well, but against me he was lost. All the rage and agony of the last day gathered themselves together. I was lifted up and cried aloud in the joy of having someone on whom to wreak my vengeance. I felt as if I had against me the whole world and were pouring out my hate at the end of my sword. My fury lent me the strength of a devil. I drove him back, I drove him back, and I fought as I had never fought before. In a minute I had beaten the sword from his hand, and it fell to the floor as if his wrist were broken, clattering down among the cups. He staggered back against the wall, and stood there with his head thrown back and his arms helplessly outspread.

' Ah, God, I thank thee ! ' I cried exultingly. ' Now I am happy.'

I lifted my sword above my head to cleave his skull, my arm was in the swing—when I stopped. I saw the staring eyes, the white face blanched with terror; he was standing against the wall as he had fallen, shrinking away in his mortal anxiety. I stopped; I could not kill him.

I sheathed my sword and said,—

'Go! I will not kill you. I despise you too much.'

He did not move, but stood as if he were turned to stone, still terror-stricken and afraid. Then, in my contempt, I took a horn of water and flung it over him.

'You look pale, my friend,' I said. 'Here is water to mix with your wine.'

Then I leant back and burst into a shout of laughter, and I laughed till my sides ached, and I laughed again.

I threw down money to pay for my entertainment, and went out. But as I bestrode my horse and we recommenced our journey along the silent roads I felt my head ache worse than ever. All enjoyment was gone; I could take no pleasure in life. How long would it last? How long? I rode along under the mid-day sun, and it fell scorching on my head; the wretched beast trotted with hanging head, his tongue lolling out of his mouth, parched and dry. The sun beat down with all the power of August, and everything seemed livid with the awful heat. Man and beast had shrunk away from the fiery rays, the country folk were taking the noonday rest, the cattle and the horses sheltered by barns and sheds, the birds were silent, and even the lizards had crept into their holes. Only the horse and I tramped along, miserably—only the horse and I. There was no shade; the walls on either side were too low to give shelter, the road glaring and white and dusty. I might have been riding through a furnace.

Everything was against me. Everything! Even the sun seemed to beat down his hottest rays to increase my misery. What had I done that all this should come to me? I clenched my fist, and in impotent rage cursed God. . . .

At last I saw close to me a little hill covered with dark fir trees; I came nearer, and the sight of the sombre green was like a draught of cool water. I could no longer bear the horror of the heat. From the main road another smaller one led winding up the hill. I turned my horse, and soon we were among the trees, and I took a long breath of delight in the coolness. I dismounted and led him by the bridle; it was enchanting to walk along the path, soft with the fallen needles, and a delicious green smell hovered in the air. We came to a clearing, where was a little pond; I watered the poor beast, and, throwing myself down, drank deeply. Then I tied him to a tree and advanced a few steps alone. I came to a sort of terrace, and going forward found myself at the edge of the hill, looking over the plain. Behind, the tall fir trees gave me shade and coolness; I sat down, looking at the country before me. In the cloudless sky it seemed now singularly beautiful. Far away on one side I could see the walls and towers of some city, and to it in broad curves wound a river; the maze and corn, vines and olive trees, covered the land, and in the distance I saw the soft blue mountains. Why should the world be so beautiful, and I so miserable?

'It is, indeed, a wonderful scene.'

I looked up and saw the monk whom I had spoken with at the inn. He put down his sack and sat by my side.

'You do not think me importunate?' he asked.

'I beg your pardon,' I replied, 'I was not civil to you; you must forgive me. I was not myself.'

'Do not talk of it. I saw you here, and I came down to you to offer you our hospitality.'

I looked at him questioningly; he pointed over his shoulder, and looking, I saw, perched on the top of the hill, piercing through the trees, a little monastery.

'How peaceful it looks!' I said.

'It is, indeed. St Francis himself used sometimes to come to enjoy the quiet.'

I sighed. Oh, why could not I have done with the life I hated, and also enjoy the quiet? I felt the monk was watching me, and, looking up, I met his glance. He was a tall, thin man, with deeply-sunken eyes and hollow cheeks. And he was pale and worn from prayer and fasting. But his voice was sweet and very gentle.

'Why do you look at me?' I said.

'I was in the tavern when you disarmed the man and gave him his life.'

'It was not for charity and mercy,' I said bitterly.

'I know,' he answered, 'it was from despair.'

'How do you know?'

'I watched you; and at the end I said, '"God pity his unhappiness."'

I looked with astonishment at the strange man; and then, with a groan, I said,—

'Oh, you are right.　I am so unhappy.'

He took my hands in his, and with the gentleness of the mother of God herself replied,—

'"Come unto Me all ye that are weary and heavy laden, and I will give you rest."'

Then I could suffer my woe no longer.　I buried my face in his bosom, and burst into tears.

EPILOGUE

AND now many years have passed, and the noble gentleman, Filippo Brandolini is the poor monk Giuliano; the gorgeous clothes, velvets and satins, have given way to the brown sackcloth of the Seraphic Father; and instead of golden belts my waist is girt with a hempen cord. And in me, what changes have taken place! The brown hair, which women kissed, is a little circlet in sign of the Redeemer's crown, and it is as white as snow. My eyes are dim and sunken, my cheeks are hollow, and the skin of my youth is ashy and wrinkled; the white teeth of my mouth have gone, but my tooth-less gums suffice for the monkish fare; and I am old and bent and weak.

One day in the spring I came to the terrace which overlooks the plain, and as I sat down to warm my-self in the sunshine, gazing at the broad country which now I knew so well, and the distant hills, the wish came to me to write the history of my life.

And now that, too, is done. I have nothing more

to tell except that from the day when I arrived, weary of soul, to the cool shade of the fir trees, I have never gone into the world again. I gave my lands and palaces to my brother in the hope that he would make better use of his life than I, and to him I gave the charge of seeing that heirs were given to the ancient name. I knew I had failed in everything. My life had gone wrong, I know not why; and I had not the courage to adventure further. I withdrew from the battle in my unfitness, and let the world pass on and forget my poor existence.

Checco lived on, scheming and intriguing, wearing away his life in attempts to regain his fatherland, and always he was disappointed, always his hopes frustrated, till at last he despaired. And after six years, worn out with his fruitless efforts, mourning the greatness he had lost, and pining for the country he loved so well, he died of a broken heart, an exile.

Matteo went back to his arms and the reckless life of the soldier of fortune, and was killed bravely fighting against the foreign invader, and died, knowing that his efforts, too, had been in vain, and that the sweet land of Italy lay fallen and enslaved.

And I do not know whether they had not the better lot; for they are at peace, while I—I pursue my lonely pilgrimage through life, and the goal is ever far off. Now it cannot be much longer, my strength is failing, and soon I shall have the peace I wished for. Oh God, I do not ask You for crowns of gold and heavenly raiment, I do not aspire to the bliss which is the portion of the saint, but give me rest. When the great Release comes, give me rest; let me sleep the long sleep without awakening, so that at last I may forget and be at peace. O God, give me rest!

Often, as I trudged along the roads barefooted to gather food and alms, have I wished to lay myself in the ditch by the wayside and die. Sometimes I have heard the beating of the wings of the Angel of Death; but he has taken the strong and the happy, and left me to wander on.

The good man told me I should receive happiness; I have not even received forgetfulness. I go along the roads thinking of my life and the love that ruined me. Ah! how weak I am; but, forgive me, I cannot help myself! Sometimes when I have been able to do good I have felt a strange delight, I have felt the blessed joy of charity. And I love my people, the poor folk of the country round. They come to me in their troubles, and when I can help them I share their pleasure. But that is all I have. Ah! mine has been a useless life, I have wasted it; and if of late I have done a little good to my fellowmen, alas! how little!

I bear my soul in patience, but sometimes I cannot help rising up against fate, and crying out that it is hard that all this should happen to me. Why? What had I done that I should be denied the little happiness of this world? Why should I be more unhappy than others? But then I chide myself, and ask whether I have indeed been less happy. Are they any of them happy? Or are those right who say that the world is misery, and that the only happiness is to die? Who knows?

Ah, Giulia, how I loved thee!

> O Ciechi, il tanto affaticar che giova ?
> Tutti tornate alla gran madre antica,
> E'l nome vostro appena si ritrova.

> *Blind that ye are! How doth this struggle profit you?*
> *Return ye must to the great Antique Mother,*
> *And even your name scarcely remains.*

THE END

Colston & Coy., Limited, Printers, Edinburgh.

T. FISHER UNWIN, Publisher,

SIX-SHILLING NOVELS

In uniform green cloth, large crown 8vo., gilt tops, **6s.**

Effie Hetherington. By ROBERT BUCHANAN. Second Edition.

An Outcast of the Islands. By JOSEPH CONRAD. Second Edition.

Almayer's Folly. By JOSEPH CONRAD. Second Edition.

The Ebbing of the Tide. By LOUIS BECKE. Second Edition.

A First Fleet Family. By LOUIS BECKE and WALTER JEFFERY.

Paddy's Woman, and Other Stories. By HUMPHREY JAMES.

Clara Hopgood. By MARK RUTHERFORD. Second Edition.

The Tales of John Oliver Hobbes. Portrait of the Author. Second Edition.

The Stickit Minister. By S. R. CROCKETT. Eleventh Edition.

The Lilac Sunbonnet. By S. R. CROCKETT. Sixth Edition.

The Raiders. By S. R. CROCKETT. Eighth Edition.

The Grey Man. By S. R. CROCKETT.

In a Man's Mind. By J. R. WATSON.

A Daughter of the Fen. By J. T. BEALBY. Second Edition.

The Herb-Moon. By JOHN OLIVER HOBBES. Third Edition.

Nancy Noon. By BENJAMIN SWIFT. Second Edition. With New Preface.

Mr. Magnus. By F. REGINALD STATHAM. Second Edition.

Trooper Peter Halket of Mashonaland. By OLIVE SCHREINER. Frontispiece.

Pacific Tales. By LOUIS BECKE. With Frontispiece Portrait of the Author. Second Edition.

Mrs. Keith's Crime. By Mrs. W. K. CLIFFORD. Sixth Edition. With Portrait of Mrs. Keith by the Hon. JOHN COLLIER, and a New Preface by the Author.

Hugh Wynne. By Dr. S. WEIR MITCHELL. With Frontispiece Illustration.

The Tormentor. By BENJAMIN SWIFT, Author of "Nancy Noon."

Prisoners of Conscience. By AMELIA E. BARR, Author of "Jan Vedder's Wife." With 12 Illustrations.

The Gods, some Mortals and Lord Wickenham. New Edition. By JOHN OLIVER HOBBES.

The Outlaws of the Marches. By Lord ERNEST HAMILTON. Fully illustrated.

The School for Saints : Part of the History of the Right Honourable Robert Orange, M.P. By JOHN OLIVER HOBBES, Author of "Sinner's Comedy,' "Some Emotions and a Moral," "The Herb Moon," &c.

The People of Clopton. By GEORGE BARTRAM.

11, Paternoster Buildings, London, E.C.

T. FISHER UNWIN, Publisher,

WORKS BY JOSEPH CONRAD

I.

AN OUTCAST OF THE ISLANDS

Crown 8vo., cloth, **6s.**

"Subject to the qualifications thus disposed of (*vide* first part of notice), 'An Outcast of the Islands' is perhaps the finest piece of fiction that has been published this year, as 'Almayer's Folly' was one of the finest that was published in 1895 . . . Surely this is real romance—the romance that is real. Space forbids anything but the merest recapitulation of the other living realities of Mr. Conrad's invention—of Lingard, of the inimitable Almayer, the one-eyed Babalatchi, the Naturalist, of the pious Abdulla—all novel, all authentic. Enough has been written to show Mr. Conrad's quality. He imagines his scenes and their sequence like a master; he knows his individualities and their hearts; he has a new and wonderful field in this East Indian Novel of his. . . . Greatness is deliberately written; the present writer has read and re-read his two books, and after putting this review aside for some days to consider the discretion of it, the word still stands."—*Saturday Review.*

II.

ALMAYER'S FOLLY

Second Edition. Crown 8vo., cloth, **6s.**

"This startling, unique, splendid book."
Mr. T. P. O'CONNOR, M.P.

"This is a decidely powerful story of an uncommon type, and breaks fresh ground in fiction. . . . All the leading characters in the book—Almayer, his wife, his daughter, and Dain, the daughter's native lover—are well drawn, and the parting between father and daughter has a pathetic naturalness about it, unspoiled by straining after effect. There are, too, some admirably graphic passages in the book. The approach of a monsoon is most effectively described. . . . The name of Mr. Joseph Conrad is new to us, but it appears to us as if he might become the Kipling of the Malay Archipelago."—*Spectator.*

11, Paternoster Buildings, London, E.C. c

T. FISHER UNWIN, Publisher,

PADDY'S WOMAN

BY

HUMPHREY JAMES

Crown 8vo., **6s.**

" Traits of the Celt of humble circumstances are copied with keen appreciation and unsparing accuracy." *Scotsman.*

" . . . . They are full of indescribable charm and pathos."—*Bradford Observer.*

" The outstanding merit of this series of stories is that they are absolutely true to life . . . . the photographic accuracy and minuteness displayed are really marvellous." *Aberdeen Free Press.*

" ' Paddy's Woman and Other Stories' by Humphrey James ; a volume written in the familiar diction of the Ulster people themselves, with **perfect realism and very remarkable ability. . . . For genuine human nature and human relations, and humour of an indescribable kind, we are unable to cite a rival to this volume."** *The World.*

" For a fine subtle piece of humour we are inclined to think that 'A Glass of Whisky' takes a lot of beating . . In short Mr. Humphrey James has given us a delightful book, and one which does as much credit to his heart as to his head. We shall look forward with a keen anticipation to the next ' writings' by this shrewd, ' cliver,' and compassionate young author."—*Bookselling.*

11, Paternoster Buildings, London, E.C.

T. FISHER UNWIN, Publisher,

THE GREY MAN

BY

S. R. CROCKETT

Crown 8vo., cloth, **6s.**

Also, an Edition de Luxe, with 26 Drawings by
SEYMOUR LUCAS, R.A., *limited to 250 copies, signed*
by Author. Crown 4to., cloth gilt, **21s.** *net.*

" It has nearly all the qualities which go to make a book
of the first-class. Before you have read twenty pages you
know that you are reading a classic."—*Literary World.*

"All of that vast and increasing host of readers who
prefer the novel of action to any other form of fiction
should, nay, indeed, must, make a point of reading this
exceedingly fine example of its class."—*Daily Chronicle.*

"With such passages as these [referring to quotations],
glowing with tender passion, or murky with horror,
even the most insatiate lover of romance may feel that
Mr. Crockett has given him good measure, well pressed
down and running over."—*Daily Telegraph.*

11, Paternoster Buildings, London, E.C.

1

T. FISHER UNWIN, Publisher,

A DAUGHTER OF THE FEN

BY

J. T. BEALBY

Second Edition. Crown 8vo., cloth, **6s.**

" It will deserve notice at the hands of such as are interested in the ways and manner of living of a curious race that has ceased to be."
Daily Chronicle.

" For a first book 'A Daughter of the Fen' is full of promise."—*Academy*.

" This book deserves to be read for its extremely interesting account of life in the Fens and for its splendid character study of Mme. Dykereave."

" Deserves high praise."—*Scotsman*. [*Star*.

" It is an able, interesting . . . . an exciting book, and is well worth reading. And when once taken up it will be difficult to lay it down."
Westminster Gazette.

IN A MAN'S MIND

BY

JOHN REAY WATSON

Crown 8vo., cloth, **6s.**

" We regard the book as well worth the effort of reading."—*British*

" The book is clever, very clever."—*Dundee Advertiser*. [*Review*.

" The power and pathos of the book are undeniable."—*Liverpool Post*.

" It is a book of some promise."—*Newsagent*.

" Mr. Watson has hardly a rival among Australian writers, past or present. There is real power in the book—power of insight, power of reflection, power of analysis, power of presentation. . . . 'Tis a very well made book—not a set of independent episodes strung on the thread of a name or two, but closely interwoven to the climax."
Sydney Bulletin.

" There is behind it all a power of drawing human nature that in time arrests the attention."—*Athenæum*.

11, Paternoster Buildings, London, E.C.　　　　*m*

T. FISHER UNWIN, Publisher,

NANCY NOON

BY

BENJAMIN SWIFT

Second Edition. Cloth, **6s.**

Some Reviews on the First Edition.

" ' Nancy Noon ' is perhaps the strongest book of the year, certainly by far the strongest book which has been published by any new writer. . . . . . Mr. Swift contrives to keep his book from end to end real, passionate, even intense. . . . . If Mr. Meredith had never written, one would have predicted, with the utmost confidence, a great future for Mr. Benjamin Swift, and even as it is I have hopes."—*Sketch.*

" Certainly a promising first effort."—*Whitehall Review.*

" If ' Nancy Noon ' be Mr. Swift's first book, it is a success of an uncommon kind "—*Dundee Advertiser.*

" ' Nancy Noon' is one of the most remarkable novels of the year, and the author, avowedly a beginner, has succeeded in gaining a high position in the ranks of contemporary writers. . . . . All his characters are delightful. In the heat of sensational incidents or droll scenes we stumble on observations that set us reflecting, and but for an occasional roughness of style — elliptical, Carlyle mannerisms—the whole is admirably written."—*Westminster Gazette.*

" Mr. Swift has the creative touch and a spark of genius."—*Manchester Guardian.*

" Mr. Swift has held us interested from the first to the last page of his novel."—*World.*

" The writer of ' Nancy Noon ' has succeeded in presenting a powerfully written and thoroughly interesting story."—*Scotsman.*

" We are bound to admit that the story interested us all through, that it absorbed us towards the end, and that not until the last page had been read did we find it possible to lay the book down."—*Daily Chronicle.*

" It is a very strong book, very vividly coloured, very fascinating in its style, very compelling in its claim on the attention, and not at all likely to be soon forgotten."—*British Weekly.*

" A clever book. . . . . The situations and ensuing complications are dramatic, and are handled with originality and daring throughout."—*Daily News.*

" Mr. Benjamin Swift has written a vastly entertaining book."—*Academy.*

11, Paternoster Buildings, London, E.C.

T. FISHER UNWIN, Publisher,

THE MERMAID SERIES

The Best Plays of the Old Dramatists.
Literal Reproductions of the Old Text.

Post 8vo., each Volume containing about 500 pages, and an etched Frontispiece, cloth, **3s. 6d.** *each.*

1. **The Best Plays of Christopher Marlowe.** Edited by HAVELOCK ELLIS, and containing a General Introduction to the Series by JOHN ADDINGTON SYMONDS.

2. **The Best Plays of Thomas Otway.** Introduction by the Hon. RODEN NOEL.

3. **The Best Plays of John Ford.**— Edited by HAVELOCK ELLIS.

4 and 5. **The Best Plays of Thomas Massinger.** Essay and Notes by ARTHUR SYMONS.

6. **The Best Plays of Thomas Heywood.** Edited by A. W. VERITY. Introduction by J. A. SYMONDS.

7. **The Complete Plays of William Wycherley.** Edited by W. C. WARD.

8. **Nero, and other Plays.** Edited by H. P. HORNE, ARTHUR SYMONS, A. W. VERITY, and H. ELLIS.

9 and 10. **The Best Plays of Beaumont and Fletcher.** Introduction by J. ST. LOE STRACHEY.

11. **The Complete Plays of William Congreve.** Edited by ALEX. C. EWALD.

12. **The Best Plays of Webster and Tourneur.** Introduction by JOHN ADDINGTON SYMONDS.

13 and 14. **The Best Plays of Thomas Middleton.** Introduction by ALGERNON CHARLES SWINBURNE.

15. **The Best Plays of James Shirley.** Introduction by EDMUND GOSSE.

16. **The Best Plays of Thomas Dekker.** Notes by ERNEST RHYS.

17, 19, and 20. **The Best Plays of Ben Jonson.** Vol. I. edited with Introduction and Notes, by BRINSLEY NICHOLSON and C. H. HERFORD.

18. **The Complete Plays of Richard Steele.** Edited, with Introduction and Notes, by G. A. AITKEN.

21. **The Best Plays of George Chapman.** Edited by WILLIAM LYON PHELPS, Instructor of English Literature at Yale College.

22. **The Select Plays of Sir John Vanbrugh.** Edited, with an Introduction and Notes, by A. E. H. SWAEN.

PRESS OPINIONS.

"Even the professed scholar with a good library at his command will find some texts here not otherwise easily accessible; while the humbler student of slender resources, who knows the bitterness of not being able to possess himself of the treasure stored in expensive folios or quartos long out of print, will assuredly rise up and thank Mr. Unwin."—*St. James's Gazette.*

"Resumed under good auspices."—*Saturday Review.*

"The issue is as good as it could be."—*British Weekly.*

"At once scholarly and interesting."—*Leeds Mercury.*

11, Paternoster Buildings, London, E.C.

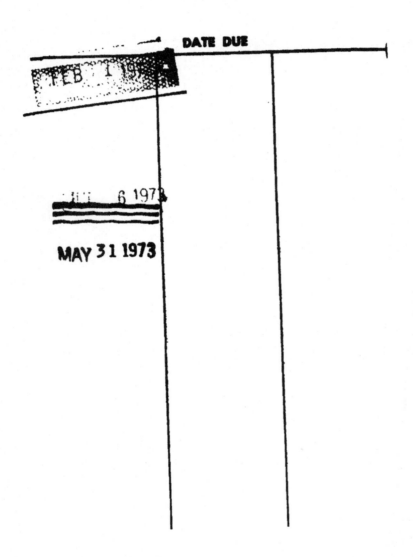

CPSIA information can be obtained
at www.ICGtesting.com
Printed in the USA
BVOW09*0514011217

501502BV00009B/35/P